In Session

Stephanie Leigh Moses, PhD

In Session is published under Imagine books, sectionalized division under Di Angelo Publications INC.

IMAGINE BOOKS

an imprint of Di Angelo Publications In Session. Copyright 2019. Stephanie L. Moses, PhD in digital and print distribution in the United States of America.

Di Angelo Publications

4265 San Felipe Road #1100

Houston, Texas, 77027

www.diangelopublications.com

Library of congress cataloging-in-publications data

In Session. Downloadable via Kindle, iBooks and NOOK.

Library of Congress Registration

Paperback

ISBN-10: 1-942549-36-9

ISBN-13: 978-1-942549-36-9

Layout: Di Angelo Publications

Cover: Savina Deianova

Developmental Editor: Elizabeth Geeslin Zinn

1. Fiction

2.Fiction ——— Women's Fiction ——Therapy——United States of America with int. Distribution.

Dedication

Influence is an invaluable notion. This book is dedicated to all of the wonderful people who have an influence on me. My family has always been my biggest support system. My friends (six-pack and beyond) have challenged me to grow personally. My colleagues challenge me to never stop achieving.

It is for those who allow me to serve them therapeutically and challenge me to be a lifelong learner. For these influencers, I am forever grateful.

Table of Contents

Part I The Unknown

Andrea   5
Cori   18
Sophie   35
Vivian   52

Part II The Fallout

Andrea   61
Cori   93
Sophie   114
Vivian   135

Part III Sessions

Andrea   164
Cori   206
Sophie   229
Vivian   278

Part IV The Truth

Andrea   307
Cori   314
Sophie   318
Vivian   326

Part I

The Unknown

Andrea

Andrea shook with anger. Her whole body felt like it was about to burst as the words came flooding out of her like the waters of a broken dam. "I absolutely hate you, and if you think, for one second, that I can't live without you, then you have me fucked up." Andrea heard what she was saying, and she knew the words were powerful, but she didn't feel bad about them. It was true she could live without Daniel, and she didn't need any more snide comments from him about what she did when she got off work and how long she did it.

The truth was Andrea simply just didn't care. She wasn't the type to care about other people's feelings above her own, regardless of who they were. She had done everything for herself up until the point that she met

Daniel. He was, for all intents and purposes a great guy, but she didn't need anyone breathing down her neck about what she did when she got off of work. Her job was stressful. It took a lot of energy and drive to get where she was, and she deserved to be able to enjoy the time she had off the way she damn well pleased. She spent her days at the firm, or in court, litigating and advocating for other people's divorce needs—now she felt her mind preparing arguments for her own.

"Dre, really? It's three in the goddamn morning," Daniel hissed in a whisper that still somehow managed to echo off of the walls around them and hit her ears with a sting. It didn't matter how important she felt, he had a way of getting to her with his insults. "It's like you don't want to be with your own children, or me. You don't love any of us, what the hell do you expect me to say when you come in like this, wasted, looking like a tired whore…what do you expect?"

"Tired *whore*? What the hell, Daniel? I spend all day working, working my ass off and making more than you and taking care of all of us. I don't hear you complaining when those bonuses hit the bank. If I want to go out and have a good time, I think I'm entitled to it… to whatever I want. What, are you too manly to have to watch your own kids because I want to take a break? Is it *my* job because I'm the woman?"

"That's not the point, Andrea. You should *want* to be here with them, with us," Daniel interrupted, eyes wide with rage. "Who have you been with? You have eye makeup smeared all over your face. You look like a goddamn raccoon, and you smell like you bathed in whisky. Your shirt is untucked, your hair is a mess. Did you screw someone else? You don't look like a mother, that's for damn sure." Daniel closed the door to their bedroom, locking Andrea out.

Her head spun as she slid down the side of the bedroom door and sat. *Who in the hell does he think he is?* She was seeing double when she heard a sound down the hallway.

"Mami? Is that you?" It was Ezekiel, her five-year-old boy. He rubbed his eyes and came walking down the hall to her. She couldn't quite focus on him. Although sitting, she felt like the entire room was spinning. It was a merry-go-round from which she couldn't escape.

"Hey baby," she said, letting out a heavy sigh.

"Why are you sitting on the floor Mami?"

"I…I need to sit for a minute, Zeke. I was feeling sick."

"Your tummy hurts?"

"Yeah, baby. Mami doesn't feel good."

"You want me to sit with you? Do you need messinin?" he asked, sweetness spilling forth from each word and little mispronunciation.

"No, no baby. I need to go to the bathroom," she groaned, feeling her stomach churn and her palms sweat in the unmistakable signs that she was about to upchuck the bottle of whisky she'd taken in.

"Why was daddy yelling?" Zeke asked, looking down and fiddling with his pajamas. He was a precocious child, and whenever something like this would occur in their household, he knew what was happening consciously, but didn't have the vocabulary to articulate the circumstances. His eyes conveyed the message to his mother that he knew more than he could say.

Andrea thought for a second and looked at Zeke. She could see that he was about to burst into tears, his fear with the situation mounting. She knew Daniel was on the other side of the door listening. She didn't want to give him any ammo against her.

"Daddy wasn't yelling. He was just worried because I was sick," she lied. Zeke had heard their arguments

7

before and was aware of their verbal abuse to one another.

"Daddy was yelling. I heard him. You were, too. Why are you fighting with daddy?"

"Baby, it's way too late for you to be up, you have school in the morning. Go back to bed," she said, her voice slightly stricter.

"I can't sleep now," he whined stretching out each word. Zeke had a way of stringing his words together like nails on a chalkboard.

"I don't care," she snipped. She didn't have any more energy to tell him what to do again. "Do what mami says. Go back to bed, now!" Zeke jumped a little with her final emphatic word; Andrea could instill fear into her children. She almost felt bad about it, then reminded herself that her children needed to have respect for her and she slowly stood up and shuffled to the guest bathroom.

As she hunched over the toilet, vomiting up every drop of liquor she'd spent her money on, she felt the pressure in her head cease a little. She curled up into a ball on and took comfort in the coolness of the tile floor, all went dark as it always did when she started to black out. She didn't have court in the morning, she thought to herself, so she could be a little late and it wouldn't matter, and she passed out.

The sound of an electric coffee grinder snapped Andrea up. She blinked and realized she'd slept with her contacts in. Her head pounded, and her body ached from the unnatural position in which she'd slept on the floor. She looked to her right, she'd made a mess of vomit on the floor.

"Christ," she said, standing up and evaluating her face in the mirror. "I got three hours, three fucking hours of sleep!" She examined her overweight and disheveled frame, her round face sunken in. Her hair, very dark and shiny needed a good wash and blow out. She evaluated everything she needed to do at bare minimum to make herself work ready. Down the hall she heard Daniel chattering to the children and getting them ready for school and daycare.

Andrea tried to sneak into her bedroom to take a shower, but Daniel stopped her before she could make it down the hall from the guest bathroom.

"Did you piss yourself again?" he asked.

"Fuck you, Daniel."

"Really? Because you don't anymore. That's a pretty ironic statement."

She turned around, knowing her ass and legs were not what they once were, thinking about how he used to grab at her in jest as she walked by instead of hate on her. She had practically ruined her skin from all the stress of work, late nights out and sleeping in makeup, but she held her head up high. "You know what? Maybe if you had a little more respect for me and what I do, things would be different. Maybe if you didn't turn on that ridiculous coffee grinder at six thirty in the morning, every morning, I could get some more rest and have energy."

"Someone's got to get up and be responsible," he replied. He huffed a sigh of irritation, rubbed his hand over his deliberately and meticulously shaved head, cracked his neck, and walked past her to their kitchen.

"You could do it the night before," she said loudly to ensure he heard her.

In the shower, Andrea tried to wash off the filth of the smells that were stuck to her. Cigarette smoke— something she only did when she drank—but she drank all the time, the smell of vomit, the feeling of being coated in a layer of filth from the bars she'd been at. The cab ride home that Frank had paid for. *Frank*, she thought, *at least he doesn't judge me. I can talk to him about things without catching hell about anything.*

She had worked with Frank for some time now at the firm, and she thought of him as a good friend, somewhat of an equal. Not like Daniel. Daniel wasn't her equal. He didn't know what it took to do what she did. He may have been handsome and chivalrous, something that drew her to him in the first place. But he didn't understand life at the firm, the way she had to think, the level of education she had and the knowledge she had to keep fresh, ready to spout at any moment. He didn't know any of those things. He bitched about responsibility, but did he even really know what that meant? He probably thought she should be home, with the kids all day. She shook Frank from her mind, knowing that she was going down a dangerous path.

Her thoughts drifted back to her husband. When they met, she thought he had wonderful morals and values, but now Daniel was too old school. She knew he'd probably prefer her to be home barefoot and pregnant, while he worked for them, providing a mediocre lifestyle. She couldn't have that. She made good money, and her income secured them a home within the confines of a gated community. The house was a plantation style estate home, with Italian marble floor in the foyer and 13-foot ceilings. In the back, she had the walls knocked out and rebuild it with ceiling to floor windows, so that they could have a beautiful overlook of the infinity edge pool she had installed. Ezekiel attended the best private school in the city and it was all because of Andrea. She knew Daniel wouldn't have been able to do any of that. Zeke would be in a public school, getting head lice while sitting in oversized classes.

Fresh from the shower but still appearing like a haggard banshee from having no sleep and no hydration, Andrea wrapped herself in her robe and padded into the kitchen. Zeke and Anna were seated at the barstool. Lilly, only a year old and was seated neatly in her high chair.

"Good morning, babies," Andrea said, her voice sounding a bit hoarse.

"Mami!" her two-year-old, Anna, shook her sippy-cup and smiled at Andrea. Anna slammed it down on the countertop.

"Oooh, baby don't slam that. It's too loud," Andrea winced as she poured a huge glass of orange juice for herself.

"You gonna leave any of that for the kids?" Daniel squawked, watching Andrea chug.

She didn't respond, she just looked at him with a glare and kept drinking, then poured another glass. She needed toast. She started looking for the bread. She just bought it two days ago.

"Where's the bread?" she said as she checked the pantries and counter tops.

"It's gone, I made toast yesterday and today for all of us. Plus Zeke's sandwiches for school," Daniel snapped back at her.

"Fuck," she mumbled under her breath. She just needed some avocado toast. That was all it would take to make her feel human enough to go to work and function.

"Watch your language around the kids, you don't want them talking like you, I definitely don't," Daniel scolded, immediately setting Andrea off.

"I'll say whatever I want, Daniel. I need some fucking toast. But fine, we don't have any. I'll just go to the drive-thru," she hissed. Lilly started to cry, adding more painful noise to Andrea's already throbbing skull.

"You upset the baby," Daniel growled, walking over to Lilly's high chair and picking her up. "It's okay baby, Daddy's got you. You're fine, you're fine," he coddled, lifting his eyes up and shooting daggers at Andrea.

"Mami, are you still sick?" Zeke asked, kicking his feet gently up against the wall space beneath the breakfast bar in the kitchen.

She ignored his inquisition. "Zeke, don't kick the wall, you're gonna leave marks," Andrea snapped sharply. Zeke stopped and looked down at his plate of crumbs, with a look of shame for speaking to his mother. Everything that made his mother upset was somehow because he was a bad boy.

"God you're just a ball of sunshine this morning," Daniel said smugly. "Let's go kids. Come on, Zeke, Anna, let's get in the car. Zeke, don't forget your backpack."

He loaded Lilly up in her car seat and hauled her out the door with his forearm flexed. It was his smug tone that Andrea felt was increasingly penetrating her consciousness when she was around him. That's why she excused herself whenever she became so irritated with him and did as she pleased. His words, his tone, his gestures—they were all just insults. And who was he to insult her? No one. He was no one.

The door to the garage closed hard behind them as they left. It made Andrea clench her teeth. She started digging through the medicine cabinet for naproxen sodium, and some leftover hydrocodone. She needed everything she could get in order to make it through the day.

She put herself together a bit haphazardly, squeezing into a skirt and tucking in her shirt. Her pooch in the front just couldn't be hidden. Her suit jacket wouldn't button up around it. "Dammit," she said, almost crying. She had always been very poised, and impeccable in a pencil skirt for work. Her metabolism was slowing down, and her suits just didn't quite fit right.

She rubbed makeup on her face and tried to hide the immense hangover she was feeling with concealer. It made her look more like a corpse at a morgue than alive and well. On her way to her office in her black luxury sedan, shiny and perfect, she kept glancing at herself in her mirror and trying to adjust her hair. It looked oily and she'd forgotten dry shampoo. She pulled into the drive-thru at McDonald's and ordered a greasy breakfast sandwich and black coffee. She dumped three packets of sugar into it and stirred it quickly. Without being able to wait a moment longer to eat, she took a bite of her food and the steaming hot egg burned the roof of her mouth, making her spit it out. Her blouse was grease-stained now. It was too late for her to go home and change.

After a bout of cursing rage in the car as she drove, she pulled up to the high-rise building that housed her firm, parked her Mercedes in a haphazard manner, and walked into the lobby of Park & Zimmerman, the most esteemed law firm in the area. The firm was several generations old and handled high profile criminal, family, and civil law. Andrea had once loved the place; the look, the smell, the energy and action. When she first started, she had her sights set on making partner and wanted an office on the top floor.

"Hi Andrea." She looked up to see the friendly face of the security guard downstairs. She looked like she felt, and she felt like shit.

"Hey, Mike," she said halfheartedly.

"You okay?" he asked, noting her overall appearance, but not saying anything.

"Yeah, yeah I'm fine. I was just up with one of the kids last night—the little one's sick again."

"Oh, I know that's hard. I hope she gets to feeling better," he said as she waited for the elevator.

"Thanks, Mike," she waved and pressed the button to close the door on the elevator as fast as she could, multiple times.

She pushed away the twangs of guilt she felt for letting herself lie that one of her children was sick. It was something she never thought she'd let herself do, and now the words came out of her as naturally as giving an acquaintance a greeting. She felt the pull of the elevator up to the 20th floor. It made her woozy. She was still drunk. She had to switch on that floor and take the next elevator up to the 37th floor. She sucked in a deep breath and walked to the next set of elevators.

"Hi Andrea!" chirped a familiar voice. It was Jackie, the newbie of the firm. She was like Andrea once was, young, Latina, gorgeous and smart. She had on a form fitting outfit that would make anyone take a second glance at her, and her red lipstick made her lips pop. Andrea felt envious of her youth and energy but wouldn't dare show it.

"Hey, girlie, you look cute today," Andrea replied with false enthusiasm.

"Aw, thanks. I really wanted to go out with you guys last night. Did you have a good time?"

"Sure!" Andrea said, "You should come, we always have a great time."

"I would have but I had my yoga class, you should come sometime!" Jackie chirped. Her naturally, shrill, high pitched tenor drove nails through Andrea's scull. Yoga was the last thing Andrea wanted to go do. She knew Jackie would realize, in time, that their job wasn't all it was cut out to be by society. The pressures were real, the stress was real and the pay, although glamourized as fantastic by society, didn't quite make up for the mental toll the job took on a person. Jackie had made it a habit of advertising her entire life as some sort of campaign for Latina women to succeed and Andrea just wasn't about that. She had done it alone, without letting the world know through social media or any other means how awesome she was to do it all on her own and for that fact, she had even less respect for Jackie.

"Oh cool, thanks, I'll see," Andrea said as she moved away with quick steps.

Making it past anyone else who might talk to her, Andrea sped to her office and closed the door hard, the sound of it thudding adding an extra pounding to her temples. Leaving the lights off, she went to her desk and made sure her window blinds were down. There was absolutely no way she could function with the hangover she had. Feeling nauseated again, she laid her head down on her large, organized desk and let the quiet sink in. Thinking about her schedule, she began mentally plotting how she could rearrange client meetings and hearings. She wasn't feeling up to it—up to anything. It was happening again. She didn't understand it, but she knew she had to go away.

A knock on the door interrupted her thoughts and she straightened herself up, clicked around on her desktop and called for the person to come in. It was Jim, her partner on the White divorce case. She told him good morning and they went through the pleasantries of typical office greetings.

"You did well in litigation on Monday, Andrea, really well. I wanted to make sure you knew that. You are extremely articulate, and you don't miss a beat, you

15

have what it takes to keep growing in this firm," he said with an honest tone.

"Wow, Jim, thanks. I've worked really hard, and that means a lot to me. You've been a great mentor."

"Glad to hear it," he smiled. "Look, I know things can get exhausting, but I need to make sure you're on board one hundred percent of the time. I'm going to tell you this as a friend, okay? Not as some sort of warning, or anything like that. Just friend to friend, okay? Hell, it happens to all of us from time to time, our job gets rough," he started. Andrea's heart fluttered with anxiety.

"What...what is it Jim?"

"Last month, you missed a lot of work, and I get it, I really do, I've been there myself, but you have to be able to pull it together in this type of job. It's a dog-eat-dog world. I *want* you to succeed. You're my fighter. I'm putting you and Frank on the Carson case that's coming up, and that's a big one, but I need to make sure you don't have another—moment."

She knew he was referring to the bout of downtime she'd had several weeks ago. She'd taken some time off because she had found it physically and mentally impossible to function. Out of nowhere, she couldn't even get out of bed. She'd passed her cases on to other people, taken paid sick leave and stayed home in a state of utter fear and anxiety, spending most of her time under the covers of her bed. She was too down to even drink. Thinking about it bothered her and she pushed the memories quickly out of her mind, she was back up and running, ready for anything.

"Oh, Jim, I know. Look, I know how bad that must have seemed, but I'm past that. I'm ready for this. I've read up on the Carson case and I'm ready for it."

"Good, good. I'm glad you got the help you needed. I know it's a confidential thing, but that doctor I referred you to, Doctor Evanston, he's the best around. We all need to talk to someone, a professional someone, from time to time. Shit, I know I do. Especially with the things we see and deal with day to day."

"He was great, Jim, he helped me a lot. I can't thank you enough. I'm so excited about this opportunity on the Carson case and thanks for this, I appreciate you coming to talk to me like this," she said with her cunning and sweet smile, masking her pounding head.

"It's my pleasure. You're my go-getter," he said, standing up and straightening his suit. "I'll see you in the break room."

When the door closed, Andrea lay her head back down on her desk and closed her eyes. She'd never gone to Doctor Evanston and she never would. She didn't need a shrink trying to dissect her thoughts and problems. She could handle them on her own, like she always had, coming from nothing to something. Besides, she was smarter than they were anyway. Therapists were for other people, weak people, and white people on TV. Not her.

Cori

"Mr. Ellington, you're going to be fine. I listened to your lungs, I don't hear any wheezing, but if you want to go in for a CAT scan, we can have it arranged." Cori smiled gently at the older man. He was recently retired and was in great health. *Why doesn't he believe me? He's fine,* she thought to herself. And he was. He simply didn't have anything better to do but to feel old and sick.

"Maybe, maybe I will. Let me think about it, doc," Mr. Ellington said, leaving the examination room.

"I can have the nurse arrange the scan, and we will notify you of the date and time," she reminded him. Thinking to herself, she couldn't decide if he was second-guessing her, or if she was second guessing herself. She'd done everything she was supposed to do. She did everything by the book. Certainly, she wouldn't get a call that Mr. Ellington was hospitalized with pneumonia because she had missed something. She covered everything.

"He's healthy, he's just bored, anxious," she mumbled to herself as she collected her things to prepare to see her next patient. Checking her phone, she saw it was 1:00 already. *Thank goodness,* she thought, just four more hours.

She heard her nurse, Karla, knock on the door where she was lost in thought.

"Mrs. Yancy is here for her three month," Karla said, nodding her head to encourage Cori to go on to her. Ashley Yancy could be one of the most difficult patients. She'd talk too much, hold Cori back, and back up her schedule. She had a way of making the people around

18

her feel obligated to listen to her, as if anything she had to say was of the utmost importance, when in reality she could be talking about the behavior of her dog while walking it. One wouldn't realize it until after the conversation was over and time had disappeared. But she was also a loyal patient; always wanting Cori's opinion before starting a diet or exercise routine, touting Cori to be the best general practitioner in the area and bringing in a lot of business for her. Ashley's clandestine demanding demeanor could be stressful at times. Cori had to remind herself that she was the one in charge of the patient before she walked into the room.

She knocked and entered the room where Ashley sat, cross legged, on the end of the examination table. Her perfume filled the room with a sort of glorious stench of pretentiousness, and the red bottoms of her shoes indicated to Cori a sense of one-upping. Ashley was examining her manicure when she looked up to see Cori.

"Hey, doctor!" she chirped, smiling at Cori and flipping her overly-curled blonde hair over her shoulder.

"Ashley, how have you been? I see you're here for your three month—"

"Oh, yes. Oh my God, did you look at my chart yet? I gained five pounds. *Five* pounds!" Ashley interrupted, eyes wide with astonishment at her own words.

"I see that," Cori mused, going over the updated paperwork. "But what have you changed in your routine that you think caused that?"

Ashley shook her head. "I don't know. You know? I just don't know." She motioned with her hands almost as if she was fanning herself. "You know, Charlie, my husband, he has been gone a *lot*, lately. I mean, at first it was all business and I get that. I mean, he brings home the bacon and all and I never have to ask for a *thing*, the money is just there—but I started to feel really bad about myself, like he was maybe lyin' a little," she confessed, letting her southern accent break through her real-housewives of OC appearance.

Before Cori could question her on that, Ashley continued. "And once I get something in my head, I just can't shake it and I started stressin'. I started having a glass of wine every night. But then on those nights he was gone or worked late, it turned into two glasses or sometimes three. I know that's what's been doing it to me. It's all that sugar! And a girl like me, in my thirties, my metabolism just isn't the same. I have to work extra hard just to get those calories off—and it's not fair. You, know, in college, we used to have wine parties every Sunday and watch the new *Sex and the City* episodes— God that was a long time ago. It never made a dent, all that alcohol. My trainer doesn't know about the wine. He just keeps me working on the same routines. What do you think?"

"Well, Ashley, I get that you're stressed and with your husband being gone, wine can relax you, but I have you on, let's see..." she flipped through the chart to her medication, "...you're on a relatively high dose of diazepam as needed, and then we started 30 milligrams of Cymbalta six months ago for your pain and depression. I have to advise you not to drink while you're on these medications. When I took you off of the Klonopin last year, you weren't drinking then, were you?"

"Oh, Cori, you know how it is. I'd have one every now and then, but not every day," Ashley started.

"Yes, but the last time we saw each other you wanted to begin learning to cope with your anxiety in a more natural way. You told me you were going to start Barre classes and meditate. Drinking with these medications—it's really dangerous."

Ashley rolled her eyes playfully and smiled. "Okay, doc, you know best. I promise I will stop. TONIGHT!"

"You can start halving the diazepam tablets, as well, so that your body begins becoming less dependent on them," Cori instructed.

"Okay, I'll do that. But the other thing I really wanted to ask you about was Adderall."

Cori's eyes widened a little and she looked at Ashley, compelling her to finish her thought.

"My weight...I can't let it get out of control. I just, I can't," she cracked, putting her head in her hands. "I already have all this anxiety. If I start to get fat," her words choked a little bit more, "Charlie could leave me. He's already gone so much and making me worry, like I was telling you. And he's not that much older than me, he's still young enough to find someone.... I've seen the way other women look at him," her voice trailed off and she sniffed hard to try and stifle her crying.

"Adderall for your weight?" Cori asked. "Ashley, you gaining five pounds in three months, most likely due to your intake of alcohol, is not the reason to prescribe Adderall. I know some doctors prescribe it...."

Ashley cut her off again. "Yes! Look, if we're being honest, I used to take it in college and focus really hard before my exams, it basically saved me. I didn't really want to stress eat either while I was on it. Listen, I was at the Junior League meeting last night and an old friend of mine was telling me *her* doctor prescribed it to her and she'd lost 10 pounds in just a few months. She doesn't even want junk food, she just wants to focus on whatever it is she's doing. She is getting tons done; she is like the energizer bunny! It sounds perfect for me. I could focus more on what I have to do with the kids and at home, and I wouldn't worry about Charlie as much, hell, I may even focus more on him! And I wouldn't want to eat so damn much."

Cori took a deep breath. "Ashley, I know that Adderall can help people the way it helped your friend, but with your anxiety and the headaches you get, I just don't think it's a good fit for you. I have to think in your best interest," she glanced at the clock. They were already going over scheduled time.

"But…," Ashley began to protest.

"Adderall is essentially amphetamine salt…it's like legal speed, Ashley, that's why people don't eat and focus like machines when they're doing something. It's only to be given to people who have ADHD and have trouble concentrating. You don't have a diagnosis to warrant the meds Ashley. I can't…It's a controlled substance and regulated very closely."

"Look, Cori, I trust you, but I really, at the very least, want to *try* this. I don't want to have to go to another doctor to get their opinion. Meghan gave me her doctor's card, but *you're* my doctor," Ashley said, leaning in with expressive blue eyes that flashed wildly from the red veins around them from her crying.

Cori had a rush of thoughts hit her all at once. What if Ashley left and went to the other doctor? What if she took her friends with her? What if Ashley stopped coming altogether? It wouldn't kill Ashley if she took Adderall…it wouldn't really hurt at all. It wouldn't be the *best* thing for her, but neither were the benzos she'd been on for so long. Perhaps, thought Cori, Ashley was right. It might ease her mind to not eat when she felt anxious and be focused a little more on something else.

"Fine, Ashley, I'll put in a script for you to your pharmacy. It will be a one month supply, but you can*not* drink with this, do you understand? The side effects are horrible. You could get more headaches, your anxiety can spike, you can essentially blackout have no control over what you're doing.

"Ok but can I have three months? Just until my next appointment? Please doctor? Three months and no more."

"I will write it for 10 milligrams daily of Adderall; one prescription for each of the next three months but no more. Ashley, you need to understand that even social drinking with Adderall is impermissible."

Ashley nodded her head in agreement. "I won't, promise. When Charlie takes me to those social things for work, I'll just order club soda or something. No alcohol."

"Also, you can't take this with the diazepam regularly. You're going to need to take half a diazepam at night for two weeks, then quarter it for two weeks, then take a quarter every other night, until you're weaned off. You can call me if you feel that isn't working. Let me know if you have any questions. You have to call me if you feel like something is wrong in *any* way with these meds. I'm typing all of these instructions into the system and they'll print it out for you at reception."

Ashley nodded and pursed her lips.

Cori wrote out the prescription reluctantly and handed it to Ashley. "I'll see you in three months, take care. Remember, call the office and have them patch you through to me if you have any questions, let me know if you have any side effects."

"Bye, doc, you're the best, you're a life saver," Ashley said emphatically, strutting quickly out of the office to the front to check out.

Cori went to her office, knowing she was behind on patients, and thought about what just happened. She felt overwhelmed, like she'd just been through a whirlwind that swept her up and took her away from her true self. She felt her heart begin to pound in her chest and in her ears. She had gone against everything she knew, even what her gut was telling her, and given Ashley a stimulant—and Ashley had no diagnosable condition to warrant the need for *that* substance. What in the hell was she thinking? *Lots of doctors do it,* she told herself. But Ashley—she was so manipulative. She manipulated Cori into writing the script. It was like Ashley had come in and taken complete control of the entire situation. It didn't matter how much Cori said, or how much knowledge she spouted to Ashley, she caved and gave her drugs that she didn't need.

Cori felt lightheaded and put her hands in her heard while trying to slow her breathing. Karla knocked on her office door. "Jim Sherman cancelled, you've got an extra 15, but I just wanted you to know that it's a bit behind, so you might just want to take the next one," she said through the door.

"Thanks, Karla, I'll be right out," Cori said in a sweet tone. She didn't want Karla to think she was having a moment.

Taking a long breath to calm down, she looked at herself in the decorative mirror that hung in her office. Her dark, velvety complexion had just the right shine on it today. That new tinted moisturizer she bought was great, she thought. Her cheekbones were high and naturally highlighted and she admired them from both angles. But her nose. She looked at it more closely. *Good God, could my nostrils look any bigger today?* she thought. "Ugh, I'm going to have to start contouring. That'll take an hour out of my morning," she whispered to herself as she pushed the side of her nose in to see what it would look like if it were different. Ashley's poise earlier had set Cori off, too. She wanted to be *that* poised and confident all the time.

The rest of her day, she saw patients come in and out, treated them, checked them, prescribed things to them, and by five, after the last patient had left, she went to the reception area and just sat with Karla. The other staff members she employed left at 4:30 since it was Friday, and Karla was there, as the lead nurse, finishing charts and straightening up.

"Karla, what are you going to do tonight?" Cori asked, causally shifting back and forth in the receptionist's rolling chair.

"Funny you ask! I have to get home and cook, my boo's birthday is today and his mom and them are coming...I have to prove to her I can make *arroz con pollo* the same way she does. I mean, it's basically an imaginary pissing contest. If I can't cook, it doesn't matter how many degrees I have."

Cori laughed out loud and leaned back. "Oh my, and so the fact that you're a registered RN working on becoming a nurse practitioner isn't good enough?"

"For this woman? No. Hell, she'd prefer me to be home, if we were married, having kids and making food all damn day. I don't have time for that! I can cook, I always had to for my little brothers when I was growing up. But now, I've got a career, a life! I mean, thanks to you, too. You've helped me so much, I don't think I would have even gone back to start the nurse practitioner program if it wasn't for you," Karla said with a big sigh, getting her purse together to leave.

"Well, it's because I knew you could do it. It's not all that different than med school, if you ever decide on that. You've got what it takes."

"I don't know what I'd do without you, Cori. When I told his family what I do, they seriously looked at me and

25

said that back where they came from, it would be useless because they had their babies at home and they had a local shaman. I'm not kidding," she sighed. "I'm gonna head out, I have an entire traditional Mexican meal to prepare with a smile," she quipped sarcastically.

Cori knew Karla was waiting on a ring, too. Karla had been dating her boyfriend for two years and they practically lived together at that point. She knew Karla deserved a good husband and a happy family.

Cori and her husband Stephen met in college. Stephen was a very successful CPA. He was a few years older than Cori, which she once thought made him very mature. He had always been supportive of her; late nights studying while she was in med school, long hours at the office while she worked to build her private practice. They remained close through all that, even now with her recent detachment, he never questioned it. He let Cori be herself truly and completely. She smiled thinking of him as she went to gather her things from her office.

Sitting in her car, she turned the heated seat on to warm her. It was a bit chilly outside, but mostly she liked how it relaxed her back. She pulled out of the garage where her practice was housed and decided to take the side roads home. She could already see the back up on the freeway. The sound of sirens started to crescendo into her ears as they approached the ramp onto the freeway.

"A wreck, that explains it," Cori said to herself as she glanced at the stagnant traffic on the elevated freeway. She went underneath it to take all of the side streets home. A few red-lights certainly beat sitting in a parking lot on a freeway any day.

Cori let her mind wander towards those familiar yet blackened waters of the mind in which she couldn't swim. Her mind seemed to jump there involuntarily with a sharp reminder, like the sound of the service vehicles frantically trying to get to the accident.

How had her brother suffered, she wondered, when he died in his car accident? It had been a little over a year. Her brother, her sweet baby brother, Benjamin, had been hit by a drunk driver. They said he was killed instantly, but Cori, as a doctor and as the family member who went to identify him, thought too much about what all could have transpired.

He had to have known, he saw it coming, she thought as she sat at a red light. She thought of the drunk driver. He had survived...probably didn't feel a thing when he was slung out of his windshield. But Benjamin—sweet Benjamin and his wife, Jaimie, they had to have felt everything. She couldn't get images out of her head. It was something no one should ever see. It didn't matter how many cadavers she had seen and cut into in med school, identifying her brother was the worst thing that had ever happened to her. He was unrecognizable in the face, a distorted version of a human. She closed her eyes and winced. A car behind her honked, shaking her thoughts and making her jump. The light had turned green and she was just sitting there. She stepped on the gas pedal a little too hard and made her car thrust forward. Her thoughts still tarried. Jaimie had been life-flighted to the nearest hospital, but she didn't make it. Internal bleeding from the impact had killed her. Why do I continue to relive this over and over, she thought? As tears streamed down her face. "They're with God, now, Cori," she reminded herself. It was through her faith that she comforted herself the best.

She parked the car without going into the garage. All she had to do was push the button, but she didn't want anyone to hear the sound of it opening. She just needed a few more minutes alone. Her heart began to pound again. This time the more she tried to breath the more the pounding increased. "Please, Lord, let me go in and let me get through this evening," she prayed. She felt so apprehensive about going inside. Stephen was home with the kids—Benjamin and Jaimie's kids. Cori had taken them after the accident. It was what seemed right. She was the aunt, her mom was getting older and Cori and Stephen hadn't had any children of their own yet because they were so career-driven. Cori was 37, she was still young enough, but now that she had Anthony James, or A.J., as he was called, and Alexis, sweetly nicknamed Lexi, and she didn't want to try and have her own. She was their mom, now.

She opened the front door and was greeted by Stephen, who was sitting with A.J. on the sofa, helping him with his homework. He was still just a baby to them. At seven he was a sweet, smiling, angel. They both looked up at her and smiled.

"Hey Aunti Cori!" A.J. grinned. "You're finally home!"

"Hey babe, what took you so long, it's a half past six?" Stephen asked, but he wasn't overly concerned.

"Yeah, there were a few late patients, I was talking to Karla afterward, then there was a—" she paused and looked at A.J., "there was a lot of stalled traffic on the freeway, I took the back roads home."

"Well, no worries, I ordered Chinese for us. I figured it's Friday, we made it to the weekend, who wants to cook?" Stephen laughed.

"I got sweet and sour chicken!" A.J. grinned, showing an adorable smile with his front teeth peeping through in the gaps from baby teeth had fallen out.

"Where's Lexi?" Cori asked, feeling she already knew the answer.

"She's in her room, she said she's not hungry," A.J. responded promptly. He loved to be the one to give any news, good or bad, about his sister.

Cori looked at Stephen, searching his face for any clue of what might have transpired before she got home. Alexis didn't respond well to anything. Cori felt her heart in her throat as she considered going into Alexis' room to talk to her. She just didn't know if she could handle her today; but she had to. *"Who else will do it if I don't?"* Cori asked herself, which was her go-to pep talk to herself to motivate her to do those things that caused her to choke on her own breath. There was no sign from Stephen of anything in particular having transpired prior to her arrival, so Cori forced herself down the hall and knocked on the door.

She heard Alexis approach it and open it, without a word, returning to her bed fit for a pre-teen princess. Alexis plopped back down on her neatly made bed with her tablet, not making eye contact with Cori and unpausing a YouTube video that was playing entirely too loud.

"A.J. said you weren't hungry; did you order anything?" Cori asked over the sound of the video, making sure her tone was sweet.

Alexis sighed and without lifting her eyes from the screen, spoke starkly. "Why would I order anything if I'm not hungry?"

Cori blinked hard and thought for a brief moment about how to react. She didn't want to jump down Alexis' throat, but she wouldn't have ever been allowed to talk to adults like that. Then she was pulled back and forth with the concept of loss and the psychological trauma Alexis had experienced. She reacted softly.

"Honey, I just wanted to make sure you had something to eat. You need to eat a good dinner. Let me know if you're hungry, you can have some of mine," Cori said, then she turned and left the room, barely making a sound with her steps on the soft carpet.

"Stephen, did you order Lexi anything?" Cori asked as she rummaged through the brown paper takeout bag for her box of General Tso's chicken, her favorite.

"Yeah, I got her the usual, I put it in the fridge for later. She didn't want to eat," he said, clicking on the large television mounted on the wall. He didn't seem phased by her behavior. He didn't seem to find it odd. Cori wished she knew if he thought something was wrong with Alexis.

Cori didn't understand how Stephen did it—how he could be so cool, calm and collected about everything all of the time. She could feel tears wanting to pour from her eyes, and an overwhelming sense of dread take over. It wasn't that big of a deal, though. She knew it. She knew that she shouldn't be panicking over Alexis and her attitude. Alexis was going through something, Cori had known it would be a challenge from the first day. She felt if she tried to speak, she would only be able to cry. The crying wouldn't bring her relief though, it would only make everything that more complicated. A.J. would see her cry and be confused, Alexis would roll her eyes and think it was pathetic, Stephen would tell her everything would be alright and pat her back to calmness. But would it? Would everything really be alright? Cori took her food and without putting it on a plate, opened it and began eating almost voraciously. She didn't realize how hungry she was. She took large bites and remained standing at the counter as she ate. She could see Stephen and A.J. from the kitchen; the house was a large, modern, open concept design, and she hoped they wouldn't turn around and see her stuffing food in her mouth. No, she only wanted to eat and get ready for bed. It was only almost seven, but she was ready to lay down and read.

She looked down at her mostly-eaten box of food. She realized no one else had eaten yet. They'd been waiting on her. "Oh, God, guys, I'm sorry," Cori mumbled. "You were waiting on me to come home, I just realized. I just started eating...I'm so sorry," she said hurriedly and started putting A.J. and Stephen's food on plates for them and setting them at the table in the kitchen nook.

Stephen laughed a little, and made a little joke about how hungry Cori must have been, comparing her to some animal. Cori didn't really hear it, but she knew it wasn't malicious towards her, he only meant to make A.J. giggle, and A.J. did. She was focused only on getting the food set nicely. They sat down at the round table together and began eating. Cori's guilt consumed her. She felt so awful for having started eating without them. Her internal dialogue scolded and scolded, relentlessly reminding Cori of how careless she was being.

"How was your day?" Stephen asked in between bites. They had always been able to talk. Cori could actually say she'd married her best friend. They got along very well considering. She told him everything, but at times questioned if he did the same. Now the lump in her throat seemed to prohibit her; it filtered her ability to communicate thoroughly.

"It was...it was good. Yeah. I had a full day with patients. It went by quickly," she replied, blowing her next bite of food to cool it, although it wasn't hot since she'd opened hers before everyone else's.

"Good, glad to know you're keeping them booked, well, hopefully just for checkups," Stephen smiled, "I don't want people to actually be sick," he finished.

"They weren't. For the most part. Most of my patients have minor illnesses, or they're coming in routinely to get refills on their medications or flu shots. I had one man, an older man, I think he's been googling his symptoms too much...it was almost like he *wanted* to be sick," Cori thought out loud.

A.J. laughed. "Who wants to be sick?"

Cori chuckled, swallowing a bite. "It's not that they really *want* to be sick, it's just that they feel something is really wrong with them, if their tummy hurts or their chest hurts, they think it might be more serious than it actually is," she explained to him.

"What if they are, though?" Stephen mused.

Cori looked up at him, lifting her eyebrows a little, wanting him to finish his thought.

"What if someone comes in with, say, a chest pain, you check them out, then you send them on their way because you didn't find anything—but they have something else wrong, something you couldn't detect?" he asked.

Cori felt suddenly challenged in some way. Sudden irritation poured into her body, making her head tingle and become hot. She replied defensively. "Well I don't take their symptoms lightly. If I think a patient needs an X-ray or an MRI, anything, I send them for one. I am not careless you know. I just mean that some of these patients come in already having diagnosed themselves with something from reading about it on the internet, then it becomes psychosomatic, they create their own symptoms. A patient might not have even thought they had a tingle down their arm until they read about it, then they begin making themselves feel that way. It happens all the time." She felt like she'd just given a statement of defense.

Stephen didn't seem to notice. "Oh, well, that's good that you don't have too many of those, babe. I can't imagine dealing with people coming to my office and telling me they already know everything about their taxes," he said, getting up to get a beer out of the refrigerator. "Well, sometimes they do, but a few tax-jargon words from me and they shut up about it and listen."

"You're drinking tonight?" Cori asked, but making more of a judgmental observation.

"It's a beer that I definitely earned today. I've been looking at numbers all day, and having to tell these kids straight out of college to get their ass in gear, the firm doesn't hire just anyone. It's like they take it for granted. They were given this great opportunity for a paid internship and they act like they deserve an award just for showing up."

Cori nodded, and didn't make eye contact. She really didn't understand why he needed to drink every night. This earned beer of which he spoke was something that he seemingly awarded himself every night. She had really come to despise drinking. Her parents hadn't been drinkers, and so she never really drink either. She tried in college, and it always resulted in her being hungover and feeling horrible anxiety the next day. It made her dislike everything about it, and by default, dislike the idea of her own husband feeling it was some sort of pleasure.

"Oh, that reminds me," Stephen interrupted her intrusion of thoughts. "The firm is having the annual fundraiser gala Saturday night. We have a good table, with the Smiths, you remember them, right? Bob, he's a little older, and his new wife Angie, a few other people will be at the table, I can't remember who all Bob mentioned."

"Aunti Cori, can I have more juice?" A.J. asked, giving Cori time to process everything her husband had just said. She smiled in the affirmative and took his glass, walking over to the refrigerator to pour more juice for him. She hadn't remembered the fundraiser. It was around the same time every year... with the same people, and the same questions, and the same dreadful pretentiousness. This year would be worse, people knew about their situation—her brother.

"Why don't I just stay home with the kids?" Cori suggested, handing A.J. his juice.

Stephen furrowed his brows and looked at her. "You're joking, right? I gotta have you there, by my side. My beautiful, successful wife. I'm the doctor's husband, after all. You have upgraded me and I want to prove it!"

Cori forced a small smile, curling her lips ever so slightly. "I know babe, it's just that the kids...we don't have a sitter."

"I talked to Ed from across the street. His daughter, Vanessa, she's 15. You've met her, right?"

Cori nodded yes, swallowing her water.

"Vanessa can do it. Fifteen dollars an hour. Not bad for a teenager. So, we pay her about 75 dollars, leave her some pizza money, and we've got a good date set up!" he said with his smooth tone and a wink at her. He was obviously excited about the event. He had worked out all of the details. He loved getting dressed up and going out on the town with Cori. She could see his eyes sparkle with his visions of how the night would be for them. Cori couldn't think of other excuses to get out of it. She'd just have to go. She had a few days to prepare, at the very least.

Sophie

Sophie blew her nose hard and took a good, long look at her face in the mirror. Her eyes were swollen, effacing her eyelashes from her face, and her lips were puffy, but not in a pouty, sexy way. She looked like she'd been in a prize fight. Her normally golden complexion was almost jaundice-like with red rimming her nose and eyes from the crying. Dark circles colored the skin beneath her eyes giving her a sickly, perpetually exhausted look. She turned on the cold water and cupped her hands in it, letting it fill up and overflow. She dipped her face down into it, her nose gently blowing out air bubbles.

Taking a towel from the cabinet in her bathroom, Sophie gently dabbed her face dry, making sure not to rub it. She didn't need to look any more miserable than she already did. She dug through her drawer for her face cream and applied it gently, taking care to cool off the puffs underneath her eyes, hoping they'd subside, and possibly lighten the appearance of the purplish circles before Will got home.

If he sees me like this again today, God knows what he'll say, she thought to herself, wanting to be able to snap her fingers and look normal again. She saw no point in putting on a full face of makeup, and she also didn't see the value in using her expensive makeup during the day when she really didn't have anywhere to go. If she ran out, she'd just have to ask Will—or even worse—her mother, for a shopping trip. She had on a pair yoga pants from last year, but they were just a bit too tight around her waist. Her baby weight wasn't shedding so easily—but she wasn't really trying either.

She didn't feel that she could. Her pregnancy had been a mess. She'd put on much more weight than she expected, and she had twins to boot. The bedrest that had been enforced upon her had broken all of her good health habits and she lost most, if not all of her motivation to get them back. The only thing that would remind her of the need to recover what she had lost in herself were moments like this...moments where she felt insecure and none of her clothes seemed to fit in a flattering way. It was symbolic of how nothing in her life seemed to fit in a flattering way. She pulled down her sweatshirt and examined herself in the mirror, knowing he'd be home soon. She wanted to be able to pull off that flawless, carefree yet still sexy yoga-mom look, but it wasn't working out for her. It had never worked out for her after she'd had the twins. Each day seemed to drag her down a little more, into a depth of recurring self-judgment.

Her phone buzzed, and she checked it immediately. It was a message from her mother.

"Sophia, call me. We need to have lunch this week," it read. It was more of a command than an invitation. Sophie's mother, Cordelia, was the epitome of perfection. Although worlds different from each other, Cordelia and Will had much in common when it came to Sophie and judging her. The difference was that they also judged each other harshly and Sophie was perpetually stuck in the middle refereeing.

Cordelia never called Sophie by her short name, it was always Sophia, and Sophie was always reminded that her name meant wisdom, and that she had ironically never used any of it. She had wasted everything that had been handed to her on a silver platter for love, and she'd flushed down a perfectly good career to stay home and raise her children, just as her husband wanted.

Cordelia saw it as a true waste of a life that had so much potential. She threw it out for love, and to Cordelia, love was merely a notion that had no real value beyond companionship and loyalty. Those who believed they were in love, in her eyes, were young and inexperienced, incapable of understanding the rationality of true companionship.

It was all true, except for the part about wisdom. Sophie wasn't inept, she simply had made different choices than her mother had wanted. Cordelia had felt that since Sophie was able to rise up and attend Princeton, of all universities, and acquire a degree in Architecture, and be offered a position in an extremely respectable firm, just to have to resign to have children, Sophie was out of her mind. Her father, dominate in her life up until her choice for a husband, barely spoke to her. He had been such a stable and important figure to her and she'd always been daddy's girl, doing everything in her power to please him, but now he barely acknowledged her. He had, of course, helped Sophie rise up through the ranks to acquire her degree, outperform her peers and be able to work in such a prestigious architecture firm. He had been proud of his ability to help her rise.

But Sophie didn't think she had risen up; it had all been laid out for her. Her father was a respected attorney, a white man with a suit, and her mother a perfectionist African American lady, who had the taste of a queen and the demeanor of an evil step mother. Sophie was always held to a higher standard than everyone she knew—even the other wealthy children at the private school she attended while growing up. She didn't choose Princeton because *she* wanted to go to school there, her mother had chosen it long before and had prepared everything for her. Her paternal grandfather had gone to Princeton, so Cordelia felt it was only natural that Sophie attend as well, and continue the family tradition, even though her own father had chosen to study elsewhere—something that had embedded itself underneath Cordelia's skin about Sophie's father.

Noise distracted Sophie from her self-deprecating thoughts, and Will came through the door, covered in dust and dirt from a day's work as the foreman at a construction site. He slid his dirty pants off and left them near the front door, mindlessly. Sophie went to fetch them and admired him. The man knew how to work with his hands and he was good at it. In their early days of dating, they joked that Sophie would design the buildings and he would build them. Now he was just building, and Sophie was home.

"Hey baby, what's for dinner?" he asked immediately, without hesitation to ask after her or what she'd done that day—which had been essentially nothing of great importance—at least not to her. She didn't think he wanted to hear about meals, snacks, walks in the park or diaper changes.

"I thought I'd make those Thai noodles you like, and then cook some fish to go with them," she said, picking up little toys and putting them away, looking around and noticing she hadn't put much of a dent in cleaning for the day.

Will's expression changed from enthusiastic to somewhat flat.

"Fish," he murmured.

"Well, yes, unless you want this ass to keep getting bigger," she joked. "We said we'd start eating healthier…I need to, at least," she said, making her way to the kitchen with him. He started scrolling through his phone, most likely checking his messages and checking his social media now that his hands were clean.

"Well, baby, I don't know about you, but I got my workout today on site. It was so damn hot with the sun out... I did some heavy lifting," he smiled, revealing his movie star grin and flexing his bicep to be funny. It didn't make Sophie laugh, but she forced a slight smile. She was exhausted of thinking about her imperfections. He still had the body of his youth. Having grown into it in his thirties, he was well built, with a broad, muscular chest, abs, and a muscular rear that would have any woman take a second look when he walked by. He was perfectly fit.

He straightened his posture and looked at her. "Can't I have some fried chicken to go with my noodles? Or can you batter the fish? I just want to feel full after I'm done eating," he declared, then went back to scrolling through his phone.

Sophie was immediately put off by him. Usually able to make him laugh and say something witty, Sophie was at a loss. She felt the knot in her throat and the tears well up in her eyes. She wanted to run off and cry—cry hard. But she couldn't. She had been crying enough already. He hadn't noticed the puffs around her eyes this time, but she feared him seeing her emotional would set off a storm of words.

"Sure—sure...," she stuttered a little, her pretty eyes fluttering. She didn't want to make two meals. She didn't want to eat anything fried. Losing weight wasn't going to happen if she ate like that. Will had absolutely no regard for the needs of her physique. She knew Will's family ate like that almost every day. He had grown up in a traditional Black family where his mom fried everything, cooked the beans with large chunks of ham hocks and it was all delicious, but terribly

39

unhealthy. His father had died of heart complications just two years earlier. Will was lucky, he got enough physical exertion along with his typical workouts to be in excellent shape. He could eat whatever he wanted. He didn't understand why Sophie didn't want to cook that way, and he didn't understand why she really didn't want to make two separate meals for them. To him, it was completely abnormal that she'd been home all day and didn't have a meal waiting for him, set and ready to go.

She threw the idea of the noodles out of her mind. "How about I put on some green beans and make some breaded chicken, and I'll make some mashed potatoes," she offered.

His eyes lit up a bit, but his words crushed the moment. "It's not ready? I mean it's almost six. I was really hoping it would already be ready when I got here. I'm starving."

Sophie panicked internally for a moment. He didn't seem to follow that she didn't have anything ready, she had just been talking about making noodles. His distraction was annoying. She hadn't planned dinner, hadn't thought much about it at all. Now the potatoes would take over an hour to make, the beans needed to simmer in the bacon she had, the chicken needed to be breaded and that would take some prep time. *Oh shit,* Sophie bit her lip, the chicken was frozen.

"I can have dinner by seven," Sophie said apologetically. Will looked at her with an expression of dissatisfaction, and went to go play with the twins, who had been quietly watching TV and eating baby-food snack crackers from a large bowl Sophie had given them earlier when she felt her meltdown encroaching.

He disappeared from her sight to the next room where the kids were. The house wasn't a modern one with the open concept Sophie wanted. It would be nice

40

to be able to peek over the stove as she cooked and see the kids. No, this house had been built in the fifties and although it was in a lovely, quaint little neighborhood, it wasn't remodeled, and each room was separate from the other, creating walls and a maze to walk through to find where the twins might have toddled off to. It was not the style of home in which Sophie had been raised, but she was content. The school district was great—one of the best around. She wouldn't have to worry about a private school or tutors. They had easy access to everything in the city, and their neighbors were all old-timers who had owned homes there for years. They could afford the home on Will's salary, and it was a pleasant, original place to be, unlike some of the newer neighborhoods where developers put as much clunky house on the land as they could, leaving little yard space and a proximity so close to one's neighbor that one could practically reach out from an open window and knock on the neighbor's wall.

She started running the chicken under hot water and scrubbing the potatoes, getting all of the dirt off of them. Then there were the beans. She didn't have any fresh or frozen ones; she'd have to use canned beans. They were organic, at the very least, she thought that would offset something about the disaster she had created by simply not planning ahead for dinner. She hadn't ever had to think about it until she'd married Will. Her mother cooked occasionally, but they also had someone come in and cook every so often, plus they frequently ate out. She had never had to prepare her own food until college, and even then, she ate out most of the time. Dating Will, they went out a lot, and it wasn't until they'd actually moved in together had she had to learn how to prepare full meals.

Cooking had been a trial by error experiment for her. She used recipes and watched YouTube videos on how to properly do things, but she often times made a horrible mess of all of it. The first time she tried to make lasagna, there was absolutely no layering to it. It was just a mess of ingredients sloppily dumped together in a casserole dish, and Will had awkwardly tried to eat it, but she could still vividly remember scraping his uneaten portions into the trash. She had felt like such a letdown.

She sang to herself quietly while she began boiling the potatoes and beans. She took bacon and sliced it into little chunks to add to the green beans. She may not have had ham hocks on hand, but at the very least, the bacon would give some extra flavor. She seasoned them with salt and pepper. The chicken was slowly beginning to thaw and she shut the water off to let the cutlets sit in a bowl of hot water for a moment as she prepared little bowls of flower, egg and cracker crumbles for the breading.

"Sophie, the kids, babe...," Will snapped her to attention from her quiet singing as she worked.

"What is it?" she asked, washing her hands off.

"They dumped those cracker things everywhere in the living room. They're all squashed into the carpet. Jaylen's diaper is overloaded. Javion was trying to change the channel on the TV, but his hands were covered in like, goo I guess, from the crackers and slobber and it's all over the damn screen."

Sophie dried her hands and looked at him, almost blankly. Did he realize, she wondered, that she couldn't cook and keep an eye on them at the same time? Her mind started racing, she'd have to vacuum, then get out the wipe spray for the LED screen and clean it properly. Maybe have to scrub the carpet a little depending on how bad the mess was. She walked past Will, who was holding Javion, and went to change Jaylen's diaper.

It was filled to the brim. She hadn't realized it and felt horrible. She repeated the mantra she always repeated to herself when she was cleaning up their biggest of baby messes. *No one else is going to do it for them, it's only me. If I don't do it, nobody else will.* She said this to herself in a caring tone, knowing they were just sweet, helpless babies who needed her. She cleaned up Jaylen and cooed at him, listening to his two-year old babble as she chattered at him. She evaluated the mess on the floor. It was just as bad as she imagined. She ran to the bathroom and got a towel and a cup of warm water. She shuffled back into the room and began pouring the water onto the chunks of goo and crumbs smashed into the carpet. Jaylen started crying. Sophie felt herself pushing the towel more rapidly into the carpet, in pressing back and forth motions. She just wanted to go back to the bathroom and close the door. Jaylen got louder. He mumbled something about being "stirtee" and she knew she'd have to make him a sippy cup. Then she thought of the kitchen. She'd left everything sitting out. It had only been a few minutes, but it had already put dinner behind schedule.

"Hold on baby, mommy's cleaning the carpet," she said in a forced tone of sweetness.

After tossing the towels back into the laundry hamper in the bathroom, she grabbed the vacuum out of the hall closet and began sucking up all of the crumbs and other little pieces of debris that had been sitting on the floor for more than a week. Things rattled and snapped into the chamber of the vacuum as she went over the carpet, trying to make linear patterns that looked professional and nice. Glancing at the TV, Sophie realized it truly *was* smeared with the paste they had managed to make out of the baby crackers. She stopped vacuuming and went to retrieve the spray and the wipes from the kitchen. Will had taken Javion to the bedroom, she could hear them down the hall. She sprayed the screen and started wiping, making the whole TV shake as it wobbled on its stand. Jaylen protested for her attention, his pitch becoming louder with irritations as he demanded his drink. Sophie could feel her tears returning, but she forced them back. She swiped the screen one more time to get the last mark off and went back to the kitchen, all the while muttering in her light, fluttery mommy voice that she was getting Jaylen his drink.

She opened the refrigerator for apple juice. There was about half a cup left in the bottle. She needed to go to the store. She hadn't done that during the day either. She despised going to the store. It was another thing she'd never really had to do. When she and Will first got married, she didn't mind going with him because they did it as a couple. Then slowly, he distanced himself from those types of outings and left it all to Sophie, who sometimes simply didn't know what to buy, and definitely didn't know how to budget, so, she avoided it since going was an anxiety attack waiting to happen.

She poured the last bit of juice into the cup and added a splash of water to make its contents seem more acceptable for Jaylen. It would be better for his teeth, too, she noted, justifying the dilution of flavor. Handing it to him, she whipped back around and began breading the chicken, which hadn't quite fully thawed. The beans were fine, she put them on a low heat to simmer. Taking a knife, she sliced into a potato to see how cooked they were—not nearly cooked enough; the knife wouldn't even go all the way through the potato. Cursing the whole situation in her mind, she continued to bread the chicken, pouring olive oil into a pan to fry it in.

Jaylen had realized his juice didn't taste quite right and waddled into the kitchen, holding up his sippy cup in a motion of objection. His toddler jabber was hit or miss from one word to the next, but he made it quite clear to Sophie that he was displeased with the flavor. She told him that she'd fix it and took the sippy cup to the refrigerator, pretending to do something to the drink, hoping that she could give him a dose of the placebo effect to make him believe the drink was different. He took the cup eagerly, sipped it, and then threw it on the ground. Sophie disregarded it. She couldn't deal with the dinner, Jaylen's juice, a tantrum and her overall sense of being overwhelmed all at the same time. Putting the first piece of chicken cutlet into the oil, she jumped back as it popped and hissed. Her arm already had a grease burn scar on her dainty, creamy café ou lait complexion and she didn't intend on getting any more. Returning to the potatoes, she made sure they were boiling on high and put a lid on them. Cheese, milk and butter were then pulled from the refrigerator to add to the potatoes once they were soft enough. Lining up all of the ingredients, she made a mental note of the items she needed from the store.

Will walked into the kitchen and stepped on the sippy cup, which was just a snap on lid. It popped off and sent juice all over the floor. Sophie gasped in frustration and grabbed a wad of paper towels to wipe it up.

"What in the hell was that doing there?" Will barked.

"Jaylen threw it down," Sophie said from her crouched position on the floor.

"Why?"

"I don't know. He didn't like it. I added some water to the juice to make it better for his teeth…they both drink

45

too much sugar, they're used to that now and they don't want what's better for them," she said begrudgingly. Will had been the one to give them sugary juice in the first place. He'd let them try soda, too. She didn't want them to be sugar addicted little ADHD brats, but that seemed to be his secret plan. He wasn't the one who stayed home with them all day, so how would he know anything about what was good for them? He just got to come home and be the fun dad. Sophie had to do all of the dirty work.

"Well don't yell at me, I'm not the one who left it in the middle of the floor," Will said, leaning back on the counter as Sophie finished wiping up the mess.

"I wasn't yelling, I was just telling you...," she let her words trail off. It didn't seem to make a dent.

"Dinner almost ready?" he asked, sniffing around the pots.

"No. I'm still working on it."

"It's almost seven."

"I know, I'm busy."

"But you had all day...."

"I didn't know what you wanted," Sophie turned from the trash disposal and snapped, this time with a quivering voice.

"What were you doing? Talking on the phone? Watching TV?"

She froze, upset that he'd think she'd just sit and do nothing.

He saw her eyes well up with water, but he didn't say a word. He didn't understand why she was so upset. She got to do what every woman wanted to do, he figured. Stay home and raise the babies. He did everything he could so that they didn't want for anything. He despised crying. It was a sign of weakness to him and anytime he saw anyone cry, something inside of him

46

felt twisted and awkward, and he just couldn't be around them.

"Well don't cry," he said, almost mockingly.

"I'm not," Sophie sniffed.

"Then what is wrong," he asked as if he was talking to a child.

"Nothing, nothing. I'm just trying to get this cooked as fast as I can. Can you watch the boys? They're going to get into something. I can't watch them and cook three things at the same time," she said.

"Well, my mom did it. There was me, Tommy and Denise. We're all just a few years apart. She did it every day," he said. He didn't realize what the words coming out of his mouth conveyed to Sophie.

Sophie's blood boiled. She wasn't his mother. She wasn't a house wife like that. She was never really meant to be one. It wasn't how she was raised. She was doing her best, but that wasn't ever seen. He was so casual about it, too, as if his words would somehow motivate her. Instead, they shrunk her desire to be the perfect stay at home mom into a wad of resentment. She just looked at him with wide eyes that slowly watered. She didn't speak because she knew intrinsically that anything she had to say would be negative, and if she began saying negative things about his mother or his upbringing, it would only lead to an argument and hateful words between them. So, her tears began to drip, as each one represented a different argument she wanted to make but just couldn't. Then some of the tears represented a pure emptiness—one that she couldn't quite define but knew was there.

Will saw her and only knew that she was crying again, and he couldn't pinpoint why. But his upbringing and his natural disposition toward tears didn't allow for him to feel any emotion towards it. His mother had never cried in front of him. She had never once shown she was hurt or that she was in anyway weak towards anyone's words. For this reason, Will looked at Sophie with a somewhat confused expression that Sophie only interpreted as horrible and wicked of him. There was no pity in his eyes. It wasn't that she wanted to *be* pitied, she wanted him to simply *care*. Even if Will did care and wanted to help, he didn't know how to begin. He had no experience comforting a crying woman and he certainly had never lived with one.

Sophie hadn't even been like this until recently. She had always been upbeat, fun, and ready to go out with him anywhere. They were both beautiful people that lit up a room. When they walked into any place, a restaurant, or a party with friends, people immediately noticed and smiled at them either with admiration or a hint of envy for their façade of perfection. Now, Sophie couldn't cope with any of her emotions and she felt as if they were all coming at her at once. It was like being thrown a barrage of balls and trying to catch them all, but each one coming harder and faster.

She didn't feel as beautiful as she used to, and most of that resentment she put on Will. Never flamboyant, but always classy, Sophie was used to being the center of everyone's attention. As of lately, the more she festered on her imperfections, the more she blamed him. She had sacrificed her body for his children, and now he had no desire to at least support her in eating well enough to shed some weight. She knew her body was judged by his eyes so she didn't need him to verbally say a word. She had sacrificed a fine career to stay at home and raise his children, and for that he gave her no accolades. He acted as though it was a reward in and of itself. When she spoke to other mothers at the park or on play dates, she would try and touch base with the real world by talking about college or her former career and find that most women either hadn't finished their degree or felt no regrets at all in staying home with their kids. It was the battle that had been raging since people began openly talking about it.

"Oh, I wouldn't want anyone else raising my kid," a friend would say when the idea of working again came up.

Sophie would concur, but only because she was non-confrontational, and usually thought back on her own upbringing and how her mom had brought in a French tutor when she was 10 and left her alone with her to study with her during the days in the summer. People like that hadn't raised her; they'd educated her. As a child, Sophie was able to mix and mingle with adults and children alike and speak in English and French. When she was five and attended a premier private school, she remembered a teacher comforting her after she'd fallen and scraped her knee. What was wrong with that? These women seemed to think that there was something *wrong* with another person helping develop a child. Sophie would nod as they discussed such matters at the park or at birthday parties, but she didn't agree. None of these women seemed to understand the value of a cultured, varied upbringing. Now Sophie was stuck with them, categorized with them, and labeled as one of them. For this, she also blamed Will.

"I don't want some stranger changing their diapers," he had said when she'd brought up the idea of going back into the architecture firm.

In the beginning, she had tried to reason with him that it was completely normal, but he wouldn't hear anything about it. She was so in love, and so obsessed with proving to her mother that their love was real enough for her to dedicate herself to him, that she hadn't argued much more about it with him and she'd made the decision to go along with him and his ideal of a family. She had a vision in her mind of how they could be and how they *would* be, and that was the driving force behind her dedication to him. She wouldn't fail.

Now she found herself feeling overweight and in tears for just about any reason. She turned her attention back to frying the chicken. The pieces were browning nicely, and she stuck a meat thermometer in them to ensure they were thoroughly cooked. The potatoes were softening, and the water was evaporating, so she added milk, butter, salt, cream and cheese and began mashing them by hand with a masher, creating a delectable smooth buttery pot of potatoes. The beans were done and ready to be eaten. She began serving everything on plates, cutting up the chicken cutlets for the boys so they could eat them like finger food, as well as the long green beans.

That night, after she'd cleaned up dinner (which the twins had mainly pushed around and played with rather than eaten), bathed them and herself while Will went to the gym, and vacuumed and mopped, she curled up in bed beside Will and let her mind drift. She thought of how her life was before she got pregnant. She wasn't an extroverted person, but she had a small group of friends that she now felt she hardly saw. She wondered what they truly thought of her. She knew good friends would always understand everything, but doubt crept into her mind and it lagged there until she thought further about the plans she still had. She wanted to travel so badly. She hadn't been back to Europe since she was a teen and she wanted to go with Will and the kids so they could all experience it together. Will kept shooting the idea down, saying it was expensive and pointless, but she knew it wasn't. *I've completely lost myself,* she thought. She had lost the person she once was.

Will rolled over to her and touched her breast softly, indicating his intentions. In the dark, Sophie felt she could perform a little better, not worrying so much about her body. He began to kiss her on her neck and breasts, heating things up under the covers. Sophie began to feel uncomfortable, like she didn't want to be touched. The feeling snuck in slowly and she tried to fight it off. Will noticed it though, because she was laying there like a dead body. Without talking, he stopped, rolled over, and sighed heavily. Sophie knew she couldn't let him down. She rolled over to him and reached around his body, stroking his abs and pulling him to roll back over, which he did. She didn't feel like being the dominant one, her libido had essentially flat lined, but she could act, and so act she did. She pulled him on top of her, kissed him back, and forced him to go through all of the motions and do all of the work.

She felt mechanical, and without the actual desire to get into the act, she knew she couldn't orgasm. As much as she hated it, she knew she'd have to fake it, so she started in on the act of pretending to climax. She made gentle moaning sounds and grabbed him all over, acting like she was about to lose control of herself as he kept on, then she clenched his back tightly with her hands, digging her nails into him, and tightened her body, making herself shake gently, like she had just peaked and she was satisfied. *Did he buy it?* she wondered, looking at his silhouette in the darkness of the room. He seemed to, as he kept going, moaning and mumbling, moving her to her side so that he could finish. She felt good knowing that it would end soon, and that she could go to sleep without worrying about it anymore.

Vivian

Vivian clicked the end button to cut off the FaceTime session she'd just had with her daughter. It hadn't gone as well as she would have liked for it to go, but she wasn't quite sure precisely how it should have gone. There wasn't an instruction book for it. Her daughter was technically an adult, but she was still just a kid. Vivian felt that Carly didn't know what she was doing and that she wasn't taking her studies serious enough. She'd let her go to the University of Texas against her own motherly wishes of Rice University and had let Carly find out who she was. Just then, seeing her on FaceTime, Carly was showing her new blue hair and a bull nose piercing.

"It's cute, right?" Carly joked, shaking her shaggy bob of Smurf-looking hair at her camera. Vivian just smiled and said something that she now couldn't even recall... just something nice to placate her daughter and keep the peace. She knew how easy it was for Carly to get offended and disappear for days at a time without communicating, and that just wasn't acceptable for Vivian. That's not how she was brought up in her Vietnamese culture, and it wasn't how her and her husband had raised Carly or her brother, Joshua. They had raised them to be respectful, studious, and aware of both of their cultural heritages, but ever since the split between Vivian and her husband, just a few years prior, Carly had begun acting out. It was like the separation had opened up a door that Carly discovered, learning how to escape through it and test the limits of Vivian's self-control and trying to keep the attention of her father after he had run off with a younger, whiter girlfriend.

He had done the stereotypical break and run by finding a younger woman who was harshly made over, bleach blonde with fake breasts and a basic Louis Vuitton bag dangling from her arm at all times. Vivian knew it, and was deeply saddened by it, but Carly took it as a grand insult to not only her mother, but herself. This girlfriend of her father's, who was coincidently named Carlie but spelled with the "ie", was the quintessential mid-life crisis girlfriend. Carly being half Vietnamese and half white took it as an even harder hit because she just couldn't ever be what this girlfriend was, and she couldn't get the kind of attention her father was giving this woman at a time when she so desperately needed it, and to add insult to injury, they had the same name. She thought it was sick that her father could be with someone only slightly older than his own daughter and call her the same name.

Therefore, Vivian was left in the middle, tediously balancing emotions and outspoken rage between Carly and her growing hatred toward her father, Joshua and his senior year of high school studies, and an IT business that she'd grown with her husband from scratch that was now overwhelming her to the point she was ready to wash her hands of it all and sell. In order to sell, her husband, Michael would have to agree to it, too. Every time she thought about approaching the subject with him, she felt her chest grow tight and her heart speed up. She couldn't bring herself to dial the number. She froze until the feeling subsided, then found something else to do. She piddled in her car in the parking lot of a shopping center for a moment. She wanted desperately to call Carly back, and tell her that she loved her, and that she wanted her to come home and visit—it was just a two-and-a-half-hour drive—and that Carly could bring a friend if she wanted. She wanted Carly to know she was always welcome home and that Vivian was accepting and not judgmental mother...but too much had transpired in those delicate formative teen years right before Carly had chosen which college she wanted to attend and how she wanted to live her young adult life without Vivian hovering around.

Vivian had been heartbroken and cold for a while, and very harsh in judgment towards her children. She didn't have a problem with the University of Texas a whole, it was a Tier I school and one of George W. Bush's daughters had graduated from there. It was fine, but she had always wanted Carly to go to Rice and they'd gone to so many baseball games and other events when Carly was growing up that Vivian really didn't expect that Carly would have anything else in mind. Then she realized that Carly needed to get out of Houston, whether Vivian wanted her to or not. Vivian needed Carly but didn't realize how much of her own self-worth and value she had wrapped up into her children and how they behaved toward her. Carly was a part of how Vivian reflected upon herself. Now Carly was a wild thing, flying around her university, experimenting with friends and lifestyles, and going against everything with which Vivian was comfortable. Vivian couldn't help but feel conservative about certain things. She was 42 now, and some ideas just become ingrained within a person to the point that there is no changing of one's mind.

The difference now was that Vivian didn't have control, and Carly could do as she pleased, which gave Vivian moments where, like today, she couldn't breath and felt choked, and thought that maybe she was having a heart attack.

She ate well, exercised, and looked fantastic for her age and having had two young adult children, but she lost so much of herself in her split up with Michael that it didn't matter much to her if she looked like a model or a vagabond, she was out of sorts. And poor Joshua... he was lost in the mix. With the craziness of his sister, the madness of his father splitting up with his mother and dating a lady with the same name as his sister, he just shut himself out of it all and did whatever he had to do, keeping his head down and trying his best to stay out of everyone's business. He'd go to whichever college his parents wanted him to just so long as it kept everyone calm. Vivian appreciated him for that but knew that he was internally tortured to an extent. It was a painful existence for all of them—especially since Vivian and Michael weren't *actually* divorced, just separated. Texas had no legal "separation" of marriage like many states, so technically they were still married by law, by God, and by any other means that marriage made a difference in their lives like taxes. The other trouble was with the inquiries of people in general. All of their close friends realized they had split up, but none talked about it much. Many friends had chosen sides and would go out with Michael and Carlie to the hotspots in town, leaving Vivian cast aside and alone.

Vivian didn't date. Even if she'd wanted to, her own mother would have snapped her in half like a twig. It didn't matter how old Vivian was. Her mother, Ngoc, didn't come to Houston during the fall of Saigon, change her name to Nancy, and raise her family, spending her time in a nail salon while her husband ran a small restaurant just for Vivian to divorce and look dishonorable in the eyes of her parents and their friends before the divorce was final.

So, Vivian had to simply live by an imaginary honor code of what a mother should be and do, all the while watching as her husband was philandering around, parading his new mistress for all to see, making Vivian seem meek and easily manipulated. She knew her old friends would gossip about her, and about Carly and her lifestyle, too. But what could be done? It wasn't as if Vivian could call anyone she thought might be talking about her up and say, "I know what you're saying, and you can just come straight to me and ask me if you want to know something." No, that would be too rude, too outlandish. She'd been taught to be classy and quiet, and so she remained that way.

There was one good friend, Kathleen, who stood by Vivian's side regardless, and who would come over for a drink or meet her for a meal, and was always at Vivian's beckon call, especially if a situation arose where Vivian simply could not call her own mother and bring her into it. For instance, there was one particular day where Vivian had gone to the grocery store and run right into Michael and Carlie in the wine isle. She was mortified. They met eyes with one another and Carlie let out a snicker at the irony of seeing her there. Vivian looked at them with wide, horrified eyes and scurried off to the parking lot and into the safety of her car. If she had called her mother, Ngoc would have been a judgmental mess about the entire thing and possibly driven over there to confront Michael herself, feeling obligated to protect Vivian in such a horrific situation. She would've undoubtedly made a scene, and when Vivian stopped to think about it, the entire reason Michael met Carlie was partly Ngoc's fault.

Carlie had been a client at Ngoc's nail salon for many years, and Michael and Vivian had stopped by one day to visit. Michael noticed Carlie, tan and glowing, getting her nails refilled and approached the desk of the nail technician, asking about what she was doing to her long, plastic gemstone laced acrylic nails and how the science of it all worked—all a strange yet clever ploy to get closer to the beautiful young woman. Vivian hadn't noticed because she was choosing a nail color from the vast wall of selections, wanting a pedicure for herself. Ngoc had been oblivious and had introduced Michael to Carlie, going on and on about how Carlie, her mother and grandmother had been great customers for years.

Carlie mentioned she was looking for a position as a receptionist or some sort of job while she finished her degree in Finance, and Michael gave her his business card, his and *Vivian's* business card, under the ruse that she could interview for a position at their firm, and it had all unraveled from there. Thus, Ngoc felt she had every right to accost Michael and Carlie, who was no longer a customer at the salon, if she saw them in public flaunting their relationship. She often talked about what she would do if she saw them, much to Vivian's horror.

So, in times of extreme distress, Vivian called Kathleen, who was levelheaded and understood the dynamics of the entire situation in which Vivian was having to live. But now, she was feeling ill. It was an entirely different thing, new to her, and she thought about who would be best to tell. "Should I call her, or not?" Vivian asked herself. "She's probably home, and she likes taking care of me. It'll make her feel important," she thought of her mother.

She bent her head and looked down at her phone, scrolling through her contacts. Perhaps she would just call Joshua and see what he was doing. He would be home at that time anyway, and she could talk to him about something mundane to calm herself down. She FaceTimed him instead of calling. There was something soothing about seeing her children's faces instead of just talking or texting them.

The phone made its special ringing noise and Joshua answered. As far as she could see in the back ground, he was home and in their living room. His face smiled as he saw her, and she tried to mimic his face with the same genuine happiness. He asked her what she was doing and she began telling him she'd just talked to Carly and she wanted to know what he'd been doing.

"But when are you coming home? I'm hungry," Joshua said, almost child-like for an 18-year old. She'd made him too dependent on her. She hadn't meant to, it just happened that way. One child was a rebellious independent, and the other one wouldn't make a move without her. She thought for just a moment about things she could and probably should tell him to do, like make himself a sandwich or learn to cook eggs properly. But she didn't want to scold him, it brought up a fear inside of her that he wouldn't want to talk to her.

"I'm at the store, I'm about to go in, I can pick you something up. Do you want one of those sandwiches, the one with the chow chow?" she asked. He replied that he did and asked for a specific drink to go along with it. Now Vivian had to go inside, the same store where, ever since she had seen Michael and Carlie together, she had to work herself up to enter. She inhaled deeply, closed her eyes, and opened her car door, clenching her purse tightly and pulling her cap down over her eyes. She felt like she had to be in disguise just to shop. But what did *she* have to hide from? She hadn't done anything wrong. She had been the victim in all of this. Her mind rushed and she felt her stomach flutter as she approached the automatic doors and chose a small sized shopping cart. When she entered, she immediately began scanning the area with her eyes.

Michael was a tall man and had a head full of blondish-red hair. She could spot him if he was around. She acknowledged that he probably wasn't there and continued on with her shopping, but not without the debilitating paranoia that always remained in the back of her head.

Going straight to the sandwiches, she found the one Joshua requested and found the drink, too. After that, she went straight for the basics she needed and hurried to the checkout line, annoying other people with her fast steps and determined rush to get down isles and past people. She looked like she was an arrogant woman who had no time for courtesy. What no one around her realized was that it was taking every part of her being to even be in the store. She could feel her heart again and sweat began to make her palms feel disgusting. She nervously wiped them on the side of her yoga pants and proceeded to check out. Mindlessly ignoring the clerk and her attempts at friendly customer service, Vivian got her things and scurried out of the store and back to her car.

Once home, she ate some fruit and watched as Joshua happily ate his food. She'd done at least one thing well, she thought. Joshua was happy. He began telling her little things about his day, funny stories about friends and teachers. She smiled with him and then realized she needed to check the mail, which meant leaving the house again. She just didn't want to be outside. She didn't want to see anyone, for any reason. She started out the front door toward the mailbox.

Inside the box sat the letter she'd been dreading for some time. It was the letter that officially stated the sale of the business that she and Michael had owned together. They had a buyer. It was done. She stared at it in a bit of disbelief and had mixed emotions about the money she'd earn from it. It would be a lot—plenty to live off of. She could essentially retire at 42. Then she grew angry and resentful. Michael made the whole deal happen behind her back, without her. It was their joint company, so it should have been their joint business deal. She feared Michael was ripping her off or would find a way rip her off somehow. Scowling, she retreated back into the comfort of her home and slammed the door. Joshua looked at her a little strangely but continued eating and scrolling mindlessly through their Netflix account for something to watch.

Vivian passed by him without saying anything and closed the door to her bedroom. There, she crumbled to the floor with the papers and sobbed. This was where it really hurt. This was what they had built together, and if their business was dissolving—being sold off—then she knew what was coming next. There was no hope for reconciliation now, and she knew it. Next, she'd be served with divorce papers.

PART II

The Fallout

Andrea

Sitting in her car after a long day of litigation, Andrea thought about what to do. A week had passed, then another, and she'd been going out and returning home late each evening. She'd hired a woman to come and cook three times a week and look after Lilly once Daniel had gotten everyone home, and that had helped curtail many problems, at least in her mind. It was one less stress for Daniel, and no one would complain about there being no cooking, as the woman was a sweet, older woman named Silvia, a relative of her mother's friend, who had come from Mexico without papers.

She was too old to do strenuous work, and the pay was agreeable, so the position was a perfect fit. The food was authentic, and she genuinely cared about baby Lilly. Andrea didn't have to worry about Daniel flirting with her because she was so old. It was a win-win for everyone.

But now, Friday had come again, it was five in the afternoon, and Andrea didn't want to go home. She felt a rush of excitement pulse through her veins. She called Silvia, "¿Podrías hacerme un favor? Si ayudas a poner a los ninos a domir por favor?", asking if she could stay a little later and settle all of the kids down that evening, explaining that she had to work late and wouldn't be home, and that Daniel would be grateful for the help, but he wouldn't want to say anything to her. She told Silvia that if he asked, to tell him that they had discussed it as a possibility earlier in the week and it had all been worked out. She'd pay her extra for her time. Silvia agreed, and Andrea ended the phone call, letting a smile curl her mouth into a fixed position of delight.

Lying to Silvia was as easy as lying to a doctor who was obligated to ask if she'd ever done illegal drugs. No, of course not, was always the answer or the box she'd check just as most people would. She checked her messages, and Frank had sent her a message asking her if she was going to the Road Bar with everyone. Their recent work together on the Carson case was going well, but it was stressful work and at the end of the day, they both needed a release from the stress.

"Of course," she replied to his question, adding emojis of smiley faces…but in her rush, she accidently hit the emoji of the face that blew a heart kiss. She didn't see it until she'd already sent it. It was too late now, she couldn't take the text back.

Frank replied quickly, with an emoji of a face winking. Andrea felt her heart beat fast. Her accident perhaps wasn't such a bad thing. She felt wonderful, suddenly. She felt like she mattered, her presence would make a difference, and most of all, she felt desired. Frank was so much fun to talk to…he never put her down. He saw her as a true equal. She put her car into gear and drove quickly to the Road Bar. It was a step up from a trashy bar, but not quite a classy one, either. It was famous for its happy hour, which included margaritas made with Everclear. Typically, after a few drinks made of Everclear, a person would be completely inebriated and possibly very sick. Andrea couldn't wait to get her hands on one.

She saw the group as she entered the bar. There was Frank, Jim, the receptionist Katie, and Jackie. *Wow, the bitch made it,* Andrea thought to herself upon seeing Jackie smile and take a sip from a long straw into a frozen daiquiri. *Amateur,* she thought. No self-respecting woman would drink a frozen daiquiri. They weren't little girls with slushies. She sat down and ordered a top shelf margarita on the rocks, with salt, and requested that it be made with Everclear. The waiter took the order and promptly turned around to have it made. As soon as it was brought out, between the chatter of the group and discussing all of the little things people discuss after having worked together all week, Andrea sucked the margarita down to the bottom.

"Woah, slow down there speedy," Jim laughed, noting how fast Andrea had finished it.

"Shut up," she joked, "it's been a long week, I needed to knock one back first and get it out of the way. That was for yesterday," she laughed.

"We were here on Wednesday, you mean you didn't get enough that night for Thursday?" laughed Katie. Everyone but Jackie had been there on Wednesday and frankly, they were all surprised that Andrea had made it into the office on Thursday.

"I ain't no punk," Andrea laughed, ordering another one. She noticed Frank, who sat beside her in the large round booth, let his eyes linger as he looked at her. She remembered their texts and she felt herself blush.

As they all drank, their talking and laughing became louder, more boisterous. They discussed leaving and hitting up a bar not too much farther down the road but decided to stay put. They ordered appetizers and shots.

"Jaeger bombs!" Jackie squealed upon seeing the round sat down at the table. "I haven't had one of these since college...they're like cough medicine," she laughed, picking hers up.

"Yeah cough medicine to get you lit, this'll put a little hair on your chest," Andrea replied, lifting her glass. She was three margaritas and two shots in and had ignored her water to the point that all of the ice had melted and the glass was filled to the brim.

"Fuck it, let's take it," Jim lifted his glass. "To being fucking lawyers!"

Katie laughed and reminded them of her position.

"Okay, to being fucking lawyers and putting up with lawyers," Jim corrected with a smile.

They all slammed the Jaeger bombs back, wincing a little at the sting of the shot. Everyone except Andrea. She didn't want anyone to think she was punking out on drinking the hard stuff. She didn't let her face change at all. Her head buzzed with the euphoria of intoxication— the beautiful point where she had not yet begun to feel bad, or sloppy, or disoriented, but that threshold where the feeling was so perfect that to stop drinking would make it all slow down and go away, and was, therefore, out of the question. She had to keep it going. More rounds of margaritas were ordered and the group continued on with their meaningless sound and fury.

Phones came out and soon they were all taking pictures together and Snapchatting them. Jackie had three margaritas and was clearly intoxicated, and said she'd take an Uber home and get her car the next day.

"Oh my God what a little bitch!" Andrea exclaimed, laughing at Jackie. "Take it like a man, honey, or you're never gonna cut it in this world. You aren't gonna drive home?"

From Andrea's words, a cloud of awkwardness filled their immediate environment. Aware that she was being taunted, but trying to remain professional, Jackie replied that she didn't want a DWI and that they should all be careful that night.

Andrea couldn't resist though. Now she had nothing holding her back, and the others weren't stopping her. "Jackie, you're not gonna make it in this business if you can't man up—it's a man's world. It's always gonna be this way," she said sloppily. "You have to show them you're not a little bitch, or you'll get your ass kicked. You think you know this job? You don't know shit. You haven't seen it yet. Everything they told you in law school? Most of it's bullshit. They don't explain how to get through it all, to make partner, to actually be successful. You keep on like you are, you'll be everyone's little bitch."

Everyone sort of stopped and looked at Andrea. Jackie bit her lower lip and looked down. She thought about leaving it. *No, no, I can't just let myself be talked to by her like that,* Jackie's inebriated internal dialogue told her. *Tell her what you really think, she probably won't remember anyway.* Jackie straightened her posture and looked down at Andrea, whose leg was now touching Franks, and everyone sat in silence waiting for what was coming.

"Andrea, I really wanted to like you. I did, but now I see just as I suspected that you're an alcoholic with low self-esteem. You don't like me because I threaten you.

I don't have to be a man to be successful, I'm sorry your brain is still stuck in the 1930s. The way you're going, the way people talk about you—and the sad part is that you don't even know it—you'll be lucky if you last another year. You can call me whatever makes you feel better. I came out tonight because I wanted to try, at least *try*, to get along with you, but alcohol changes things, which definitely let me see you for what you are. Pathetic.," she quivered with her words. She turned around and walked outside to get into her Uber.

"Fuck her," Frank said, breaking the tension. Katie looked down and tapped her long acrylic nails on her margarita glass. It was around midnight. Andrea felt the weight of what Jackie had just said sink into her. She was riding a high that she simply didn't want to get off of. She wasn't going to let Jackie ruin it.

"Yeah, fuck her," Andrea mumbled. "She'll remember what I said. It is a man's world in this business."

Katie started laughing and said something about just being the receptionist, making everyone laugh and further breaking the tension. Her brown eyes sparkled beneath her cute, shiny brown bangs and she, wanting to fit in with all of the lawyers, tapped Andrea's leg with her foot underneath the table.

"Come to the restroom with me," she said. Andrea scooted out of the round booth and followed her, walking now with the swaying unevenness that inevitably happened when she'd drank enough to put down an elephant.

They both entered stalls and began to pee and Katie asked for some extra toilet paper from Andrea, seeing that her stall was out. Andrea passed her some under the wall of the stall and they exited about the same time. Katie was recently divorced, younger than all of them, and very sarcastically funny. Andrea liked her. She needed a friend. She felt nervous about Frank. He wasn't sexy—he didn't even compare to Daniel—but he was charismatic and very charming. He talked to her, listened to her, and made jokes that were actually funny. He stood at 5'10 with broad shoulders and blue eyes. He had perfect teeth that, even though he was a bit chubby in the face, made up for some of his less attractive features, like his receding hair line. He made her forget about how cruel Daniel was to her.

As they washed their hands, Katie noticed Andrea seemingly lost in thought. "Hey Dre, you okay?" she asked.

"Yeah," Andrea lied. "I'm just super tired from the past few weeks." She really wasn't tired at all, she felt a powerful adrenaline that kept her going, burning through the alcohol and keeping her functioning each day. She was irritated by Jackie and was thinking of ways to get revenge.

"I've got a little something," Katie whispered, and she pulled out a little bag full of white powder.

"Is that…that's coke?" Andrea asked, unsure since she'd not used it before.

"Hell yes," Katie laughed. "How else do you think I make it through the day sometimes? Coffee just can't cut it."

"Well, cut that then," Andrea smiled.

"No, look, here in the bathroom, use your pinky nail. Come into the handicap stall with me."

They scurried into the stall and Katie opened the little package. With her long fake nail, she scooped up the powder and snorted it into her nose. Her eyes opened a bit wider and she smiled broadly with satisfaction.

Andrea, being a cocaine virgin, felt some hesitation, but followed suit, using her pinky nail to scoop up some and snort it. Immediately she felt a beautiful sensation run throughout her. She felt awake and like she could do *anything*. Her eyes sparkled with the immense pleasure the feeling of unstoppable immortality brought to her. The rage she felt for Jackie melted into a feeling of flippant disregard.

"Get it, girl," Katie giggled, taking another bump. Andrea took another turn. It was the most amazing feeling she'd ever had.

"That's enough for now, but you know who's got what you need now," Katie winked as they left the bathroom.

"What is it that girls do together in the bathroom?" Frank laughed as they came back to the table. Katie and Andrea looked at each other and began laughing hysterically, tears coming to their eyes.

"Look at you," Jim smiled at Katie, and Andrea saw him put his arm around her waist. "I don't think you should drive home tonight," he said, winking at her.

Feeling absolutely capital, Andrea ordered another drink. Her notion of how much control she had over herself had changed. She was more alert and more in tune; the cocaine had taken the sloppy edge off of the alcohol enough for her to make more sense and feel more in tune with everything and everyone. She wished she would have already had it when Jackie was still there.

She began talking to Frank very confidently, straightening her posture and pushing out her breasts toward him. He smiled and talked to her, but Andrea, although focused on him, wasn't paying attention to his words. She was paying attention to how close he was getting to her. She wasn't stopping him, but she had never come this close to crossing the line.

There was a pause in their intimate conversation and they looked over at Jim and Katie, kissing. It was something Andrea had never experienced in office culture but had always heard of. Jim was married and about 15 years older than Katie. He had a golfer's tan on his face, and he was flushed from the alcohol which only enhanced his red tanned cheeks in comparison to his white forehead. Katie wore sexy office attire and made no attempt to hide her cleavage from day to day, so the attraction must have been building for some time. Andrea watched, almost with envy, as Katie's tongue massaged Jim's. She wasn't envious of what they were doing, she was envious that she hadn't had anything like that happen to her. Underneath the table, she knew where their hands were from the position of their arms, and she could see that they were going to leave together. She didn't feel sorry for Michele, Jim's wife, because she didn't feel sorry for anyone. She was not born with the ability to empathize.

Frank and Andrea looked away, so that it would be less awkward, and continued to talk. She could see in his eyes that he wanted, but he wasn't touching her, and she wasn't was a little uncertain about this. She liked being wanted. Daniel made her feel like she was still a little girl in ESL class most of the time. Frank laughed at her jokes and appreciated her position at the firm. He understood the intricacies of what she did each day and the issues with her cases and he didn't mind listening to her when she needed to vent. He wasn't judging her. He didn't mistake venting for bitching.

Jim closed out his ticket, paid for Katie's, and ushered them out the door with a wink and a smile goodbye toward Andrea and Frank. Andrea wasn't sure where they were going, but she knew they weren't going their separate ways.

"And that's how quickly it happens," Frank noted as they walked away. Andrea's head buzzed with the fuel of cocaine and drunkenness. She felt like she was left with a choice…like Katie had paved some sort of moral pathway for her and she could follow it with Frank or she could hold back and see what she should do in spite of her mental state.

"I see," Andrea noted. "But what do you think will happen on Monday?"

"They'll probably keep flirting and act like nothing happened tonight. But you, you're the one who's got beef with Jackie now," he laughed. "That's not going away Monday."

Andrea straightened up a little. She had all but let the memory of what had just transpired between her and Jackie fade away. Would it be that bad, she wondered? "I don't have anything to worry about," Andrea retorted. "Jackie had it coming."

"You have to admit, you were a little hard on her," Frank nudged her with his elbow. "It's kind of bad moral for you two at the firm. Maybe apologize?"

"Well, she has to learn somehow. You can't just chirp your way through life with your shrill voice and make everyone respect you. Do you know how hard I had to work to get to where I am? Do you know how many men I had to go up against to get where I am? Do you know how many times I was told that since I'm a woman *and* I'm Latina that I won't succeed, or that I should be home with my kids? It's exhausting. It's a constant battle," Andrea huffed air, releasing her words and emotions all at once.

"You've got a supportive husband, certainly he's helped along the way," Frank said, coaxing Andrea to tell some hushed truths about her marriage. It worked.

"Yeah, Daniel and I…we aren't doing so well. Sometimes with these cases, where I'm dividing up assets, arguing on behalf of one spouse or the other, I can actually imagine it being me and Daniel. Sometimes I want it to happen," she confessed.

"Why?"

"Just to get it over with. If it's going to happen, it just needs to happen. Why wait? Why wait for our arguments to get worse," she rested her head on her hand, elbow on the table.

"You married him for some reason," Frank asked.

"Because we were young. He was hot, so was I, we had our future in front of us...."

"You still are," Frank admitted, and touched her hand. She felt herself lean into him and felt the touch of his lips on her cheek. She turned ever so slightly towards him, and let his lips touch hers. She pulled back.

"I should go home."

"It's early still, but if you want to leave why don't we head to my place" Frank said, expecting a denial.

With a sly smile Dre nodded in agreement and followed Frank to the parking lot. She pulled up to his townhouse. The place was nice—perfect for a single guy. She wasn't sure what all the night would entail. As they walked through the door she felt Frank's gaze on her backside. He walked to the kitchen to pour her a glass of wine and handed it to her, his face coming close to hers, his nose brushing against hers.

She drank her glass of wine quickly, letting the effects kick in, and he walked over to her after pouring them another. "I want you," he whispered.

Her heart pounded. She could feel her body tingling as her pantie became filled with moisture. It was so wrong, she knew, but it felt so good—too good to stop. *No one has to know*, she thought. It was as if he read her mind. "No one has to know but us. I can't stand seeing you each day in the office and not being able to grab that ass."

"Grab it then," Dre dared, biting her lip.

He did as she instructed, and pulled her close, kissing her sloppily. He hissed so different than Daniel... harder and with less pull. She matched his style, reaching to unzip his pants.

It was happening fast, but she didn't want to stop it and she didn't want to miss a second of the high she was on from it.

"The couch," she whispered breathlessly.

Taking off his clothes and tugging on hers, he sat down on the couch and Dre climbed on top of him, the feeling of his erection tantalizing every part of her insides. She had not experienced the depth or breadth of a man this size. She squealed with pleasure while riding him until both of them had accomplished their goal.

"I can't even explain how good that felt," Frank said, out of breath and smiling.

"I know I'm good," Dre replied, moving off of him and pulling up her panties. In this moment all of her insecurities subsided, knowing that she had just had complete control of the moment.

She checked the time. It was half past midnight. She kissed Frank on the forehead, sure he was to pass-out, naked on his couch from the excessive orgasm rather than the alcohol and let herself out. She was completely intoxicated now, teetering as she walked. She got into her car and turned on the ignition and using her cameras she backed out carefully and felt herself as though she were out of her body driving home. Her car drifted and she scraped her rims of her passenger side up against the concrete curb. She cursed and yanked the car back into its lane, causing a passing driver to honk wildly. She sneered at the driver and honked back, causing her to jump another curb, and this time scratch the right side of her car against a light post. She didn't stop. She couldn't risk getting a DWI… she just hadn't felt this out of sorts ever, and the adrenaline rushes of anxiety she had about going home were starting to overcome her gut.

When she pulled up to her house the lights were off and she stumbled out of her door, falling into in the grass and vomiting. She walked around to see the damage she'd inflicted onto her car. The scratch had dented the door, and her front passenger side rim was mutilated. Not noticing the messages on her phone, she went inside and sat all of her things down on the counter, leaving the phone out and forgetting about it. She made her way into her master bathroom. Daniel was probably awake but ignoring her. She showered quickly and slipped into something comfortable to wear and managed to get into bed beside Daniel without him saying a word to her, but she could tell by his breathing that he was awake.

After racing thoughts, she drifted into a disturbed, spinning sleep. In her dreams, she saw flashes of the bathroom stall and Katie, and saw Zeke watching her snort bumps of coke. Frank was there, too, but he was just sort of a background figure. The location changed to a strange version of her childhood home, and the dream changed as dreams so often do to a surreal scene that was almost impossible to articulate. Daniel was her father, and he had a gun in his hand, and she was trying to explain to him why she needed to do something in particular that she couldn't quite articulate, but as dreams go it was only clear to her that he couldn't understand her and he was angry, and she fought to try and move, feeling like she was trapped in molasses, fighting to open her eyes, scared that she was paralyzed somehow, and she'd never be able to wake up. It was suffocating, it was impossible to move.

She woke up to daylight, and the sound of her children in the kitchen. She sat up quickly and a pain pierced her head, and practically knocked her back down into her pillows. She moaned and rolled over to her bedside drawer and scrounged around for any bottle of pills she had handy. She swallowed two old Vicodin pills and four ibuprofens; a cocktail that was sure to help her recover faster and made her way into the kitchen.

This particular morning the juice and other food items were fully stocked and she was able to drink juice without the fear of drinking all of it, and make herself eggs and toast without worrying that there wouldn't be any for later. Daniel had made the kids microwave pancakes, something that disgusted Andrea, but she was nonetheless grateful that they were eating. She kissed each one of them on the head and looked around. Daniel was sitting on the luxurious white leather sofa, holding her phone. His face was pale, and she could see it beaded with sweat.

Approaching him slowly, she looked over his shoulder to see what he was looking at with such contempt. Her stomach churned. There was a message from Frank; a dick pic with a message saying he woke up in the middle of the night with a hard after their late-night fuck fest. She gasped. Daniel looked up at her, his eyes red with the pain of rage and hurt. He opened her photo album and began scrolling through the multiple pictures and selfies of her and Frank, as well as Jim, Katie and Jackie. It looked bad.

"You're fucking Frank?" he gritted through his teeth.

She couldn't breathe. She felt her knees weaken and she gripped the sofa hard to sturdy herself. "No, Daniel, no."

He gripped her phone with all the strength in his hand, then threw it hard against the wall, denting the dry wall and shattering its screen. The kids stopped eating and looked over at them. "Then what the fuck was that all about?" he whispered through clenched teeth.

Tears welled up in her eyes. The messages, she hadn't asked for them. Frank had sent them in his own drunken stupor. It wasn't *her* fault. It was Frank's fault. It was Daniel's even. He'd looked at her phone before she'd had a chance to see what had even been sent to her, and certainly she would've just deleted Frank's messages, and the stupid pictures before anyone could have seen them. It was just Frank being drunk.

"You gave him head," Daniel spat, a little louder than a whisper this time. Andrea glanced with fear towards the children.

"No, I mean, he wanted me to, but I didn't...I wouldn't...," Andrea stuttered. The Vicodin was kicking in now, mixed with her breakfast, and she was able to think better. The tiny hit of euphoria from the pills gave her the energy she needed to try and explain, begging Daniel to follow her into their room.

Daniel didn't want to follow her into their room, he had seen enough. He had seen the messages about meeting at Road Bar, and the emojis. He'd seen what happy hour *really* looked like. He had seen everything he needed to see. Working in a bar for as long as he had, he scolded himself internally for not thinking of any of it before. He'd seen it happen to other people time and again. He thought to himself of all the messages he'd probably never seen that she had erased. *But she was too drunk this time,* he thought. *I caught her before she had time to delete anything else.*

"I guess I should have listened to them when they told me not to get serious with a ho I met at the goddamn bar," he sneered at her.

She begged him in pleading whispers to come into their bedroom. Her eyes dripped with heavy tears as she tried to explain what happened. She heard herself talking but her mind continued to search for better words to use to try and convince him that she wasn't lying about Frank. It was one moment. A weak drunken moment. She hadn't let another man touch her. She remembered his lips on hers, the cocaine had stopped her from blacking out in her Everclear-infused state.

Finally relenting, Daniel followed her into their room. He stood tall, with his broad chest flexed and his arms crossed. She could tell he'd awoken early and had shaved his head—he kept it bald on purpose—and had readied himself for anything. He looked at Andrea with loveless eyes. "How long has it been going on?"

Andrea shook her head no, and she went up to him and tried to hug him. "Daniel, please, baby, please, it's not…I never did anything with him or anyone. I don't know why he sent those pictures." She began heaving with sobs. "Daniel, please, just please, hold me!"

"Don't!" he stepped back from her, letting her collapse to her knees onto the carpet floor. "Don't try this shit, Dre. I saw the other messages, I know how you've been acting. For two months now you've been going out, drinking, fighting with me; it all makes sense now."

Between heavy sobs and uncontrollable gasps for air, she begged him to listen, to understand that she didn't want Frank, that they only talked after work and that he had been drinking and sent the messages completely unsolicited. She was so accustomed to being able to argue her point well, and for people to listen to it, that the frustration of not being able to get through to Daniel was enough to make her want to scream. At that moment, it didn't matter how smart she was or how much better she thought she was than anyone, she just needed Daniel to *listen* to her.

Zeke and Anna had walked to the door and were listening through it. Anna started for the handle, but Zeke took her hand and stopped her. She whined a little, but not loudly enough for Daniel or Andrea to hear her. Zeke looked hard at his sister, at only the age of five, and said to her, "Mami and Daddy are fighting, shhhh!" hushing her. He took her by the hand and led her upstairs to her room. He went to his room, feeling a churning of anxiety in his gut, and hid in the corner. Their fights caused him to feel like he was enduring the winds of a hurricane, and even though he wasn't in any physical danger, it made him feel like he was in between a dangerous crossfire, and that he had to protect himself and his sisters. Realizing that Lilly was still in the kitchen in her high chair, Zeke nervously went downstairs to get her.

Lilly had smeared pancake mush all over the white table portion of her high chair and clapped her hands joyfully at the sight of little Zeke. She was eager to get out and cooed at him for help. Zeke was tiny as it was, but he managed to get his hands underneath her arms and pull her out of the high chair, but it tumbled over and fell as he pulled her out. Hearing the crashing noise it made, Lilly was startled and started to cry.

"Lilly, no!" Zeke tried to hush her, but she was a baby and couldn't be reasoned with. The noise brought Daniel and Andrea out of the bedroom and into the kitchen.

Andrea felt desperate, completely desperate and sad. She was losing. She hardly every lost. She argued for a living, and she made her money by winning those arguments. Now she couldn't fight for herself, for her own life. Daniel snatched up Lilly from Zeke without saying a word to him and took her up to her room. "Zeke!" he yelled, and Zeke followed his voice up to Lilly's room. "Stay in here with your sister, make sure she doesn't get into anything. Play with her," he commanded, his voice shaky and demanding.

Andrea paced back and forth. It was almost 11 in the morning, and she felt like her entire world was collapsing. She thought about ways to convince Daniel that she wasn't having an affair. Different scenarios passed through her mind. She was guilty of some things, and yes, she did have a night of indiscretion, but it was one time. She needed to blow off some steam and Daniel certainly had not been helping in that way. She didn't have to answer to anyone, only herself. It wasn't the way she was brought up, through Mexican Catholic tradition, but not much of what she did was anyway. Truly, she realized if she was going by tradition and by all of the things she *should* do then she wouldn't be at the crossroads she was with Daniel now. Divorcing him would be a horrid embarrassment to her family, and she could be excommunicated from the church, but she no longer attended anyway, so she didn't see what difference it would make besides utterly humiliating her family. She wasn't a 24- year-old girl any more. She was a 35-year-old attorney who could make her own decisions and her own money.

Who were her parents, who hadn't helped her at all attain a law degree, to tell her what to do? Who was Daniel, who judged her so harshly he wouldn't even hear her out, to tell her what to do? Who was anyone at work to tell her? They were all essentially her peers. Even the older ones with more tenure at the firm—they were only over her because they were simply older and had been there longer. Andrea couldn't reason why the fact that someone's age automatically gave them some sort of God-like control over anything. Everything spun in her head. She was a *good* mother, she told herself. She did what was best for everyone and they should all be thanking her, but they weren't. They couldn't see what she had sacrificed to be where she was and to be able to do what she did. Her kids didn't have to deal with what she had to deal with in school—being the little Mexican girl in ESL, not knowing correct English, being poor and not having the best things—hell, not even having parents around most of the time.

Daniel walked upstairs and went into Lilly's room. He noticed Zeke was sitting with her, building blocks. Tears watered in his eyes. He couldn't understand how a boy of only five was capable of such love, such understanding. He needed them more than he could ever tell them. They were what held him down, what kept him glued to his family. He knew they'd already seen so much fighting and it made him feel sick. They all needed a break from it; it didn't matter if they had to leave the comforts of their oversize house—all it seemed to equal to him was oversize fighting. He pulled a bag out of Lilly's closet and began gathering clothing and diapers out of drawers and putting them neatly into her bag.

"Daddy, why are you packing Lilly?" Zeke asked, as Daniel knew he would.

"We're going to go stay with Abuelita," he said gently, trying not to show any emotion in his voice.

"But she lives in San Antonio…isn't that far?" Zeke said, stretching out the word "far" for emphasis.

"Not too far, buddy. About four hours. It won't take any time. Go to your room, buddy. I want you to get your bag, too. Pack clothes and make sure you pack underwear. Pack clothes and pajamas for five whole days, can you do that? That means a shirt and pants and underwear for each day, and PJ's," Daniel instructed, wondering if the instructions were overloading his little, curious mind.

"Okay Daddy. Is Anna coming?" he asked so innocently.

"Of course, of course she is. I'm gonna help her pack in a little bit."

"What about Mami?"

Daniel paused and squeezed the clothing he held in his hand. "She's got to work," he replied with an indefinable emptiness in his voice.

Daniel had never not loved Andrea. He chose her. He chose her before she even knew it. He had been working nights bartending at a local university bar. Andrea had come in with her friends when she had first started law school. He was young, buff, clean cut and had his choice of women, but there was something different about Andrea from the moment he saw her. He just knew she was for him. She wasn't like the other college girls. She glowed with the brilliance of confidence and complete control. She had the perfect body, and she had the attitude of not caring what he or anyone else thought, and he loved that about her. He could see her that night, in his mind's eye, jet black shiny hair, a dazzling smile, and cleavage that made his heart skip a beat. She had on jeans that fit her perfectly, and he thought about how badly he wanted to come from around the counter and kiss her. He remembered asking for her number that night, and she, licking her red lip stick and winking at him, telling him that she didn't give her number out to *chuntaros*. It was an insult in Spanish, but it was a joke intended to lure him, too. She may have been playing hard to get, but she was attracted to him. She liked the attention. She didn't realize he already had his degree and had applied for a job in insurance, which was where he worked now. He had just given his two week notice to the bar, sure he would get the job, which he did. He smiled his big, handsome grin at her and asked her why she thought he was a chuntaro, to which she replied that no bartender ever made her a margarita with *that* much tequila and that he couldn't possibly be Mexican enough to deal with her family if he wanted to date her, and with the shirt he was wearing, he had to be a chunt. She said to him in Spanish, "Prove me wrong and I'll give it to you." Laughing, they joked about the meaning of the derogatory word, which essentially meant wetback, and how he was actually a very accomplished young man and was finishing his days bartending so that he could start his corporate career. She left the bar that night saying she didn't believe him, but underneath the napkin on which her drink had been sitting, she had left a card with her number. She had hidden it, so that if he hadn't looked closely enough, he might have missed the chance, but she knew somewhere down deep that he'd see it.

From then on, they dated, they had a long, beautiful engagement, and had a full Catholic wedding. He had even given her a three-karat ring...something none of her family had ever seen. They traveled through Mexico on their honey moon and spent their first few years in perfect wedded bliss before having kids. They had both had their moments of crazy drunkenness, and in arguments she'd shoved him around a bit, but it was after they had Anna that he noticed Andrea began to change so drastically. With each folded piece of clothing he put into a bag, he remembered something that made him feel like stopping, but he knew the environment was toxic. Andrea was up and down constantly, hadn't been herself in months and months, and now, had cheated on him. It was beyond reparable. It was beyond forgiveness. He couldn't imagine forgiving that sin.

He checked on Zeke, who was packing one bag full of his clothes and another with his favorite toys, then went to check on Anna. He started putting her things in a bag and continued to wonder about what the future held and what could possibly be wrong with Andrea, the woman who he thought had it all.

Meanwhile, Andrea lay on the bedroom floor sobbing. Her sobs had puffed her eyes up to the point that she could barely see and her voice was so hoarse that she didn't even sound like herself. It didn't matter what all she could buy or how impressive her career or bank account was, Andrea felt like a complete failure. Everything she had felt like absolutely nothing. She went into her closet and started knocking down her wall of expensive purses. She chunked Louis Vuittons and Hermes bags down on the floor of the large closet and kicked them. They were just things to her now. Next were her shoes. Louboutins and Jimmy Choos were chunked on top of the bags, and she looked down and cried some more. She bought all of these things to impress, to fill a void...but the emptiness was still there. None of the thing she owned actually made her feel any better except for brief superficial moments where maybe someone complimented her. Within her, deep down below the first few layers of her surface, there still existed that insecure little Mexican girl who stumbled with her English, wore handmade dresses to school— whose parents drove an old pickup truck and worked on someone's land handling cattle and cleaning houses to make ends meet. She worked so hard to be leaps and bounds beyond that life in which she had been raised, yet she was still with a controlling man that made her feel the need to escape, a *machismo*, the style of man she so desperately never wanted to be with.

She thought of Katie kissing Jim. Katie was the receptionist, who probably made only $40,000 a year. She couldn't afford any of these fancy things Andrea had, yet she was young, fun and desirable. If Jim left his wife for Katie, Katie would have it made, without ever having to work for it. What was it she had that Andrea didn't…being white? Being more fun? Being in a lesser position, thus, less of a threat? Andrea felt completely useless and defeated now. It didn't matter that Frank had sent those messages; the timing had been off and now her world was crashing in on her.

She opened her bedroom door and noticed the silence. Her heart fluttered in sudden anxiety. She heard a drawer close upstairs and instinctively knew what it meant. She ran up the stairs as fast as she could and swung open the door to Zeke's room.

"Baby what are you doing?" she said in a loud, cracked voice.

Zeke, feeling his little heart flood with anxiety, answered his mother politely. "Daddy said to pack clothes, we're going to stay with Abuelita."

Andrea gasped and turned away. *No,* she thought, *no that son of a bitch is not taking my babies away and not to his mother!* She scrambled down the hallway to Lilly's room and saw her sitting, playing with blocks and other large infant toys with her TV playing mindless baby cartoons. She ran from Lilly's room to Anna's and saw Daniel packing Anna's things, with Anna toddling around and touching one thing to another gently, dragging around a doll and a stuffed animal.

"Daniel!" she screamed. Anna stopped what she was doing and looked at her mother with wide, frightened eyes.

"I'm packing us up. We're going to my mom's," he replied, trying to keep his tone emotionless. He wasn't going to be the emotional one in this fight. He wasn't going to call names anymore and try to get her to see the error of her ways by verbal abuse. He saw that it didn't work with her. She was incapable of being reasoned with. He waited for her predictable response.

"Hell no! You're not taking *my* kids to *your* mother! What would...why would you think that was okay? What in God's name would make you think that was okay?" she roared, now terrifying Anna to the point of trembling tears. Zeke had come out of his room and peeked through the doorway at the chaos unfolding.

"Andrea, they're our kids; my kids, too. They don't need to be around this constant fighting. You? You're out of control, I don't know if you realize that, but this can't go on. I can't go on. I need some time away, and I can't leave them with you...especially not when you're never here to take care of them."

"Excuse me?" Andrea challenged, stepping up to him. "I take care of everything you fucking have, Daniel! I pay the bills! I make sure we have the best of everything! I make sure that my kids don't ever have to suffer like I did! That they don't have to be the poor little kids who don't know English and get made fun of and get accused of spreading head lice to the class or any of the other bullshit I put up with as a kid! I pay Silvia so that we can all have extra time for ourselves! Time *my* parents never had because they were working to make some stupid white family's life better!"

Daniel looked at her condescendingly, something he knew how to do so well. Ignoring her other points she had made in her rant, he skipped right to the chase.

"No, let's be real, you pay Silvia so you can stay out late, drink 'til you pass out, and do whatever the hell you want, like fuck Frank."

With those words, uncontrollably, Andrea's hand came through the air and popped Daniel in the mouth, leaving him speechless. This wasn't the first time she had put her hands on him, but he was not the type of man to retaliate against her in the same way. He could make things worse by his ability to control a situation better than she could with all her wit and intelligence. He looked at her, telling her with his eyes that she had just crossed a line; that she had done a thing that could never be forgiven.

Horrified with herself, Andrea stopped and looked at her own hand, then tried to apologize. Hearing herself talking and bumbling out words, she realized none of what she was saying could make the situation better at all, and that she'd just done it in front of both her son and daughter. Regardless of the rational cognizance hidden somewhere within her, she kept on at Daniel. She used every insult about his family, his mother especially, that she could think of. It had the opposite effect of making Daniel want to stay home and keep his children away from his mother, but Andrea couldn't pause the barrage of abhorrent words that flew from her dehydrated lips.

"You can say whatever you want about my mother, your children's grandmother, Dre, you can call her whatever you want, you can insult her in every way possible, but that's not going to stop me from taking the kids and getting the hell way from you. Look at this…you hit me! You think that makes you better than me? You think that makes you look like a good mother? You look like a crazy bitch, Dre," he hissed harshly and condescendingly, making her even angrier.

Andrea felt her face flush and her body rush with the adrenaline of an Olympic sprinter. She knocked Anna's clothes out of his hand and shoved him back with both hands. Daniel lost his footing a little and his back slammed in to Anna's dainty pink wall, shaking it and knocking down a beautifully embroidered framed letter A on her wall. By now, both of the children who were witnessing the argument were crying, but Andrea didn't care.

"Fuck you, Daniel, you're not taking them!" she screamed, running to Zeke's room and opening his bag of clothes, throwing them out of the bag all over the floor. "You're not going anywhere, baby, you're staying here with Mami," she said in a rage fueled fury as though Zeke was there and listening to her and comprehending her words. Instead he was in the hallway crying loudly, holding Anna as she cried, too.

Daniel stormed downstairs to his closet and began sloppily packing his own bag to leave. He figured that if she destroyed the packing for the kids, he could stop by a Wal-Mart or Target on the way and get them enough new clothes to last a week or so. They'd be fine. He wasn't destitute. He made perfectly decent money, but one would never know that by talking to Andrea. He focused hard on packing the things he needed. He heard footsteps on the stairs and stopped, walking out of their bedroom and into the living room.

"So, you're leaving me? And you don't even know the truth?" Andrea cried, desperate for him to stop. She needed him to hear her, to know she had made a mistake. She didn't realize that her binge drinking for weeks and weeks at a time was creating a miserable atmosphere. She had no idea that not touching Daniel affectionately and making him feel loved had created a fissure so deep between them that they had hardly a string to cling to between the two of them and their love. She only saw the end result. Her desperation turned to fear. She saw him packing and she screamed inaudible words of panic and hate through tears and a snot-filled nose. All three children were now at the bottom of the stairs, crying and watching the chaos unfold.

Daniel felt for them, but everything had become so out of control he didn't think to put them in a room or try and shield them from it all. They would have escaped the room anyway and come to see what was happening.

Andrea went to the kitchen and found a bottle of vodka in the freezer and poured a shot, taking it quickly, then another. She usually didn't drink at home, but her nerves were shot and she needed something else to help assuage her mental state.

"Look at you! It's not even one in the afternoon and you're drinking already! You wonder why I don't want to be here, why the kids don't *need* to be here? Do you fucking see what you're doing to all of us?" Daniel yelled, this time letting his emotions control his tone of voice. He was sick of it. He was sick of letting her hit or shove him. He'd been used to her abuse to an extent, but the combination today was all too much to bear.

"Maybe I don't need to be here then anymore, if none of you all need me. Maybe I need to go away. If this is all my fault. I'm the one who needs to leave. It seems all of y'alls lives would just be better if I wasn't in it," Andrea quivered, looking at him, spinning her shot glass around nervously.

"Maybe so, Dre, it would be a lot less trouble for me and the kids to not have to go anywhere," Daniel said angrily, imagining her hooking up with Frank at some hotel close to their offices.

"Then I should just take myself away from all of you," she said, and pulled a knife from the wooden knife holder that held all of her perfectly sharpened kitchen knives.

"What the fuck, Andrea, put that down," Daniel said with his hand out in front of him in a defensive gesture. He knew the unpredictability of her capabilities.

"Yeah, you said it, I should be the one to leave, so here, I'll just do it, just this one last thing and you won't have to deal with me anymore," she screeched, and took the tip of the knife blade and made a superficial cut, although deeper than she had intended down the wrist of her left arm.

Daniel stood still, breathless. All three kids were against the back wall of the kitchen nook, watching what was transpiring. Andrea noticed that the cut was bleeding, but not enough. It wasn't how she'd imagined her suicide before, something she'd often fantasized about. She imagined overdosing in the bathtub, slowly sinking into the water and letting the water fill her unconsciously breathing lungs. She had always assumed that would be the most peaceful and successful way to go about it, glamorizing it as the painless yet most dramatic way to make her exit. But now she was standing in front of her entire family with a large kitchen knife, scratching away at her wrist like an amateur. She didn't have what it took, she knew, to stab all the way into herself. She was too narcissistic for that. Her skin, unlike she had imagined from thoughts of wrist cutting before, was slightly tougher than she imagined, and in order to penetrate deeply enough to bleed out, shed really have to cut into it. Scratching wouldn't do the job.

Now, the entire scene began to pass as though it was happening in slow motion. Andrea tried again, knowing now that it would take much more force to make a difference, so she used the tip and dug it into her arm, creating more blood—on her, onto the floor, and frightening her children more than she could ever imagine. Daniel, realizing the totality of was happening, approached her and whipped around her to catch her from behind and stop her arms. Her strength was more than he anticipated, and in that slow, horrid moment, Andrea tried jabbing at her left arm one more time but ended up cutting into his arm instead. So, there it was. Mami stabbed Daddy. That's how the children would remember it; that's what they would tell the police when they came. Nothing else that led up to the moment would ever matter, and none of it could be taken back.

Within the next few hours, police were called, family and social services was contacted, and Andrea was driven to a local hospital where she would be treated for her wounds and undergo a complete psychological evaluation.

****

As she entered the office building, she glanced at her watch. "8:15," she said out loud. "I didn't even have time to get coffee." She sat at her desk and began checking the messages from the answering service. She heard the chime on the front door of the office as she was checking the message from a prospective new client stating that her name was Cori and she was having some issues with anxiety. She made a note to return the phone call in between her sessions.

Katherine checked her daily schedule to find that she had two new clients. She assumed the person who just arrived was one of the new clients, named Andrea. The client intake form said she had recently been released from a hospital for a suicide attempt. *Yup, definitely a*

Monday, she thought. She was getting up from her desk to greet her new client when the cell phone buzzed. She answered the text quickly from her son regarding putting money on his school lunch account then remembered that in her morning rush, she forgot to tell her 8-year-old daughter that she would not be picking her up from school and she should instead ride home with her friend. She made a mental note to email her daughter's teacher to pass along the message. She strolled down the carpeted hallway to the waiting room to great her first client.

"Andrea," she stated with a smile on her face. The woman, she noticed had natural beauty but looked much older than her age stated on the paperwork. The woman looked up and Katherine immediately noticed the emptiness behind her eyes.

"Hi, I'm Doctor Cameron but you can call me Doctor Kate."

"Hello," the woman said coolly.

Kate led her down the short hallway and noticed the woman observing the abstract painting that lined the walls. She invited Andrea to choose a seat and noticed that Andrea chose to sit in what was obviously the therapist's chair. The room was quaint and comfortable with a love seat and two matching leather chairs on one side and a cloth high back chair on the other. Kate made a point to set her laptop in the chair prior to each session as a conspicuous sign of "taken". Andrea picked up the laptop and handed it to Kate as she sat made herself comfortable in the chair.

Ok this is how this hour will go, Kate thought.

"Well good morning. Do you go by Andrea?"

"Yes. My husband and close friends call me Dre."

"Ok Dre, have you been to therapy before?"

"Only in that stupid looney bin."

"You mean the hospital? I received your discharge papers via email for you over the weekend. You were at Stanley Behavioral Health here in Houston for about a week right? Tell me about that experience."

"I don't know what you want me to say," Andrea said with little eye contact. "It was an overreaction by my husband. We had a fight and I said something that he interpreted as me wanting to kill myself. He called 911 and before I knew it, the cops took me to that nuthouse."

"Can you tell me what happened in the argument?"

Andrea rolled her eyes and mumbled something unintelligible.

"I'm sorry, Doctor Kate said, I couldn't understand what you said."

Andrea looked with obvious frustration. "Look, we had a fight. All couples fight. I know this for sure, I am a divorce attorney. We had a bad fight. We were both yelling. They took me to the hospital because I was upset."

"What was the hospital experience like for you?"

"It was horrible. They made me share a room with some 20-year-old who threw up her food during the day literally had conversations with herself day and night. I didn't belong there. I'm not crazy. And I don't belong here now. I am very successful. I'm the best female attorney at my firm—if not in the state. I don't need to talk to anyone to figure out my problems. I hit a bump in the road because of the stress of my job and my family. My husband is just dramatic. All of this is overrated and unnecessary."

"You sound agitated Dre."

"It's Andrea," she corrected Doctor Kate harshly.

"Ok. Andrea, you sound agitated. Can you tell me if you feel irritable often?"

"This is such a waste of time. I have been out of work for a week and they are telling me I need a psychological evaluation and be released to return, so can you just complete the release form? I have way more important things to do than this shit."

"I understand therapy is hard; very hard. But it's an important process that takes intelligence, patience, and strength but it works."

"Well, I'm not patient enough and I don't need this. I can figure this out on my own." With that, Andrea grabbed her Gucci handbag and excused herself from the appointment and the room. Before she exited, she handed Doctor Kate a blank form that read *Park & Zimmerman Return to Work Certification* form.

Kate watched her exit and wondered if she would be back. She walked over to her desk thinking *Lord help me get through this day.*

Cori

"I don't want to wear that stupid dress!" Alexis shouted, pouting and stomping around on her fluffy carpet in her perfectly decorated room. Cori looked at her in awe, not entirely sure what to say to her. It was Sunday and they needed to go and see her mother. It was something Cori used to enjoy, but now overwhelmed her. Cori had bought Alexis an adorable dress, perfectly suitable for an 11-year-old. It fit her the way it should, and Cori had even asked her co-workers their opinions of it before purchasing it so that she had some objective input. She'd even bought it from an expensive designer clothing website, which was too expensive for an 11-year-old, but she hoped it would make Lexi happy.

"What's wrong with it?" Cori asked, with a tone more of sheer shock than anger.

"It's ugly. And you just want me to wear it because it's Burberry. I know why you picked it. I'm not stupid."

"I never said you were," Cori countered, appalled. She looked at the dress and noticed how classy she thought it looked. She thought it looked grown up, even though there were small bows on it in certain places. It wasn't bright or ostentatious or sparkly. What did she want?

"You want grandma to think everything's perfect, and that you're perfect, and that I'm perfect, and A.J.'s perfect. Well, I'm not. I'm not perfect," Alexis sneered.

Cori didn't hesitate, she went right into trying to dissect Alexis' needs. She started asking her the usual questions: Did she need someone to talk to? Was everything okay at school? Did she need anything at all? Alexis saw straight through the questions and replied that she didn't need a shrink, she knew her parents were dead and nothing could bring them back.

"You should just stop trying to play mom. You're just *not* a mom. You're not mine, you can't be my mom. A.J. just doesn't know any better, but I do. And I know that everything you do is to try and make me feel like you're my mom. But I know you're not. So stop. I don't need anything. I don't need *you*."

Gasping a little, but holding herself together, Cori switched to doctor mode, and remembered her time at the children's hospital, during her residency, and how she would speak to the children who were angry about their conditions, some of them terminal.

"I understand everything you're saying—but I don't have to agree with it, Alexis. I know I'm not your mom, and I don't think I've ever done anything to you specifically to try and either replace her or make you think I want to replace her. I only want to take care of you. If you don't like the things I've bought for you, I'm sorry. I was just doing my best. But listen, yes, I did spend money on getting you this dress. You know why?"

Alexis looked at her and shook her head no.

"Because of grandma. And grandma is your grandma regardless of who your parents are. Grandma has expectations of us...the same expectations she had of your mom and dad, and of me. She wants to see us in our Sunday's finest. We missed church with her, she isn't going to be happy about that. So we're going to eat with her. She'll be in her best clothing, and we'll be in ours. Don't tell me you don't remember this from before the accident."

94

Alexis looked down. She didn't want to agree with Cori and acknowledge that she did remember. She wanted to be mad at someone and Cori seemed like the easiest person on whom to take out her frustrations. She wouldn't give in that she remembered.

"I was little."

"Okay, fine, but this still happened, and it's what we do. So, do me the favor of putting on the dress, even if you hate it, because it's not for me. It's for your grandmother. It will cause us all a lot less suffering in the end if we all make her happy. You lost your parents, and I'm not trying to replace that..." she saw tears well up in Alexis' eyes, but she remembered learning to speak earnestly to children in pain. "...but grandma lost her son and her daughter in- law, and she hurts, too. Doing things like this—wearing this pretty dress, even if you hate it - it will make her feel better."

Alexis conceded, but not with words—instead with actions. She took the dress and walked into her bathroom to change. Cori felt vindicated in some way. She hated to think to herself, "I won!", but of lately, it seemed like each and every day with Alexis was a battle, and each mundane, daily task that was normal for most children and their guardians was some sort of fight. From bed time to what food to eat, what Cori bought at the store—everything was something Alexis found fault with. When they started discussing planning a vacation to Disney, A.J. lit up with delight and Alexis rolled her eyes, stomping off towards her room.

Each time Alexis did something that showed her detest of every effort Cori was making, Cori felt her chest clench up and her breathing become difficult. She'd feel dizzy and sweaty, like the whole world was caving in on her and everything was wrong at the same time. She would carry these feelings with her to work, and when seeing patients, she would become less and less focused on them and more worried about tiny, minute details that didn't impact what she was *actually* doing. On weekends, like on this particular day, Cori just wanted to stay home and not do anything, but she had to get out and meet her mother, just like she had to go to the gala with Stephen last night.

As they drove to have lunch with her mother, Cori sat in the passenger seat and recalled the happenings of the prior evening. The babysitter had come just as planned. Money was left for her and Cori went over everything with her, even explaining what to do if she smelled gas. Stephen had laughed casually and joked that everything was going to be alright and that the kids wouldn't "burn the house down".

Cori had been anxious in the few days leading up to the fundraiser. She knew what the night out at the fundraiser really represented. She had to be at his side at all times—that she couldn't trust him to go alone even if it was something she couldn't attend. He hadn't done anything in years... but that didn't matter. She could only think of the things he *had* once done to her.

That goddamn bachelor party, she thought to herself and felt her adrenaline spike. Her heart pounded like she was about to skydive as she recalled the incident. Their friend Damien was getting married—primarily because he was soon to be a father—so all the guys had planned a night out for him. It was when they were still dating and in college. She pleaded with him not to go. He became so annoyed with her irrational neediness that he jumped in her face, yelling, before walking out of her apartment and slamming the door. She remembered sobbing on the floor, feeling abandoned. Damien's last night of freedom turned out to be a booze filled slut-fest, more than Cori would have ever imagined Stephen was capable of.

A couple of nights after the party, as Stephen showered, she grabbed his cell phone, a flip phone at the time with no passcode protection. She scrolled through photos and saw more than she had imagined. There were topless lap dances featuring Stephen as a very enjoyable recipient. Pictures of Stephen's hands on every exposed inch of the stripper's body were just the beginning. As she scrolled, she saw Stephen laughing as another stripper with a bad wig and log fingernails appeared to be caressing his exposed maleness which was standing at full attention. Her heart sped up as she moved to his messages. *I bet he got a bitch's number.* Her fingers trembled as she clicked. The final blow was in a text message from Justin, who she knew well, who had a girlfriend she was friends with. The text was a video of Stephen and another man with the same bad wig-wearing bitch. The footage was grainy, but she could see it well enough. The whole party had all taken place at someone's house, so rules of no touching were out the window. Stephen and the other man who sent the video were having intercourse with this woman at the same time.

Her whole body shuddered as she remembered how she felt when she'd seen it. Beneath the video, his friend had sent the message, "We hit that shit!"

Stephen had done to her exactly what she had imagined guys did at bachelor parties, and everything she had feared in him going out with all of them. She'd been cheated on, lied to, and alcohol was a factor to which she could directly point as a culprit.

When Stephen had emerged from the shower, she stopped herself from breaking the phone so she could show him what she'd seen. Much of what she said and did subsequently, she could no longer recall. Stephen attempted to invalidate her rage by telling her it was her own fault for going through his phone. She remembered bits and pieces of the accusatory and vulgar language they threw at one another, and that he ended up walking out and not speaking to her for quite some time afterward.

So now, Cori relived those emotions and thought about how the night could go if she didn't go with him. It didn't matter how much he'd changed or how supportive he'd been in her med school years. *He could drink too much and meet someone, then take them somewhere before coming home. It would all be so easy.* She knew now how easily it could all just...happen. It was always this way for her when anything came up where he might have to go out. She had to go, too, and she had come to resent him each and every time.

Once there, Stephen had grabbed a beer from the open bar and offered Cori a glass of wine. She had refused it with a twinge of disgust on her face, one that Stephen pretended to ignore, but it had gotten under his skin ever so slightly.

They sat at the table with Bob Smith and his new wife Angie, who was, I'm sure was often mistaken for a human blow up doll. Cori was tasked with sitting beside her and making conversation. Cori knew from her medical knowledge coupled with basic common sense that Angie had undergone multiple surgeries, and she noted the strange tip of her nose and how she'd had it essentially shaved off so that it would resemble that of a pixie. Angie wore a revealing, very tight silver dress that didn't fit in with the black-tie attire but did attract the attention of every man at the event including Stephen, Cori noticed. The dress revealed her large, surgically enhanced breast with her nipples that were erect although it was a nice comfortable temperature in the room. The back of the dress accentuated what was most likely a surgically enhanced ass no White woman ever naturally had that much junk in her trunk. Her blonde hair was not out of place, but seemed long—too long, like she'd had extensions sewn in. Cori tried talking to her but continued to be distracted by the way she moved her lips, and the inability of her face to move as she spoke. She'd brought up the subject of television shows, to try and find something general to talk about, and Angie had mentioned that she'd once auditioned for *The Bachelor* when the first seasons had begun.

Taking a sip of her drink at the time of the comment, Cori had laughed a little, causing her to inhale some of her water and begin to cough. It was embarrassing as it was and even more so because Angie would now realize Cori was laughing at her comment. Flushed with embarrassment and humiliation after Bob had smacked her back several times to help clear her airway, she looked at Stephen with pleading eyes, hoping he would read into them that she wanted to leave. She felt so exposed around everyone. When she got up to walk across the ballroom to go to the restroom, she felt as though she may faint, perceiving that all eyes were on her, although none were at all. When she returned, after having embarrassed herself, she couldn't think of anything else to talk to Angie about and she felt like she was hated. She began dwelling on everything she had said, mulling over each word and wondering just how much damage she had caused. She looked down at Angie's ring, a large, pear cut diamond and guessed it had to be about four or five karats. She glanced away, hoping Angie wouldn't notice.

"Cori, are you a surgeon?" she heard from across the table, snapping her out of her thoughts.

"No," Cori answered with a smile, "I'm a general practitioner. I have my own practice here in town," she answered, wondering who the man was. She knew that Stephen had introduced them earlier, but the table was large, and she couldn't remember his name—something she was normally quite good at.

"Oh, that must be nice, running your own office!" the man said, and then began asking her the sort of questions about the most interesting or the grossest things she had ever seen at work. Finally he asked why she had chosen to be a general practitioner instead of a surgeon or a more prestigious field in medicine.

Cori was aggravated by that question. She tried not to show it, but her tone came through as crass. "I like to schedule my own time, I like being able to work with a variety of types and ages. It satisfies me," she finished, with a tone that clearly stopped the man's questions. The man replied kindly, but she couldn't remember exactly what he'd said and she sat there in the car now reliving all of the emotions of the night, feeling just as horrible now as she had then.

Stephen hadn't noticed Cori's attempts to control her breathing or the tingling in her hands and legs. They pulled up to the restaurant that Cori's mother and father had chosen for lunch. It was one of those places where people go and spend a lot of time at the table, enjoying one another's company. Her mother liked the ambiance of those sort of places. She said she didn't enjoy dining anywhere that you threw peanuts on the floor after eating them or that take-out orders were allowed. Cori's father enjoyed any restaurant that would serve fresh baked bread as they sat and waited to order, so he had no complaints either way.

When they came in, Cori's mother and father were already seated and waved them to their table.

"Alexis, you look just lovely in that dress," Cori's mother noted, and Cori glanced at Alexis, who then glanced at her, and thanked her grandmother for the compliment.

"Did you pick it out yourself?" her grandmother asked, and Cori felt her stomach flutter as she wished her mother would have just left it at that.

"No, Aunt Cori did. She said you would like it and that it would make you happy if I wore it."

Cori swallowed her ice water hard and looked around. She was so angry that Alexis would say that. She thought they had had some sort of understanding, that Cori didn't have to say, "Don't tell your grandma I said that." She had definitely misjudged the manipulative little girl, and now she felt sick about it.

"Well, your aunt was right. I love it and I'm happy to see you wearing such a lovely thing. Your aunt did right by you," her mother answered. Cori didn't realize that her mother really didn't think much about the comment at all, and if anything, thought it was funny. The idea of pleasing one's grandmother delighted her and made her feel a little bit important and brightened her outlook on life. Cori couldn't know it or see it, so she just felt miserable and resentful. Alexis knew she'd said something that had jabbed at Cori and felt pleased that she'd gotten some sort of revenge for being made to wear something she hated.

When the waiter came around to take everyone's drink order, Stephen ordered a beer while the rest of the family ordered soda or iced tea. Already agitated at Alexis, Cori lightly kicked Stephen under the table after he put in his order and looked at him. He looked back at her as if to say, "What's the problem?" and proceeded to get his beer and drink it. Cori's parents noticed his beer, and then the next one he ordered after that, but didn't say anything. Cori knew they were judging him, and by default, judging her. They were probably thinking it was a bad influence on the kids, and that Benjamin had never ordered alcohol when they went out for Sunday meals. These thoughts flooded Cori's mind to the point that she didn't enjoy her food, although she'd eaten most of it. She looked over and noticed that Alexis had hardly touched her food and A.J. had made a mess of his.

"Kids! Why aren't you eating?" Cori snapped. They both looked at her with knitted eyebrows, as it was so unusual for Cori to snap.

"We *are* eating...I'm just not starving," Alexis retorted, further angering Cori. Keeping it together as best she could, she straightened herself up and looked at her father, talking to him about whatever project he was working on at home. In her mind though, she was still upset, as she was about everything. It was like a growing monster, beginning to claw its way through her brain. She wasn't fully present, and she couldn't be fully present—not feeling the way she felt. Alexis was ungrateful, and everyone treated A.J. like he was still a baby. And Stephen was turning up beers like they were water, surely to leave her parents to pay the tab.

She thought they were all discourteous and disingenuous. They only thought of themselves and no one else.

Once they arrived at the house, Cori went to change clothes and while digging through a drawer that she normally kept quite organized she felt her eyes well up with tears. She felt like no one understood. Stephen didn't get it. Alexis didn't get it. A.J. was now a baby-child that would be spoiled and ruined if things didn't change.

She put on a pair of leggings and an oversized sweatshirt. Coming out of the large closet, she ran into Stephen, who was coming into his to change into golfing clothes.

"You're going golfing?" Cori asked, irritation making its way past the façade of normalcy on her face.

"Oh yeah, Greg, just called and wanted to see if I could come, I didn't figure it'd be a problem, we don't have anything this afternoon," he said as he shuffled through his things for the right shirt and belt to wear.

I am so sick of this shit, she thought. He could just do and say whatever he wanted, and she hated it. Was he even going golfing? Did Greg really just call? Cori rolled her eyes, not attempting to cover her anger.

"Oh you didn't figure we had anything this afternoon huh? After all that you drank at lunch, you think it's a good idea to drive and play 18 holes of golf and keep drinking? So now you automatic permission to go golfing with those slutty waitresses. You know those girls are hired only because they have bit tits and just want you to buy beers. Are they going to blow you while you ride on the golf cart and slam beer after beer? Are you even going golfing? Or are you just telling me that so you can go get your rocks off and come home and shower right away without me questioning it?" she interrogated him finally yelling so loudly her voice cracked.

Cori longed for the times they'd curl up together and watch a movie or sit and binge Netflix without worrying about the world or the kids. This made her even more emotional, and she felt the tears come full on. Stephen abruptly stopped looking for his clothes and made his way over to her.

"This has to stop. That was so long ago. What have I done to you since? If you want me to stay, you have to stop. I don't hold things you've done against you for years…" Stephen said with clear frustration.

"Well I never did anything even remotely close to what you've done to me."

"Look Cori, if you are going to accuse me constantly of doing shit, you know, I mean a lot of men would just do it. And I'm not far off from thinking about it. I haven't cheated on you since we have been married and you know that. The fucked up part is that you don't even give it up any more and I am still faithful, hoping to love your black ass through whatever this going on in your head. But I can only hold on and try for so long. You may want to think about what I'm saying."

Cori's façade of composure ruptured. She told him the reason she stopped having sex with him was because it was the same thing over and over. There was no excitement not spontaneity. She told him that he could only last through three songs on the eighteen song playlist. She said she had been faking orgasms for at least two years so what was the point. She called him names that he had never heard her use in relationship to him or anyone else. She finished by saying she would be damned if he would use that as an excuse to do it with anyone else.

Stunned, Stephen thought about how he should react. She had been upset before about the past, but had never called him a pussy before. She had never even really called him a name. She had never degraded him so badly. Cori wasn't being herself. He knew she wasn't at her happiest, but this was beyond anything he'd ever seen or heard from her. "Forget you Cori. You know what you are have lost your mind. You really have. I don't know what the hell is wrong with you but I'm done. I'm out," he said sounding more defeated and hurt than defiant.

"Yes! Go!" Cori threw her arms up in frustration. "Go play golf! Go drink more beers! Go be one of the boys, the *white* boys! Those are the guys who go play golf!"

"Tiger Woods is Black," Stephen said in a deadpan tone.

Cori looked at him with rage in her eyes. "Just get out! While you are out there find somewhere else to stay. I don't want you in my house!" He didn't dare say another word; he went to the garage, got his golf bag, and left. Cori felt like she had run him off. Golf really wasn't the worst habit for Stephen to have, she realized. It was true that his golfing buddies were white, and that when she first met Stephen, he used to play basketball at the rec with some of his old buddies from college. But most of his co-workers and new friends golfed...and most of them drank beer while they did so. She just couldn't get used to it. But was that worth throwing her husband out of the house? She wasn't sure if she longed for old Stephen, her old life, or something new altogether.

The next day at work hadn't started much different for Cori than any other day. She started on time, people were showing up on time for their appointments, and her staff were all present and in good spirits. It wasn't until a little after noon that Cori's office received a phone call that was of importance.

Cori was looking in the mirror examining the aspects of her face that saw as signs of aging. She was just about to walk back out when Karla knocked, somewhat frantically.

"Cori? Cori, pick up line one," she insisted, and Cori felt in the pit of her stomach something awful had happened. Those three steps to her office phone were filled with an onslaught of thoughts that she couldn't control. She thought of Stephen, and how much she loved him. She didn't know if he'd made it to work or not. The kids—she thought of everything from an emotional meltdown to a school shooting. Her parents were old...what if something had happened to one of them?

Frantically, she picked up the phone and with a calmed tone, answered professionally. "This is Doctor Barlow."

From there, she was asked to send over the medical records for a Mr. Jacob Marlon Ellington, a patient of hers, who had just suffered a heart attack and was in a coma in the hospital. Trembling, Cori asked if the nurse minded holding and buzzed Karla, asking her to fax the medical records over to the hospital. When she clicked back onto the line with the nurse, she came to discover that Mr. Ellington had come to the hospital complaining of the exact same symptoms he had come to her with, which dismissed, and was now about to die. He was unresponsive, she was told. She said that her nurse was sending all of his information over and that if they had any further questions, they shouldn't hesitate to call her.

Hanging up the receiver, she felt a shiver of panic roll through her. She just knew his symptoms were from heartburn or maybe even stress. Mr. Ellington had *known* though, he had known something was wrong intrinsically and Cori had dismissed him, chalking it up to paranoia and him being overly concerned about his health as he was over 70.

Now he could die, and other than emergency room staff, she had been the last doctor to treat him, and he had voiced his concerns to her. It was even written up in the report of the visit that was being sent over to the hospital at that very moment. What would they think? What would they say? They'd see that she didn't recommend any testing, but that if the patient asked, he

106

would be given tests. *I basically set him up for death*, she thought to herself. All she had to do was run some tests. That was it. If she had just run the proper tests, she could've had a chance of seeing that the man's heart was unstable, or that he had some blockage somewhere, or that his levels of this or that were too high. But in her rush, in her stubbornness, she'd insisted he was fine and sent him off. Tears filled her eyes and Karla knocked again.

"Come in," Cori said, taking a tissue and wiping her eyes.

"I sent over Mr. Ellington's files," she said, closing the door behind her. "What's going on?"

"They basically called and told me he's on his deathbed. He had a heart attack, and now he's in a coma," Cori said, staring off into the space behind Karla.

"Cori, you couldn't have predicted that. Why are you so upset? They called, and yeah, they were a bit bitchy, but hospital staff can be that way."

"I may as well have killed him," Cori said. "I didn't listen to him. I did the one thing they tell you not to do before you get really deep into med school. I ignored him. I thought I knew better than him. He knew his own body."

"You cannot beat yourself up about this," Karla comforted, and although genuine, her words seemed contrived, as though those were the correct words to say to anyone in such a case, in such a situation.

"I know, I know," Cori mumbled, looking down at her desk. She sat up straight, flipped her hair over her shoulder, and thought about what to do. She thought about the family suing her, and what all that would entail. It made the pit of her stomach churn, and she felt she couldn't breathe. She knew what came with being a doctor, which was essentially that her patients would die. But she chose to go into general medicine so that she *wouldn't* have that sort of stress constantly on surgical operating tables. She wasn't an adrenaline junkie.

"Cori, I'm not going to rush you, but I wanted you to know no one's cancelled and you've got a full schedule 'til five," Karla spoke softly. "I'll do what I can, and I'll make sure Jennifer takes her time with the pre-screenings."

"Thanks," Cori said, looking up at her. Her eyes made her look like a frightened animal, large and wild—and to some extent, at that very moment, she was. She had too many thoughts happening at once, and none of them were good ones.

As she moved on to her next patient, she seemed to simply go through the motions. Her bedside manner had suddenly changed. She noticed within herself a lack of confidence that pulled her away from herself, like she was just a bystander, watching each examination. Each set of ears she looked into, each pair of lungs she listened to, represented a different error that could be made so easily.

The next day functioned much like the first one had, except people started to notice, and as one week went by, then the next, Cori noticed her patients seemed to be disapproving of her. She felt she was letting them down and to compensate for this she began writing more prescriptions for pain meds and Adderall. Be too sure of herself, and she could kill someone. Be too paranoid, and the patient would be billed if not by her, then by insurance, for the massive costs of lab tests to be run. Be too stringent with prescriptions for people that had legitimate pain and attention issues and they would find a doctor who was more agreeable. She couldn't figure it out, and she couldn't figure herself out.

At home, things weren't much better. Stephen had noticed her distance but didn't ask. She was so tired of Alexis' mouth that she had stopped trying to interact with her altogether. She loved A.J., but she was tired of babying him, and wanted him to grow up and do things for himself.

When she arrived home from a tired work day and A.J. requested a sandwich, she let out a big sigh and told him to make it himself. The thought of doing anything for anyone else, especially if they were capable, made her feel more drained than she already was. Alexis overheard, and, seizing the opportunity, told A.J. she would make it for him, since Auntie Cori was too lazy to do it herself.

It was at that moment that Cori stood up and completely lost it on Alexis. She inhaled, and then exhaled a storm of words that swirled through the room and disrupted any normalcy they'd all come to understand.

"Young lady," Cori growled through clenched teeth, taking slow steps in her direction. "I have done every single thing I can to make your life better. I have given you every single thing I could think that you could possibly want to make your life easier. I offered my home, my life, to you. And what do I ever get in return from you? Your smart ass mouth. You talk to me like I'm trash. I ask your little brother, who's about to be eight years old, by the way," she stopped and cut her eyes down at him so he'd realize he was a part of this, too, "to make a damn sandwich, and you, little princess Alexis, who complains about doing any chore we ask or anything that doesn't suit you, offer to make it for him. Do you know what that tells me, Lexi? That tells me you're a little brat, waiting for any chance to be rude to me, to make me feel bad in some way. What did I

109

deserve to get that treatment from you, huh? What was it, exactly?"

The air was thick with tension and Alexis' creamy dark complexion flushed with embarrassment and anger. She was shocked that Cori had snapped. Deep down it was what she had wanted, but she didn't know *why* she wanted Cori to be angry. She couldn't have explained to a single soul why she wanted to push Cori to that threshold of anger, but she had finally done it, and now she didn't know what to do with herself. A.J., on the other hand, was quivering and on the verge of tears.

"Go ahead, Lexi," Cori started back in on her, "tell me what you think! You always do. So what is it? What is it, huh? Why are you so quiet now? Talk, dammit!" her voice began to rise to a boiling pitch. "Don't close that smart-ass mouth of yours now, go ahead, you little bitch! Tell me! Tell me why I'm lazy because I worked all day and your brother is old enough to make himself a sandwich!"

By this time, Stephen had come through the door. Both children looked up at him, and he had heard Cori yelling, but didn't know the full context of the situation. Wanting to settle everything, he boomed in a loud voice for both of the kids to go to their rooms. They scattered like startled little squirrels and Cori collapsed onto the kitchen floor in tears. He bent down to comfort her, but she curled up in such a way that he could feel she didn't want to be touched. Her sobs were heavy, and she got up, going into her closet and closing the door. Stephen was frustrated, and he sat down in their living room with a cold beer to try and understand what had transpired.

He heard A.J. wailing and decided to go visit him, first.

"Tell me what all is wrong."

"Aunti Cori yelled!" he sobbed and proceeded to give a play by play recounting every word spoken by Cori.

Stephen moved in to hug him. "It's going to be okay, buddy. Everybody cries. Everybody yells. Maybe not all the time, but everyone has their bad days. It'll be better," he assured him, patting his little back.

Stephen walked right into Alexis' room without knocking, took her iPad out of her hands and snatched her phone off of her nightstand.

"Wha...," she looked at him in disarray.

"Don't say another word," Stephen growled, looking at her with empty eyes and an even emptier heart. "You've said enough. You've *been* saying enough. Nobody here is your enemy. We love you, Alexis." The words emerged from his mouth, but he could hear that they were empty. Ever since they'd taken on the responsibility of raising them, he had realized how totally disengaged he truly was from the parenting process. They just weren't his kids, and they weren't easy to love.

"If she loves me, why did she call me a bitch? Did you ask her that?" she jabbed.

"Your aunt made a mistake. That was not okay; but trust she does love you."

He closed her door and heard her begin to cry, but he didn't feel sorry for her. He knew what she was capable of. He'd been ignoring her bratty behavior for months, trying to be patient with her coping with her parent's death, but he also knew that Alexis had some other sort of issue—something rooted in a desire to hurt Cori, and she was clever at it.

Approaching Cori's closet door, he knocked, and knowing the door didn't lock, he opened the door slowly to find Cori curled up in the corner of the closet with the light off, gently sobbing and blowing her nose into a dirty T-shirt.

"Babe, you gotta get up off the floor. I got the kids, okay? I got them under control. Alexis is going to be grounded for a long time for what she said to you, and how she's been acting." He paused for a moment, waiting for a response from her. "I noticed how awful she's been, I did," he confessed, "but I kept giving her chances in my mind, you know? Thinking maybe she needed more time."

"Something's *wrong* with her," Cori whispered with desperation.

"Hell yeah something's wrong with her; she needs that butt whooped. She needs to learn to respect her elders."

"No, something's *wrong* with her. She needs help...and I think I do, too."

"What do you mean, help? You are a doctor. You're the strongest person I know—and the smartest. If anyone can handle Alexis, it's you."

"That's not what I mean. And you sound like my mother, she said almost the exact same thing on the phone. God, everyone can be so programmed sometimes. We need to see someone, like a counselor."

"That's for messed up people. Like, schizophrenic people...or people with money who just need to hear themselves talk and feel validated," Stephen replied arrogantly.

"No, no it's not. It's for everyone. It was part of my training. I *know* these things. I can't believe I didn't see it in myself sooner—or in Lexi. We've been needing it."

"I think it's a waste," Stephen started.

"Yeah well, you would," Cori snapped.

"Woah why are you being like this?" he asked, not piecing together her long-term changes that had happened before his eyes.

"Being like what, a doctor? A woman? A woman smart enough to realize that I need to go see someone, a professional, who can help me cope? With loss, with the sudden burden of parenthood thrust upon me? With maintaining being a good wife to you, a good daughter and a good doctor? You don't know what's been happening," her voice dropped to a whisper.

"What, what is it? I won't know if you don't tell me."

"I'm losing patients. Four have requested to have their records sent to another doctor this month. If things continue this way, I'll be out of my practice."

"Why didn't you say anything?

"It's not the sort of thing I want to come home and say," she said, her voice hoarse from crying.

"Well, I just think you need some time, but if you think you need to go to someone, then go."

Sophie

"Sophia, I've never seen you look this way. You look a *sight*. Why haven't you been taking care of yourself?"

Those were the first words out of Cordelia's mouth as she watched Sophie settle into their outdoor seat for brunch—a brunch that Cordelia had scheduled for them at one of the most high-end locations in town. The waiter came and poured ice water into a crystal glass for Sophie, and when asked what she would like to drink, Cordelia answered for her, ordering them both two mimosas.

Sophie wore her mask of perfect daughter, made up with her best attempt at makeup and smiling brilliantly as she sat opposite her mother. Although Cordelia's words cut into her like a thousand tiny paper cuts, she had grown to expect it, and waited to see if she could somehow change the subject.

"I wanted to cut out alcohol, you know," Sophie said, straightening her posture and looking at her mother as she looked down at an elegantly designed brunch menu.

"It's brunch, we'll have mimosas. We'll enjoy the afternoon. It's what we've always done," Cordelia retorted. The waiter came back with the drinks and took their order. Cordelia had ordered a dish with lox and a variety of cheeses with toasted bagels on the side. Sophie, feeling like she was being torn apart inside over the contents of a menu, couldn't decide between lox, a decadent Belgian waffle, or avocado toast on low carb bread with a side of fruit. Her head spun trying to count calories and imagine what she could do to work off what she ate depending on what she chose.

"Well, what are you having?" Cordelia interrupted her, prompting her to hurry and order.

"I can come back," the waiter said politely.

"No, she'll order now. It always takes so long for waiters to come back when they say they'll give you a few minutes, no harm to you, sir," Cordelia smiled at him, revealing a mouth full of perfectly polished veneer implants. Now they both looked impatiently at Sophie, so she made the decision to go with the waffle and avocado toast on the side.

After the waiter had gone off with the order, Cordelia took a sip of her drink. "You're not going to lose any weight with *that* order."

"It's brunch, like you said. I wanted to get something I liked."

"Well tell me now, how's the married life with William? How are my grandchildren?"

Sophie felt the question was contrived somehow to get her to reveal a hidden truth about her misery and she didn't want to answer. She also noted that her mother wouldn't say her children's names. Cordelia would do everything in the world to avoid saying Jaylon and Javion. She'd always made it clear that she believed it was a poor decision to name them twin names, and ethnic ones at that. But Sophie loved having identical twins, and she let Will help her choose names instead of dominating the decision and naming them whatever pleased her and no one else. She smiled at Cordelia and started telling her about how wonderful Will had been and how she'd called her old college friend and talked about what it was like in the architecture firms, and how she didn't miss it, but instead cherished being home with the boys.

Cordelia sipped her drink and listened, knowing it was not her daughter truly speaking—at least not the one she had raised. *How could she possibly find value in her life like that?* Cordelia thought to herself, and proceeded in wondering where, exactly, she had gone wrong to raise a daughter so perfectly only to have her choose the life of a 1950s housewife. *She's set us all back 70 years,* Cordelia laughed to herself in her mind as Sophie finished telling a story about the twins recent activity.

"That's lovely, darling. So, your father and I were thinking of getting the boys into a nice Montessori school our friends have been raving about. They say it's the best, and we'll cover the costs, of course. Then you could go back to working, make use of your talents," she said, and adjusted herself as the waiter brought out the fresh food on delicate plates and set it down in front of them, moving swiftly as to not disturb their conversation.

"Montessori school? They're so little. I wouldn't think they're ready at all."

"Of course, not now," Cordelia cut her off. "But they have to be placed on a list now, you see, or they won't get in. It's not the sort of thing you just sign up for a week before they start. You should know about this," she scolded, and took a small bite of cheese.

"Okay, well, then add them to the list," Sophie shrugged and bit into her toast, her mask of pleasantness beginning to crumble. She didn't care how fattening it was at that moment. She ordered another mimosa, feeling that if she were to make it through the meal with her mother, she'd need more liquid courage. Any chance of eating healthy was thrown out the window anyway.

"They're going to need to know about you, and William. They're going to ask a lot of questions. Of course, I can go with you to answer the questions about your father and me, but you should be prepared to tell them about your life, William's career, your career, your degree, that sort of thing."

"Okay, what else?" she could see Cordelia was holding something back.

"Nothing. It's just that… well, when they ask about William—and they will ask—you need to make what he does sound alluring, important. The way you talk about his work usually, it makes him sound like a ditch digger. Find the right vocabulary to make him sound like the *inventor* of the ditch."

Sophie set back, feeling the kick of the champagne. She dabbed at her pretty lips with her napkin and placed it back in her lap. She could go two separate ways with what her mother had presented. She could simply take her mother's words as an attempt at good, solid advice, or she could let her know that it was unendurable.

"I know you never liked him, mother. I know you hate my life. I can't reconcile that for you. But I can't sit here and let you talk about it as if it's somehow worthless just because it wasn't what you imagined," Sophie snapped. She quickly finished her second mimosa and ordered a third, avoiding her mother's eyes.

"Darling, I wanted this to be a nice meal…a getaway for you. I didn't invite you here to have it out with you, I wanted you to be able to get out, have some time away from home," Cordelia comforted. Her creamy white dress made her skin glow in the light of the late morning, and she radiated with some sort of power that seemed to affect everyone around her. Sophie felt it and hated it. She had worn a black, flowing dress that hid the parts of her body she wanted to conceal, and there at the table, sitting apart from one another, they couldn't have been more different. Black and white, day and night, they opposed one another in every way.

"Well it *is* nice of you, but some of the things you say...I can't lose weight so quickly, you know? It isn't easy. I don't have time to go to a gym, or the money. I don't have time to fix myself healthy meals and cook for the family. It's too much," Sophie confessed angrily, taking a large gulp of her third drink.

Cordelia shook her head and pursed her lips. "You make your own time, don't you? Whose schedule are you on, William's? He should be easy enough to please. Feed him meat and potatoes every day and he'll be happy. That's the easy part. God, you sound like a mid 20th century house wife. That's just not who I raised. Sophia, you make your own time, you are home and you create your own schedule. As much as I hate to say it, do you know how many people wish they could do that and would be taking advantage of it and not just sit around? You made the decisions that have led you to this point, where you're so upset about your life."

"Who says I'm upset about my life?" Sophie asked, trying to keep her voice down, relieved they were outside and that they were in an environment that tuned out voices like her own.

"*You* do. Everything about you just screams upset. You weren't raised to be what you are, and now you're learning that it's not for you. You can't take your children anywhere, because I've seen them, and the two of them together are a holy terror. That's something you brought on yourself. You're trapped at home, and that's largely due to William not wanting you to ever leave. You think I don't know? You're having an emotional crisis...it's written all over your face. I hear it when we're on the phone. I hear it when you talk about the boys. I hear it when you talk about William and what you have to do for everyone. You don't mention yourself, you leave yourself out of it. You should be taking yourself into account. You should talk to me about it, you know," she said and took another gentle bite from her cheese and lox.

Sophie felt the tears well up in her eyes but she couldn't cry there, not in public like that. "How am I supposed to talk to you if you criticize everything I do?"

She scoffed a little at that notion. "I'm not being critical, I'm being honest. There may be things you don't know about me, about my childhood, and perhaps it's time you do. But first let me say that since you and William have stopped coming to church with me, I've noticed your changes more and more. I think if you started coming again, and perhaps had a sit-down with the pastor or his wife, you might feel better."

Sophie wanted to tell her that she'd only stopped coming because the boys were so little and so much work it was overwhelming to drag them anywhere she didn't have to on a Sunday. They *were* holy terrors. But she wouldn't give Cordelia the satisfaction of being completely on point with her assessment their behavior so she sat and waited her mother's next elucidation of her weaknesses.

"I was raised with a large family, as you know. I had four brothers and three sisters, only two of which lived. Baby Diana died in infancy, I don't know if I ever told you that. My mother and father worked and worked and worked so that we could all have what everyone else had. We didn't see our parents often. I'm not sure if I ever told you that part, either. It's something I was always very embarrassed about, because everyone else seemed to have a stay at home mother. Some would say that was a bad thing that we were always by ourselves, but we learned to do for ourselves. Now,

119

there are mindsets like William's, where his mother stayed at home and did everything for him, and now he expects that of you. In his mind, that's the ideal, that's the perfect world. I know where his mindset comes from and I can clearly see what he wanted in a wife—beauty and a mother."

Sophie knitted her brows at her mother's last few words and drank another large sip.

"What you don't know about me is that growing up in poverty helped me be who I am now and helped me be independent. If I'd grown up with a mother at home, even poor, doing everything for me, I wouldn't have had the wherewithal to learn to make myself a meal, try harder in school, advance myself in life, and I wouldn't have met your father. So, what you don't know, at least I don't *think* you know, is that I think you're harming your boys by catering to them the way you do. That's why they can't go anywhere and just sit still. Look over there," she gestured at a table with two small children about five and three years of age. "Those children are sitting and coloring on the paper the wait staff provides them, we can't hear them, and they're sitting. Sitting!"

"Okay, great. Good for them!" Sophie cocked her head and squinted her eyes at her mother. "What are you trying to say? Just say it."

"They need constant stimulation because that's what you give them at home. You think it's better to do the things you're doing, but it's not. You simply don't have time for it, Sophia. Being my daughter, you will eventually feel it in your bones, but I don't want it to be too late when you do. You have to take care of yourself first. You don't have time to sit at home and eat and cry and make excuses. If you want to lose weight, you'll find a way, not just talk about it. It's obvious you didn't marry up in life, so it's up to you to do for yourself. No one else will. That's what I learned. I knew I had to work hard, marry up, and I'd be taken care of. And I was."

Sophie felt one tear escape her left eye and drip down her cheek. Her mother had said it. She'd married down. She didn't have time to wallow in her own self-pity, and furthermore, no one really cared about her self-pity. She was at a point of utter despair.

"Wipe your face, darling, people will see," Cordelia mumbled, sipping her drink and glancing around.

"No, let them see. Let them be uncomfortable. I am. Why shouldn't they be, too?"

"You're not making any sense, Sophia, I think you'd better calm down."

"I won't. I can't," by now her tears were streaming. The waiter had approached them, but backed off slowly upon seeing her face. "You don't understand me, and you underestimate me, and you think I don't want better for myself. None of that is true. I wanted a family, and I have one, and I love them, and I love Will, and you don't care for that, do you? Do you even love Dad? Or did you just see a way out in him?"

"People are looking!" Cordelia hissed in a whisper.

"Okay, so what if they do." Sophie shoved herself away from the table and ordered an Uber from her phone. She threw her napkin down in her chair and stormed away from her mother. Cordelia had picked her up and driven them, and she couldn't bare the idea of getting back into a confined space with her. Too dignified to chase after her, Cordelia sat and continued to eat, pretending to not be bothered by the scene Sophie had made.

When she got home, Will was sitting on the couch scrolling through his social media timeline while the boys played on the floor in front of him. He was sipping a beer and watching a football game. He didn't notice Sophie's tear stained face or the redness of her eyes. He said something to her about dinner and she ignored him, going into their bedroom and curling up on the floor to cry.

She couldn't pinpoint all of the things that were wrong with her, but she knew she felt lost in some way, like she was doing everything wrong and displeasing everyone. Will made his way into the bedroom to see her. He was immediately distraught at the sight of her on the floor, like a wilted flower he couldn't bring back to life.

"You didn't want to take the boys with you to brunch?" he asked, sipping his beer.

Sophie sniffed up her tears and looked at him with bloodshot eyes that made them glow wild like emerald embers.

"You...you're serious? You actually think I'd want to take them to *brunch*? At *Crêpe Dorée*? Have you ever been there? Do you know what it's like there? The boys...they can't go anywhere, they don't know how to act. I can't even take them inside a McDonalds without damn near losing control, Will. They get up, run around, nothing I say makes a difference. I *told* you we needed to start taking them out to eat from a younger age, so they'd learn etiquette...they can't eat at a place like that, but we don't even try."

Unphased by the actual point she was trying to make, he answered in a stern, condescending tone. "Babe, we have a budget. You know that, it's why you cook our meals here and we don't go eat all the time. And the boys are just little boys! Of course, they're going to run around and have fun...let them be kids, let them have fun, you know?"

"No! No, I don't know! That's not normal. Children need discipline and they don't get any other than me, and I can't do it all by myself," she snarled, wiping the snot that was accumulating from the tip of her nose.

"Well look, when I was growing up...."

"What? What happened when you were growing up, Will?" she interrupted. "When you were growing up your mom manhandled all of you perfectly fine and you didn't eat out, but if you did, you were too scared of her to misbehave? She was the perfect mother, she never dealt with anything? She probably never made a meal that wasn't above restaurant worthy, so you all never had the need to eat out?"

He ignored her insults, choosing not to engage. "We made it work on far less money than I bring in now, we don't need to go out all the time. That's what I'm saying."

"It's not about just wanting to go out. Hell, Will, I don't mind not going out, especially not looking how I want to look, how I *used* to look, but that's beside the point. The boys...we can't even take them to a fast food restaurant without them acting like wild animals. They have no concept of good behavior because we're always *here*. Kids who go to a day care or a Montessori school, they learn about appropriate behavior early. They get socialized. People tell them what's appropriate and what's not, and they bring that home with them."

Will furrowed his brows and looked at her discerningly, his tone becoming more aggressive as he spoke. "Montessori school...is that your next big plan? Have them go there? I can't afford that shit."

"My parents will pay, Will. And then I can get back to work, and we can settle, really settle into our life," Sophie explained, with pleading in her eyes. She'd never wanted him to understand her needs so badly.

"No, no, absolutely not. I'm not letting your parents pay for the boys' education. We can do it; plus they can wait for Kindergarten like every other kid and start school when they're five. I'm done with your parents' interference and mind games. Those people have no concept of reality."

He stopped, distracted by an alert on his phone, and looked back up at her. "I just got a $15 charge from Uber on my bank account," he said. Then he looked at Sophie, whose eyes began to hurt again with the pressure of oncoming tears.

"Well, I had to get home somehow," she whispered.

"An Uber? With your mother right there in her perfectly polished Jaguar, and you want to take an Uber home? I ain't rollin' like that, babe. You *have* to think about these things. You're not living like your parents live anymore. You don't live at home anymore. It's us now."

Still slightly buzzed from her mimosas, and highly susceptible to anything critical, Sophie let herself cry again. Confused by her tears but unable to comfort her, Will sat there with her uncomfortably.

"I *had* to leave, Will, I didn't want to be around her. I had an argument with her. So I left. That's how I got home, and you're going to bitch at me about a fifteen dollar charge? This is why I can't do this—I can't be your mom, a stay at home mom. I have to work, I have to have my career back and make my own money so that I don't have to answer to you every time I buy something. You said you were our earner, and it was *our* money. I feel like I'm a child...asking for a goddamn allowance! I've been on an allowance my whole damn life, Will! I'm 32, not 12, I need to have some independence. If you're going to scrutinize every single purchase I make, I don't want your money. I want my own."

Will read into her words as if she was saying she wanted space from him, but that was not her intention. She continued on through gritted teeth. "I love being a

124

mom, but if I have to hear how great you had it as a kid one more time with a reference to your mother, I'm going to fucking lose it. You don't understand how undermining and insulting that is. I can *never* be your mom, okay? I love your mom, but I'm not her. I'll never be like her. I wasn't raised like her, I wasn't taught the way she was taught...why should I have to become your mother for you? If you need to be mothered in your thirties, there's something wrong with you. Can't you see I don't have time to breathe? Can't you see that it's more than one job here at home to take care of toddler twins and mother you, too? Like, you can't even offer to make yourself a sandwich to take to work for lunch. I literally have to make it for you—and I don't think it's because you want me to make it because you like the way I make your lunch. I truly believe it's because you think it's my job, that I *owe* it to you."

He looked down, away from her. He was angry. He couldn't believe how unappreciative she was of his work. He had built a life for them, and she talked about it as if he had her trapped in a prison.

"Damn, Sophie, I thought you would appreciate me, appreciate *this*. I know so many women who wish their husbands would let them stay home and be a homemaker. You treat it like it's a jail sentence."

"Oh, you know a lot of women?" she snapped back, latching onto that one phrase, feeling insecure as it was, and her mind unable to discern anything else from his words.

"Not like that, this is insane...I know my coworkers and friends, their wives...lots of them talk about wishing they had it like you; that they could stay home and just be a mom."

"I see," Sophie said, straightening her posture and refusing to meet his eyes. "So, you don't think that I realize how good I have it? Do you know how old my clothes are? They're older than the boys, Will. I'm not 'just a mom' here, Will. I'm a cook, a maid, a babysitter, I fix shit when it's broken, I'm our accountant for groceries and bills. Do you realize I have no time for myself to go and exercise, to shed some of this baby weight? You come home and go to the gym and don't offer to take me! I'm fat, Will! Why do you think I don't want to have sex with you?"

Will's expression changed, and he looked up at her with knitted brows. "You don't want to have sex with me?"

"Not with lights on. I don't feel good about myself. I don't look the same. Your body—it's perfect. You still look the same. You haven't changed. You go to the gym, you sweat during the day. You've gotten better. Me...I don't fit in anything. I feel heavy and exhausted all the time, and it's depressing. If I don't feel good about me, then sex doesn't feel good, and you don't give me the time to go and better myself, plus you'd guzzle bacon grease if I'd let you! You have no concept of eating right. You don't help my situation, you make it worse!"

"So what do you want? How are we supposed to go to the gym together with the boys?" Will queried, desperate for a solid answer with no room for interpretation.

"I want time, for me! For me! It's not good enough to just be a mom, be here all day, go to play dates at the park and talk to women who aren't even my friends. The only thing we have in common is that we all bore children from our womb and frankly, that's not as an impressive feat to me as it is to them, and it's not much to have an intellectual conversation about, at least not when they can't hold a conversation about anything beyond tabloid gossip for more than five minutes. I want time for me

126

and me alone, where I can go and run, then go and get my hair done, or go sit and read a book alone, hell, even go to a bookstore."

He didn't hesitate to respond, almost like he hadn't been listening but instead was waiting for her to shut up so that he could rebut her remarks.

"Well just like you're not ever gonna be *my* mom, I'm not ever gonna be *your* dad. I can't afford a nanny just so you can go be your old, spoiled self. I can't do it. Why can't you just run with the stroller? Why can't you sit and read while the boys play?"

"Have you *seen* the stroller, Will? It's not made for running. I'd do it if you'd buy me one made for running, but do you remember that conversation a while back at the store? You and I debating on having two strollers? You said it was pointless. You said we couldn't afford it. But then, a month or so later, you bought that stupid cable package for all the football and sports games that cost *more* than the running stroller. Entertainment! You wouldn't buy me something I could use for the kids *and* myself, but you could buy an intangible, ridiculously priced cable package to watch a bunch of grown men throw balls around. And try reading sometime, Will. Pick up a book and try to read it with the boys right in front of you, without anyone else to help mind them, then come talk to me," she fumed.

"You want a jogging stroller? I'll get you the stroller, but this crying bullshit has to stop. I don't know what is wrong with you. I get that you said you don't feel good because of exercise and all…but I don't think you see how much I have sacrificed and what all I have to do to keep this household running. Do you ever think about that? Do you ever think maybe I get exhausted from waking up at 6:00 a.m. every morning to be on site before everyone else is, and inspect everything? Then you want to go to France—really? How do you think that's gonna work with my job, Sophie? You married me and you knew that I wasn't a backpack-through-Europe type of guy."

"I'm not asking you to backpack through Europe, I'm asking you to plan getaways for us, you and me, the two of us, no kids. People do that. It's normal. And when the kids are older, take them, too. They need to see things, Will, they are spoiled in the wrong type of way, and I can't take them hardly anywhere, it's so hard," she started to feel the tears escape her eyes again.

"What about when we have more? You always knew I wanted a big family. Do you know what it would be like to try and travel with three or four kids?"

Sophie's eyes widened and she let out a sob. "I don't want more kids, Will! Not if I don't have help from you or anyone else! I can't do it."

"Maybe you need to talk to the pastor at the church, or his wife." There it was again, twice in one day. She needed to go to church, they said. She needed counseling from the pastors.

"I don't *need* to talk to anyone. I need some time on my own to figure things out and I'll feel better," she said through tears.

"So what, you want to separate?" he misinterpreted.

"No! That's not what I'm saying! I love you!" she leaned over onto his knees, clinging to them in some sort of blind desperation.

"Then what do you mean?"

"I don't know…" she cried harder. "I told you I need to get in shape, I need to eat right. I need to feel like I have some sort of control. I don't want to be managed by you, my parents…anyone."

"I've never tried to manage you, babe, I didn't think I was doing anything like that. I'm just trying to give us a good life and enjoy it at the same time."

"Well you are managing! You just managed my Uber ride," she raged again, switching quickly between crying and yelling. "You get to enjoy the life while I get nothing!"

"I don't know how to make you happy. Nothing I do is good enough," he groaned.

"I told you what *exactly* is wrong! I didn't make you guess!" she squealed in frustration. Throwing her hands up, she continued. "How can you not hear me when I say the same thing over and over again...that you're not hearing! I think a deaf man would have figured it out by now, Will!"

While Sophie tried to articulate everything so that he'd understand, all Will could perceive was that she was crying for reasons he thought were ridiculous, and that she should be happy but she wasn't. He heard her, he understood her words clearly, but he resented her parents, especially Cordelia. He left Sophie sobbing on the floor and went back to tend to the twins, who, surprisingly, had not done anything terribly destructive while out of sight. He thought briefly of ways he could appeal to the best in Sophie, and make her see that all he did was for her, and that it was important for them not to spend money on frivolous things such as pointless Uber rides when she could have just sucked it up and ridden home with her mother, but he felt at a loss in trying to communicate with her.

Sophie's crying subsided enough for her to pick herself up off of the floor and go clean her face in their bathroom. She washed the drooping makeup off that she'd put on for brunch, an off-brand mascara she'd had to buy at the drugstore instead of what her long, curly lashes were used to from high end department stores.

She rinsed off the cheap foundation that only cluttered her skin with strange color and didn't give it the glow of something nicer that she might find at Neiman's. She dried her face in a towel that smelled of mildew and realized she needed to put almost every item of clothing or towel that was strewn about around her through the wash. More work for her, less time for herself.

Then her phone rang. It was Cordelia. Hesitant to answer, she went ahead and accepted the call.

"Yes, mom?" she hesitantly greeted.

"Sophia, I'm not going to play around with you anymore. I've tried to do everything in my power to make your life simpler for you even though you've chosen to go against your better judgement over and over again. So, it's come to this. You abandoned me at brunch, and so I'm abandoning my plethora of offers. *You* can figure it out. Figure out how to get those boys into a good school. Figure out how to get yourself back working, making use of an entirely wasted Princeton degree. I could've scholarshipped that nice young girl from church instead of paying your ghastly tuition. But instead, I made sure you had the best of everything. You can continue on like you're doing and see where it leads you—but no more mother interfering and making things more difficult for you. You know where I am and I'm not going anywhere, but forget the offer for Montessori, and forget everything else. You like making your own decisions, so make them. Pull yourself together like I had to do long before I was your age and figure it all out."

The pressure of her mother's words made her sink back down to the floor. Cordelia could hear her silent sniffles through the phone. She didn't realize that Sophie had already been having it out with Will, nor did she realize that through it all, Sophie was extremely excited to get the boys into an early age Montessori school, where they could learn how to be around other children, learn to take instruction from other people, learn how to eat in public...and long before the age of five. Now that was fading from her. She ended the call without words. The light at the end of Sophie's long, suffocating tunnel was the idea that even with using her mother and father's money and connections, she could get her life back the way she wanted. She wanted the kids and the husband, but she couldn't begin to be the housemaid, the cook, the governess and the endearing wife. She didn't think anyone actually could, and anyone who said they could had to be lying. Something had to give—either the female physique, the sex, attention to the kids, nutrition, cleanliness...it couldn't all possibly be done. "Those women are liars," she said to herself. "They don't have it all together, they *can't* have it all together."

For the next several weeks, Will and Sophie rarely spoke. She served meals of meat and potatoes, as her mother had suggested, and she didn't eat much herself. Will didn't notice her lack of food intake, and Sophie took up doing little things like burpees or squats on her own to get back in shape.

It was just as she was feeling a bit better that she saw something that disrupted everything for her. On what had been a seemingly normal day, she looked down at Will's phone vibrating on the counter while he rummaged through the refrigerator. It had an influx of alerts on the homescreen, and she picked it up. She noticed friend requests on Facebook had been accepted, and they were all women with large, tanned breasts of many ethnicities, with full faces of makeup and bodies of workout models—not the kind in the fitness competitions. These were the kind with butt implants...or maybe they were natural...who took all of their photos at an angle that showed a tiny waist and a large, round sculpted ass with no cellulite and shimmering skin.

She dug a little deeper and saw that he had comments on pictures she knew nothing about, as she had no social media. Evidently, he posted workout photos nearly every time he went to the gym and had comments from many women, and over 100 likes on the photos. In many of them, he was shirtless and had his shorts pulled low to show the v-line of his abdomen. One woman commented, "Dayyum, what are those ab lines pointing to?" He had replied with an emoji face indicating a sly face.

She began to feel herself shake and tremor. Being a cunning woman, she wanted to hide the information from him, and use it when she could. She put his phone back as it had been, and she went on about her daily activities as if nothing was wrong. For the next several days, she continued to work out harder, her inner rage fueling her, but cut back on her food intake less and less, until one day, she ate nothing at all; then the next, she'd have a few bites of something, then return to a full fast the next day. The weight was dropping off excessively, and the angrier she got at Will for hiding his online social life, the more desire she had to force away all food, and sometimes water, as well.

In her mind, she started fantasizing about him cheating, making up imaginary scenarios that she began to believe were real. They fueled every choice she made.

Will hadn't said anything to her about her weight loss—in fact, he'd been rather aloof to her altogether and had continued on with his normal routine. The only thing he'd given was a bit of praise for was her fat-filled grease meals she made sure were on the table by 6:00 p.m. each night. He didn't even notice she wasn't eating, only pushing veggies around on a plate.

It wasn't until he was driving home on a seemingly innocuous Wednesday that Will turned the corner down their street to find Sophie walking slowly. She didn't have on any shoes, and it was at that moment that he noticed how thin she looked. Pulling over, making the brakes screech, he raged at her with questions.

Where were the boys? What was she doing? What in the hell was wrong with her?

"What's wrong with *me*, Will?" she asked, not referring to her current state, but instead referring to the collection of women he was acquiring as friends on his social media, and why he possibly needed their attention instead of hers. It had eaten away at her so much that on that particular day, after the boys had both thrown a complete tantrum for her making them take a bath, she had simply walked out of the house, bemused at her life and purpose.

Will floored it the to the house and shaking with his mounting fear that the boys were injured from her lack of supervision, he found the them naked, rummaging through the refrigerator, having spilled a bottle of juice and broken a few eggs.

Turning and looking at Sophie, who had returned and stood leaning against the front door entryway, he began cursing, accusing her of going crazy. She laughed at him and only replied with, "Are you going to block me?"

He looked at her with a distorted anger, not understanding what she meant. "What in the hell do you mean?"

"You should know, you fucking cheater," she said in a low, almost hoarse voice. She turned around to walk back out the front door. He ran over to her arm and clutched it hard, ready to throw her into a chair and make her explain herself. He noticed with his grip how small her arm now felt in his hands. Startled, Sophie spun around, and a wave of dizziness overtook her, and she fell over. Panicked, will checked her all over and found that she'd passed out. He called for an ambulance, unsure of her condition.

Vivian

After staying indoors for what Joshua ended up telling her had been two whole days, Vivian realized she needed to get up, get out, and run some errands. She had to go by the post office and mail some things. She had to meet with an attorney about the business issues, and lastly, she had to go get some food from the store— the store she so desperately dreaded.

Vivian stretched and leaned over to both sides, making her back pop and trying to relax. She showered and resolutely dressed, feeling as though she was going into some sort of battle. It was 9:00 in the morning and she decided to give Carly a Facetime call. She knew she didn't have class early on Tuesdays. The odd tone of ringing began and Vivian's stomach churned with feelings of loss of control. If Carly didn't answer, Vivian would begin running a stream of events through her mind that would only serve to wreck her miniscule sense of calm that she had mustered.

There was no answer. Vivian began to think of the worst scenarios. She pictured Carly naked in bed with other girls—wild ones like Michael used to make her watch with him. She shook that disturbing image and instead imagined her being too hungover to answer and cringed at the thought of promiscuity that could be occurring. She couldn't control what Carly did there. It made her sick to think about any of it.

Setting her phone down, she went to dab on some makeup in the mirror and noticed the heavy bags beneath her eyes. The crying coupled with the stress was wearing on her and she couldn't do anything to mask them.

After a quick check of the house she stepped outside and rushed to her car, making sure she got in as quickly as possible to avoid a friendly confrontation from a neighbor. She had found she had become less and less capable of small talk and avoided it at all costs. Looking someone in the eye was like being stabbed with daggers. Suddenly she jerked to attention as her phone rang. It was Carly.

Trying to sound happy, she answered the video chat call.

"Hey mom, sorry, I was in the shower," Carly said, smiling and checking her hair in the frame of the video in which she could see herself and her mother.

Cringing at the thought of her showering with another person, she breathed in and spoke happily. "It's okay, I'm just glad you called me back." Then she noticed the tiniest of marks whoosh by on Carly's hand, on the side of her palm and pinky finger.

"What's that? On your hand?" she asked, unable to hide the frantic tone in her voice.

Carly rolled her eyes a bit, and held her hand up in a vertical salute to the camera. "It's a tattoo, mom."

Vivian felt her head spin with dizziness. This image wasn't made up, it was clearly real. She couldn't talk, her lips thinned and she tried to keep her chin from quivering as she looked at Carly, disappointment filling her eyes.

"See, this is why I don't tell you things. This is why I can't talk to you! You freak out! I can tell dad! In fact, I did! He's already seen it. And do you know what he did mom? He asked me what the writing means. So, I told him, it means 'Not all who wander are lost', but I got it in Vietnamese instead of English. You know what he said?

He said it was beautiful.   It's a Tolkien quote." She stopped, waiting for her mother to protest.

Instead of raging, Vivian let her lip go into a full quiver, and tears roll out of her eyes. She knew Carly knew how she felt about tattoos, and how trashy she thought they were. Now here her daughter was, with unicorn hair, a nose piercing, and a tattoo that couldn't even be hidden with a good shirt.

"How...how are you planning on getting a job with that on your hand?" Vivian said through tears.

"Mom, the world is different than it was when you were growing up. Calm down! Jesus Christ!" Carly sneered angrily.

"I will remind you that I am your mother! You need to have some respect for that! Your father may not care about what you do, but that's because he's in his own world, planning a *new* life, one without any of us and one that is all about him! So of course he doesn't care! You just keep finding ways to dishonor me and everything I've done for you!"

Carly looked into the screen with a blank stare, one of an emotionless void, and ended the call.

Vivian broke down harder now, digging around in her console for tissues. She couldn't believe her daughter would take her freedom in college to that level. She knew she was probably seeing girls and guys, and Vivian could live with that to some extent, but her nightmarish visions of the reality of casual college relationships coupled with her own inner dilapidation had just grown worse, and now she had no control over Carly whatsoever, and Michael was playing his cards right to make sure that he was the good parent; the one Carly could trust even though she knew Carly resented his girlfriend of the same name. It was as if Carly was willing to overlook that just for acceptance of any stupid decision she made.

"Maybe she's learning not to love me just like him," Vivian sobbed to herself. She spent several minutes crying in the car before she attempted to clean herself up and move on with the day's necessary activities.

Her first stop was by her lawyer's office. She had the signed paperwork for her business with Michael, and the selling of it, ready to hand over. When he saw her face, he was slightly taken aback. Avoiding making her feel bad, as he could tell that she was obviously in need of a moment, he asked if there was anything else he could help her with.

"No," Vivian replied in a voice of lost purpose. "I just wanted to get these to you. I'm assuming that next will be the divorce papers?"

He shook his head. "I don't know, Vivian. It looks like he hasn't filed yet. Do you want to file on him?"

The question took her by surprise. She hadn't thought of that. She didn't want to be without him in the first place, and now he was delaying the inevitable. She certainly couldn't bring herself to leave him—she was his victim, and that's how it would stay.

"No!" she gasped a little. "No, no Mr. Schwartz, I don't want to file. If he wants to do it, it's on him."

Mr. Schwartz nodded and patted her paperwork. "It's fine, no worries. I'll take care of this and I'll call you if anything comes up.

Vivian left hurriedly, getting past the receptionist with not more than a half-hearted "thank you" as she pushed through the doors. Once in her car, she knew she had to mail a form to the IRS. The stress it put on her to do the smallest of things was beginning to weigh her down like a mule with too heavy of a load on its back. She could feel the compression it was causing her. It made her neck ache and her head begin to throb. She dropped the envelope off in the drop box at the post office and continued driving. She had thought about ordering the groceries and just picking them up, but the times available for pick up weren't until later in the afternoon and she didn't want to have to wait. She needed to be able to have food for Joshua when he got home.

She parked her car and looked ahead at the store. It loomed in front of her like an evil building, warning her not to enter. She could feel her chest tighten and her breathing speed up, even her heart. She got out of the car and took a deep breath. Looking around cautiously, she saw that people were casually entering and exiting the store with no issue. *Why can't I just be like them, it's so simple*, she thought to herself, upset that she wasn't just normal.

She took one of the small carts and pushed through the automatic doors of the store, ignoring the polite nod of the greeter. Looking both ways, she passed the cosmetics section and noticed a tall man looking at shampoo. Her heart fluttered and her gut wrenched. It wasn't Michael, but the sight of anyone like him sent her into the panic of thinking it could possibly be him. She moved into the dairy aisle to get eggs. She was examining a small box of organic farmed eggs when she glanced at the person on her left. It was a blonde woman, and for a moment, she couldn't discern if it was Carlie or just a stranger. Her vision blurred and she dropped the eggs. The woman looked up, surprised by the mess of eggs on the floor.

"Oh no, are you alright?" the stranger, clearly not Carlie, asked Vivian.

Vivian couldn't breathe. She looked at the mess she made and back at the woman, a confused helplessness in her eyes. She turned away from the woman and the mess and started speed walking out of the store. She got to her car, unable to breath normally. She felt a pain in her chest.

"I'm having a heart attack!" she gasped. She didn't know what to do. She picked up the phone to call her mother, fumbling for the right places to touch the screen of the phone with her shaking hand.

"Mom, mom!"

"What is it!" Ngoc asked desperately, trying to get a clear idea of what was happening. "Where are you?"

"I'm...I'm at the store! I think I could be having a heart attack!" she gasped. "I can't breathe. I can't...I can't...." her words trailed off into a haze of dizziness.

"Hold on, Vivian, I'll be over there shortly."

Before Vivian could fully process what all had happened, her mother had called an ambulance, met them at the store, and was riding with Vivian to the emergency room, which was just a short distance down the road. It had caused a scene in the parking lot that Vivian had not noticed, as she heaved and resisted the feeling of losing all control.

She was rushed in, with Ngoc at her side, and eventually passed through triage to a doctor who could properly evaluate her. After tests were run and questions were asked, Vivian was hooked up to machines and, while lying in her hospital bed helplessly, awaited to hear what the doctor's verdict would be.

Ngoc didn't say much. She didn't understand what was happening to her daughter, but she very much wanted to. She knew Vivian had always been a bit high strung, but she simply couldn't understand why it would cause her to have a heart attack at the grocery store. She didn't think Vivian was approaching her troubles in life the right way. Ngoc had been through plenty of tumultuous times herself, and she knew that there were alternative ways to handle things that Vivian seemed to reject.

Holding her daughter's hand, she looked up with relief when a doctor came through the door.

"Vivian? I'm Doctor Carrol. I've looked at all of your test results and the read outs from the monitors. It seems that you suffered a debilitating panic attack."

"Panic attack?" Vivian gasped, almost embarrassed.

"Yes, a panic attack," he answered. "You're not the first person to come through these doors having had one like this. It's not a good feeling, I know. It makes you feel like you're dying, basically. You can't breathe, your chest feels constricted, you feel trapped in your own body, basically, and your mind feels like it's trying to attack you."

Vivian related to everything he was saying, but she felt certain it had to be much worse than a panic attack, and Ngoc agreed.

"Doctor, aren't panic attacks just like, a thing in a person's head?" Ngoc asked, skeptical of the seriousness of his description.

"Well, it's not that simple," he started. "Panic attacks usually develop after a traumatic experience has happened, and a person has been dealing with major bouts of anxiety. There are exceptions to this, but typically, a full blown panic attack in the style of the one you just had comes from a buildup of debilitating anxiety. Can you tell me, Vivian, have you felt anxiety or anxiety attacks lately?"

Vivian paused, unsure of exactly what to say with her mother in the room. She didn't like divulging her weaknesses to anyone, especially her mother, but she had to say something, and if she was going to be receiving a bill for a hospital stay, she figured she better tell him something of substance.

"Well, yes. I've actually been going through a separation," she started.

"A divorce," Ngoc interrupted.

"No, mom, we haven't filed," Vivian let out a long sigh. The doctor looked at both of them and took note of how their words played negatively off of one another.

"Okay, so you've been separated. That can be stressful. Anything else?"

Vivian looked at her mother, then back at the doctor. "Yes. My husband left me for a younger woman, who has the same name as our daughter, and he met her *because* of my mother. Now I'm left to deal with my teenage son, and my daughter is in college, and he's selling our business…I don't know what to do. I don't like going places. I don't like seeing people."

The doctor jotted down some notes and shook his head understandingly.

"Well, Vivian, these types of situations bring us to the point of severe anxiety sometimes. You've probably been getting more and more anxious, and then something today triggered a full panic attack. There are treatments, but they aren't a quick fix. I'm going to write you a prescription for something to calm you down when you feel overwhelmed, but it's temporary. I'm recommending you to a therapist. She's very good, and if you attend therapy, it can help give you the coping tools to deal with the things that overwhelm you and make you feel anxious."

"She doesn't need pills, or to go to therapy," Ngoc interrupted. "She needs to learn like I did, like everyone else does. Things happen. Stop blaming me for introducing them. Move on!"

"With all due respect, ma'am, I'm giving Vivian, who appears to be a fully capable adult woman, the things she needs to get a boost and get the treatment she'll need to feel better. Her mental health is very important, it's what landed her here today. We want to make sure she gets the best treatment to get back on track."

Ngoc huffed, upset that she wasn't being heard, and was being blamed so openly for something she truly didn't orchestrate.

Vivian took his paperwork, and she was subsequently checked out of the ER and headed back to get her car from the parking lot. As they drove together in the car, there was a silence in the air that built a wall that could only be cut through by more stinging words by one of them. Who dared to speak first was anyone's guess. Ngoc took her chances.

"Vivian, these therapists are a waste of time. They make a lot of money just sitting there listening to you, and you get to whine to them about your problems. It's up to you to fix them. You could just skip the therapy and talk to me. I'm here for you. I have lots of different things to help calm you. We have massage, I have your great-grandmother's calming tea. You don't have to do *exactly* what he said."

Vivian looked over at Ngoc with empty eyes. "No more, mother. No more. Nothing else is working. I'm going to do this and if it doesn't work, then we'll do it your way, but I can't live like this anymore. I can't wake up every day afraid to leave the house. I can't see a woman who looks like that bitch and then freak out. I can't live with the anxiety. It's horrible."

"Okay Vivian but what did you want me to do if I didn't know? How can you expect people to help you if you don't tell them anything?" The car stopped with a jolt as they parked near Vivian's abandoned car.

"I can't tell you things because you always think I'm being unreasonable. There's a limit to how much a person wants to tell someone, even their mother, if they think they're going to be judged for it."

"I'm not judging you. I'm just...." Vivian didn't let her finish. She got out of the car without thanking her and opened her own car door.

She dropped her prescription off at the pharmacy and arrived home to see Joshua waiting for her inside, playing video games.

"Where's some food, mom?" he asked, not taking his eyes off the screen to see that she still had the wrist band from the hospital on.

"You're going to have to make something yourself. Make a sandwich," she muttered, and went off into her bathroom to cleanse herself from the cold filth she felt from the hospital.

PART III

Sessions

Andrea

Session 1

As the sun came up, Andrea forced herself to shower and dress. She pulled on a form fitting dress and a pair of Jimmy Choos. She was headed to her doctor's appointment with a new primary care doctor that she found on her insurance's "Find a Doc" website. She needed someone with initials behind their name to complete her release to work form.

She was determined not to look disheveled as she did when she attended her appointment with Doctor Kate. She was convinced that her appearance must have made Doctor Kate believe that she needed help; *that* kind of help, but she didn't. She just needed to return to work to keep her mind off Daniel and the kids.

As she was unlocking her car door she heard her phone buzz in her purse. It was Frank texting to check on her. He had been the only one at the firm that was checking on her since she was out of the office. She had not told anyone of her absence, only Jim knew and that was because Daniel had sent him an email the following Monday after their fallout. Jim had simply responded with a doctor's contact information and a short note stating that he hoped she got better soon.

Andrea responded to Frank's text saying that she was still sitting on the beach enjoying the peace and quiet; a lie that Frank seemed to buy.

She started the car and headed toward Doctor Cameron's office.

"Good morning," she announced as she entered the Doctor Office. "I'm Andrea Molinar and I have a new patient appointment," she said to the receptionist, already working on sounding as clear headed and competent as possible.

"Okay the doctor will be right with you," the perky receptionist responded. Andrea noticed her long dark hair and giant boobs, coupled with her beautiful skin and perfect makeup and thought about how she so badly wanted to feel pretty again. She envied the receptionist, then did the thing she did so well and in her own mind said to herself, *why would you envy a freakin' receptionist? You're an attorney.*

She had just hit such a slump with the blow up with Daniel that she was barely able to function. Since being released from the hospital over a week ago, she would have days where she slept all day without showering or washing her hair, barely eating and refusing to talk to anyone. She had one day in which she felt like her old self again. She had not slept that night before, instead deciding to clean the entire house. As the sun came up, she went for a run, something she had not done in months. After her run she surprised herself with the natural high she was feeling. She browsed the internet and shopped on the Neiman Marcus website. She noticed that she felt so much better and used that time to call her mom. She talked incessantly about this and that and didn't seem to notice the concern in her mother's voice. When her mother asked if she was alright, Andrea assumed she meant with the separation and informed her mother that she felt great and was planning to see the kids that weekend. She hung up and called friend after friend, only to have conversations cut short.

That evening, Andrea opened a bottle of white wine and finished it off in less than an hour while working on the prestigious White divorce case that she was assigned before her sudden leave of absence. She felt like she was on top of the world and knew she would be back at work in no time, landing huge settlements for her high-end clients.

"Andrea," called a large woman in pink scrubs, snapping her out of her thoughts. She was desperate to return to that feeling. The woman in scrubs led her back to small room that did not feel like a typical exam room.

"Oh, I'm here for a new patient exam," Andrea said as the lady in scrubs was about to exit the room.

"Yes ma'am," she answered. "We begin all of the new patient visits with a short consultation first. She will be right in."

"Good morning Andrea," a beautiful, dark skinned Black woman wearing black dress with black booties and a white coat entered the room. Andrea tried to hide her look of surprise to see a Black doctor standing in front of her.

"Oh, good morning. Are you the doctor?" her surprise harder to cover than she anticipated.

"Yes I am. I am Doctor Stewart. How are you this morning?" She smiled at Andrea with a bit of smirk, suggesting that she got that question so much that she knew exactly what was being implied, but she was not offended.

"Hi doctor. I would like to establish care with you, but I mostly need you to complete a form stating that I can return to work."

"Oh okay," the doctor said as she sat down in a chair across from Andrea.

"How about if you tell me about the form and what medical condition you have that you need a release to return to work."

"Well, that's just it. I don't have a medical condition. I'm just fine actually. About two weeks ago I had a little tiff with my husband. He called the police and they took me to Stanley Behavioral Health. When I left there they told me that I needed a doctor to say I could go back to work."

"Oh I see. Ok did you follow up with a therapist then?"

"I went to an appointment yes, but honestly, doctor, nothing is wrong with me. I don't need to go back."

"Ok what did the therapist say?"

"Nothing, she just asked a series of questions about the past."

"Hmm...okay I see. Did the hospital give you a diagnosis?"

"No, actually, they just said that I wasn't suicidal any longer. But just for the record, I was never *really* suicidal."

Andrea answered more questions about her health, stating that she had healthy pregnancies, never had any surgeries, and didn't have any chronic illnesses, and was not currently taking any prescribed medications. She did her best to be chipper and sound honest as she answered "yes" or "no" to each question. She just needed to get this over with to get back to work.

The doctor then began asking about her drinking habits.

"Well, I drink socially. My coworkers and I will go out every once in a while to celebrate a big case. I am a divorce litigator and we encounter some pretty stressful cases, but it's nothing more than that."

"I see," said the doctor.

As she asked more detailed questions, Andrea began to feel defensive. She reminded herself to not get emotional and to think of it as business. The doctor then began to ask about Andrea's drug use, past or present.

"Look, I don't understand why people continue to ask me questions that absolutely don't matter. Yes, I've had a Xanax or two that weren't prescribed to me, but I know how to control myself. I'm not stupid. I wouldn't be so successful if I couldn't handle myself."

"I understand Andrea. Please know that I don't think you are stupid. These are questions that I have to ask everyone. Let's switch gears a bit. Tell me about your family."

"I'm married and I have three children, ages five, two, and one."

"Well, I bet those kiddos keep you pretty busy huh?"

"I suppose," Andrea said as tears welled up in her eyes. She knew she was withholding a lot of information from the doctor but she had a mission and she just wanted to get back to work so she could feel alive again.

Doctor Stewart noticed the tears but refrained from calling attention to it because she could see the stress in her new patient's eyes. She then led Andrea into a patient room and did a quick physical exam on her.

"Okay, so you look pretty healthy. I am concerned about you though. I know you are feeling some stress, and I think it would be a great idea for you to talk to someone. I know you don't want to hear that, but I think you need an outlet. I think you need for someone to really understand you. I want to refer you to Doctor Kate."

Andrea rolled her eyes and let out an unmistakable sigh. "Once you attend two appointments with Doctor Kate, I will be more than happy to complete your form."

With that, Andrea got up and left the room without saying a word. She had a lump in her throat so large she felt as though everyone in the waiting room could see the physical protrusion. She got into her car and let out a cry so loud it jarred her. She couldn't understand why everyone around her acted like she needed so much help. Her phone rang as she sobbed.

"Hello Andrea," said the voice on the other end of the phone. "This is Doctor Kate. Doctor Stewart's office just called and asked me to a call you."

"Hi," Andrea said through her sobs.

"Andrea, can you tell me what's making you cry?"

"I'm just so frustrated. I hate this. I don't need help. I'm not crazy."

"No, you're not crazy," Doctor Kate said with a bit of a laugh. "But Andrea, you're not happy. I could see that in your eyes when I met you."

"I just don't know what to do anymore."

"Well why don't you come and see me. I have a 1:00 p.m. opening today. Can you come?"

With slight hesitation, but knowing she couldn't deny the inevitable, she responded.

"Yes, I will be there."

At 12:45 p.m. Andrea entered the waiting room of Doctor Kate's office. Kate heard the door chime as she was finishing up a chart for another patient. As she turned the corner to the waiting room she noticed a very different looking woman sitting on the couch in front of her. This woman, although dressed immaculately, looked defeated.

"Andrea. Hi, I'm glad you came. Come on back."

Andrea followed her back down the familiar hall into the familiar office and sat in the high back chair as she had done the last time.

"Andrea, let's jump in. We didn't get to finish the evaluation last time and I have a lot of questions to ask today. Okay?"

Andrea quietly shook her head in the affirmative.

"Let's start with why you went to the hospital."

"My husband, Daniel, and I were fighting. He was packing the kids to take them to his mother's house in San Antonio. He knows I hate his mother." She shrugged her shoulders and looked down. "I freaked out. He was calling me horrible names and said he wanted a divorce. I don't know, I don't really remember what happened after that but he called the police and they took me to the hospital. The doctor at the hospital said I tried to slit my wrist."

"Do you think that is true?"

"It must be because I had bandages on my wrist."

"I see. I'm assuming it was your first time in a hospital. What was the hospital like Andrea?"

"I don't remember the first few days... not really. I just know my roommate was crazy and it seemed like everyone just wanted to talk about how much their life sucked."

"Do you think you wanted to kill yourself the night you and Daniel were fighting?"

"I don't think I cared either way."

"You don't? Have you felt like you wanted to kill yourself before?"

"Well, I just get tired of this, you know? It's like sometimes it's too much and I just want it to end and I don't care if I live or die." She paused and the tears returned.

"What makes you cry when you say that?"

"Because I have never told anyone that before. It's pretty fucked up. People look at me and think I'm so great. Sometimes I feel like I am the worst person but it's so crazy because most of the time I feel like if you don't like me, fuck you. It's constant back and forth."

"Hmmm. Tell me about your kids."

"I have three. Zeke, Anna, and Lilly. I love them, I really do. But Zeke... he drives me absolutely insane. He is such a sweet boy, and he is inquisitive. He has these really big brown eyes with these eyelashes that just steal my heart. Sometimes he looks at me as if he knows something is wrong with me. I hate when he looks at me like that."

"It's like he sees the hurt?"

"Yes," she said with tears streaming faster than she could now control. "He knows I am a mess. When Daniel and I were fighting he was covering his sisters with his body, as if he thought they were in danger."

"Wow that must be hurtful to think back on."

"It just makes me even angrier at Daniel. I really feel like I hate him right now."

"What makes you hate him?"

"He judges me. I hate that. I mean, I bust my ass working to get to where I am while he sits behind his little computer making shit money, and he has the nerve to act like he does."

"How does he act?"

152

"Like a prick; a judgmental prick. It's funny because we were both raised poor. My parents had to work for every penny and so did his. I made our life what it is now and he shows no appreciation for me. The fucked up thing is that everyone else thinks he is so great. I'm sick of it. I'm sick of him. He can go to hell for all I care."

"You *are* very angry with him, Andrea. What has your relationship been like since you returned home from the hospital?"

"He is still there with his mother in San Antonio. He's hiding like a little bitch."

"So, wait. He is still there with the children?"

"Yes. He says I'm dangerous and he doesn't trust me with our children"

"Does he want a divorce?"

"I don't know. He better not. He couldn't make it without me, but he told Zeke's school that we had a family emergency so Zeke's teacher has just been emailing his work and Daniel has been emailing it back in."

"I see. So, you came home to an empty house when you returned from the hospital?"

"Yeah, I had to Uber home."

"What was that like for you... to come home to an empty house?"

"It was fine, I guess. It gave me a chance to sleep. I can't ever seem to get any good sleep with the kids in the house. I like to be left alone. Sometimes I really don't think I was cut out to be a mother."

"Why not?"

"Because I don't think I have what it takes. I'm always frustrated and irritable. When my kids cry I get angry. When they get hurt I get angry. It's like I'm always angry."

"Always angry?" Doctor Kate asked with an inquisitive look.

"Yes, most of the time I just feel like an explosion is just under the surface."

"And the other times?"

"The other times I just want to sleep so I don't have to hear 'mommy can you', or 'mommy can I have,'" she said as she rolled her eyes.

"Why did you and Daniel have children Andrea?"

"Because he wanted to. He said it was the right thing for a woman to do, to have a family. And he didn't believe in birth control... so here we are now."

"I see."

"Well, let me change gears a bit on you. How do you sleep at night?"

"Most nights I don't sleep well at all. I'm a night owl but when I finally do go to sleep it's not for very long."

Andrea went on to describe that her sleep was often interrupted with weird dreams or that she woke up thinking of what she had to do for work. She described different situations in which she would often sleep only a few hours and wake up dragging or have a sudden burst of energy and head off to work anyway. She explained that some weeks were the complete opposite. Some days she couldn't get out of bed. She told Doctor Kate that she called into work every day for about a week and spent that time sleeping; only getting up to shower and use the restroom. When Doctor Kate inquired, Andrea explained it by saying that she possibly crashed after settling a very difficult and contentious divorce case.

Andrea continued by explaining how her appetite would fluctuate. Some days she felt as though her stomach was a bottomless pit, while other days the mere thought of eating made her feel nauseated. Doctor Kate then asked about Andrea's thoughts.

"What do you mean does my mind race? Of course it does. I have so much going on that it's difficult for me to stay concentrated on one task. It would be hard for anyone to stay focused with as much responsibility as I have. It is a lot of pressure to know that the person you are representing is undergoing a major life change and, depending on how you do, they may lose everything they have worked for or they may be able to keep the lifestyle they have become accustomed to. And don't forget the pressure that comes with being one of the best. You aren't allowed to fail. You aren't allowed to make a mistake or have a bad day. I would bet most people would crack under that pressure."

"Is that what you did? You cracked?"

"I mean yeah, I did. Why are you asking me all of these questions? What's the point of this? I just had a bad few days. I'm better now."

"Are you becoming agitated again?"

"Hell yes. I mean I'm trying to be open, I really am, but I don't know why telling you about how I eat and sleep is going to help anything. This is just ridiculous."

"I understand your frustration, Andrea. I really do. This can be very difficult to understand, but what I am doing is trying to understand how you are functioning. When I am asking about your sleeping and appetite, I am collecting information to make a diagnosis."

"Diagnosis like I'm sick? I'm not sick... I'm not sick *or* crazy. You are not about to tell me I am mentally ill."

"No, I'm not going to tell you that you are crazy because you are not. However, I will tell you that I believe you have a condition called bipolar disorder. Have you heard of this?"

"Ummm yes… and I am nothing like those crazy-ass people. Brittany Spears shaved her head, and now Mariah Carey says that's why she acts nuts, too. Please. I knew this was a waste of time."

"Well, unfortunately those stories are what we hear in the media, but let me assure you those women are not crazy and neither are you. You have a chemical condition that makes you experience symptoms— symptoms like irritability, difficulty concentrating, elevated energy followed by periods of very low to no energy, mood swings, impulsivity, and at times poor judgement. All of these are symptoms of the condition."

Andrea rolled her eyes again, but Doctor Kate could see that she was truly trying to push back the tears that were forming and beginning to fall.

"I see tears, Andrea. Please tell me what is making you tear up."

"Because, you are just trying to label me. That would make everyone happy; to know that I am crazy."

"You are not crazy. You do need treatment for this condition, but with the right treatment you could really begin to feel better. Aren't you exhausted, Andrea? Aren't you tired of feeling up one day and down the next? Aren't you tired of your mind going so quickly you can't keep up? Are you tired of wearing a mask and pretending that everything is okay when you really feel as though at any moment you will lose it?"

Andrea sat in silence for a moment. The words she was hearing were ringing true deep down but she pondered what it would mean for her career and for her life if she admitted that what the doctor was saying was true. She would now be labeled as one of "those" people. Every time she had a bad day, people would give her that look—the look she had seen so many people give her father. That look that said, "you didn't take your medication, did you?" That feeling of shame to be seen with him when he was having an episode or that look of pity given to him when he lay on the floor of the living room and cried.

This couldn't be it. She was nothing like her father. She had worked so hard to be so different from him... from her family and from the struggles they endured because he couldn't keep a job. He would either fight with someone or show up to work drunk. No, she was nothing like him.

Session 2

"Andrea. Hi. Come on back," greeted Doctor Kate with an unmistakable sound of surprise in her voice. Andrea had made two appointments over the last two weeks. One she cancelled, and one she no-showed.

Andrea replied coolly. "Hello; nice to see you again."

"Have a seat. I am happy you have decided to return for our session. I know the last session was difficult for you."

"Yes, it was not my best moment. I went back to work last week, and my boss said he strongly recommended that I keep coming. When Jim strongly recommends something, you do it."

"I totally understand that. He basically voluntold you, huh?"

"Yes," she laughed a bit. "He did."

"So, tell me your reaction to our last meeting."

"It was horrible. I left here refusing to believe you were right. I called you every foul name I could think of and later that night I got drunk."

"Wow."

"Yes, then my little one, Zeke, FaceTimed me. He told me I looked horrible. I yelled at him for being rude, and

157

he started crying, telling me how mean I was and that he never wanted to talk to me again. I was mad at first but I started sobering up and I felt so guilty. I called Daniel the next morning, and he sent me to voicemail."

"So, you haven't had a chance to talk to the kids again?"

"No, a few days later I was served with divorce papers and Daniel is seeking full custody with supervised visits."

"I could only imagine what that felt like. What was your reaction?"

"I was pissed. I'm always pissed these days. I just can't believe the size of Daniel's balls. So, that night I went out with my coworker; a really fun girl named Katie. I had a hearing the next morning, and I don't know, I think someone must have spiked my drink because I was more groggy than normal the next morning. The judge talked to me in his chambers and told me that I was on a slippery slope. When I got to my building, Jim was waiting in my office. I knew it was bad. I just started crying when I saw him. He basically told me that I had to get help or I was done."

"I see. Tell me this Andrea, how did you return to work? I mean, who completed your evaluation for returning."

"Doctor Stewart did," she said sheepishly. "I'll admit, I lied and told her I had weekly standing appointments with you and she did it... she was willing to do it though."

"Hmmm."

"What? I think most people would have done the same thing don't you?"

"No, I actually don't. You mislead a lot of people, don't you think?"

"I don't really think anyone cares. As long as I keep getting large settlements for my clients, then who cares?"

"I think it has become pretty obvious that Jim cares."

"Maybe," she shrugged. "I've just learned that people ultimately are out for themselves. No one really gives a damn."

"Let's go back to Daniel and the divorce... and the supervised visits. What are your thoughts on that?"

"I think Daniel is an asshole. I have to be honest though, I've always thought that shared custody seems pretty good. I mean it's the best of both worlds. You get your kids sometimes, and the other part of the week you get a break."

"But Daniel is seeking supervised visitation?"

"Yeah, he is crazy. He won't get it though. I know his attorney, and he is an idiot."

"On what grounds is he seeking supervised visits?"

"He says I have a drinking problem."

"Do you?"

"Look Doctor Kate, I have told you before I like to enjoy myself. I don't have a drinking problem or any other kind of problem. I am just in a funk right now. It's actually passing. I'm just happy I got back to work. I hate having nothing to do. I just become so restless and my mind goes so fast so often that I can't turn it off."

"Yes, being alone with our thoughts is difficult for most of us. Tell me about your thoughts about the condition I diagnosed you with."

"Well, I told you I was pissed. I really didn't think that I have anything like that bipolar crap."

"You didn't think so? Has that changed over the past two weeks?"

"I don't know really. I mean I know what bipolar is. I do my research, but I am honestly not like anyone I know who has bipolar disorder. I'm really not."

"Everyone with the condition doesn't behave the same. People experience different symptoms and there are different levels of severity to the condition. Some people have more depression than others. Some people have more mania. And others experience depression and mania in the same episode, that's called a mixed episode."

Andrea was studying the doctor closely as she explained the condition, listening for clues that would explain her sudden ups and downs. She was struggling to admit that she had the condition. That would be giving in. That would be losing, and she was no loser.

"You mentioned that you know someone with bipolar disorder. Who do you know?"

Andrea sat in silence for a while before she answered. "My father."

Doctor Kate sat patiently and waited for Andrea to continue.

"My father would have these crazy spells... that's what we called them. He would have days were he looked possessed and he wouldn't sleep. He would talk quickly, mostly saying things we couldn't understand. Then he would have other spells he wouldn't get out of bed for days. He would cry uncontrollably. I remember when I was eight, my mom had the priest come over and perform an exorcism on him. He seemed fine for a while after that, then it started all over again. No doctor could fix him. When I was fifteen, he was hospitalized and a doctor came and diagnosed him with bipolar disorder. My parents didn't believe in anything like that, so he didn't take the medication and the episodes continued."

"I see. So, perhaps your parents' beliefs and reactions to mental health have shaped your beliefs?"

"Yeah, maybe a bit. I don't know, it all just seems like an excuse for people's bad behaviors."

"Do you make excuses for your bad behaviors?"

"Well, no. I don't make excuses. When things aren't going well for me it's normally because of things that I can't control. Trouble seems to follow me."

Doctor Kate just nodded in response. "So, tell me this. What are you goals for our time together?"

Andrea stopped and thought for a moment. "I mean, maybe I can become less irritable. I think that would help things a lot. Also, I want to show that I am taking care of myself so I can fight this custody shit with Daniel. I don't need to be on supervised visitation. That's ludicrous."

"Okay working on your irritability sounds like a good goal. I would like to see you next week and over the next week I want you to take note and document the situations in which you feel very irritated."

"Okay, I can do that."

As Andrea left, Doctor Kate sat down to make a session note of the visit. She thought of the potential difficulties she could have treating Andrea. Andrea was still very guarded and unwilling to acknowledge the presence of her condition and the seriousness of it. Doctor Kate had treated enough people with bipolar disorder to know that those who followed a treatment plan and learned about their condition were far more successful than those who continued to blame others and excuse their actions. She was hopeful that with more time together, Andrea would let down her wall and trust her. There was more to Andrea's story, she could tell. People are not that guarded for without good reason. Typically, in Doctor Kate's experience, there were unresolved hurts that could often be frightening to talk about. Doctor Kate just had to break down that wall and get to the *real* story.

Session 3

"Hi Doctor Kate!" Andrea chirped, much perkier than the last few times Andrea had seen her.

"Hi Andrea!" Doctor Kate matched her enthusiasm. "You are awfully chipper today."

"Yep, I've had a pretty good week."

"That makes me happy to hear. Let's start there. Tell me about it."

"Well, you know that hearing for the White case that I bombed last week? I was lucky enough to get my motion to continue accepted by the judge. I stayed up late a few nights and was able to get my argument together. It was amazing. I was in the zone and the judge ruled in my favor despite being pissed at me the previous hearing. It was awesome. Mr. White walked away with all of his pension, retirement, and the savings. He doesn't have to sell the main house, but they will sell the vacation home and split the money. Tammy White just knew she was getting half of everything... the gold digging bitch. I showed her what's up. This is why prenups are important."

"Wow. That sounds pretty successful!"

"Yes it was, and the Carson case that was one that I was assigned to before my... issue," she quieted her voice with that word. "Well, Jim assigned it to someone else while I was out. So, after last week he told me he wanted me back on it. I still have to work with a colleague, Jackie, on it but that's okay. Soon she will realize that I really need to be the lead. This case is a multimillion dollar case. I just know we've got this one in the bag. Mr. Carson is a prick who can't keep his dick in his pants."

"I see. And do you get along with Jackie?"

"We keep our distance now. We had an altercation a while ago, but it's blown over. I think she is oblivious to what this life is really like. I tried to help her at the beginning, but she didn't believe me. Oh well. She will find out the hard way. I couldn't care less."

"Andrea, I notice you are speaking a bit fast right now. Are you feeling ok?"

"I told you, I feel great today. Today is a good day. Isn't it better to see me like this instead of all pissed off and depressed?"

"I'm wondering if you are experiencing a manic episode."

Andrea automatically did her typical eye roll and waved off Doctor Kate's observation.

"I don't know about all that, but I will tell you I feel great and I don't really care the reason for it. I want to enjoy it. I deserve to finally have a good week after the two months of hell I have been through."

"Have you seen Daniel or the kids?"

"Yes!" she said more excited than Doctor Kate had ever heard her speak of her kids.

"I decided on Friday after work that fuck it, I wanted to see my babies. So, when I got off work I drove to San Antonio to see them. They were so excited to see me."

"How did Daniel respond? Was he happy that you decided to come?"

"Oh I didn't tell him I was going. He was surprised, but that didn't matter. I hadn't seen my kids in weeks. He can't keep them from me. I missed those little boogers. Zeke and Anna hugged me so tight I thought I was going to choke! Lilly wouldn't let me put her down the whole time I was there. It was great. I got to feed them and put them to bed. It's crazy I didn't realize how much I had missed them until I saw them. Zeke looked like he grew three inches!"

163

"I'm happy you were able to see them. Did you get to see them for the rest of the weekend then?"

"Oh no, I never planned to do that. I drove home that night."

"You did. So, wait, what time did you leave San Antonio?"

"About ten. It was great. I got home and got some things done around the house."

Doctor Kate looked suspiciously at Andrea.

"I know you are thinking that's manic behavior and I know that it can be, but I was on a high from such a successful week at work I just wanted to see my kids to end the week perfectly and I did!"

Doctor Kate nodded and rested her hand from taking notes. "Okay Andrea, I understand that. I am concerned about your impulsive decisions. I will continue to track this behavior though. It's really important to track your episodes so we can establish if there is a pattern to them, but let's change subjects for a bit right now. Last week I asked you to jot down some things that have made you irritable in the last week. Did you do that for me?"

"Actually, I did." Andrea pulled out a blue notebook and began to flip through the pages.

"Oh Lord, yes let's start here. Last Tuesday we finished up court earlier than expected, so a few coworkers and I decided to go for happy hour. We got our normal spot a place call the Road Bar, it's your typical bar and they serve appetizers during happy hour for half price. So, we got there and I left my I.D. on my desk at work. The dumb waiter who sees me all the time refused to serve me my drink until I had my I.D. I was pissed so I had to run back to the office to grab it. All I could think of the way back was what I was going to say to the little punk. He looked all of 16, and I can assure

164

you I look way over 21. So, when I got back I threw my I.D. in his face. He looked mortified. Then I dared him to spit in my drink. I made him have someone else come and serve us so I could make sure he didn't do anything to our food or drinks." Without waiting for Doctor Kate's response, she flipped through her notes and continued.

"Okay then on Thursday night, I was driving home and stopped to get a bottle of wine from the liquor store. Some lady in there grabbed the last bottle of Rosé. When I told her that was the bottle I was going to get, she just looked at me and shrugged her shoulders. Under my breath I said, "You selfish bitch," and she heard me. She asked me what I said, so I repeated it. The manager came over and told me I needed to calm down or leave."

"How did you respond to that situation?"

"I told him to fuck off," she said shrugging her shoulders. "Then, you know what happened Friday," she said as she continued to flip through her notebook. "Oh yes, then on Saturday I met some friends at a bar, and we had a few drinks. That was fine, but one of my friends started trying to put me on blast, so I told her to watch herself and that was about it, but after that I was so pissed that she said that I couldn't stop thinking about it."

"What'd she say?"

"She said I was out of control, but what does her dumb ass know? Then Sunday... oh, that was a bad day. Oh yes, I remember Sunday now."

"Tell me more about Sunday."

"I don't know, I was really sad and nervous, but I don't know what I was nervous about. But I cried and cried. It was like any stupid commercial or lifetime movie had me in tears. But anyway and then…."

"Andrea hold on; let me slow you down a tad. Let's recap. So, it seems like you have had a lot of irritability along with normal to high energy followed by some depression and anxiety."

"I mean if you want to call it that, but really Sunday was just a bad day."

"Okay so I know you have told me before, but why are you so unwilling to discuss your symptoms as symptoms of bipolar disorder? There must be something different than just your father having the condition."

Andrea was stopped dead in her tracks. Had Doctor Kate figured it out? Did she do some research and figure out the secret behind Andrea's father? *No*, she thought to herself. *That's impossible. Doing that level of research into someone's past is something detectives and attorneys do, not doctors.*

"What's there, Andrea? Tell me why the wall? Why are you so guarded?"

"Because I found him!" Andrea shouted with a low baritone cry that she didn't even recognize. "I found him!"

"Who?" Doctor Kate asked, very startled by the quick shift in demeanor.

"My dad, Papi! I found him in his room. I thought he was sleeping covered up. I shook his arm and climbed on him and pulled back the covers, and I saw it all!" she cried out in sheer agony, piercing the well-insulated room of the office.

"What happened to your Papi, Andrea?"

She paused through tears. "He shot himself. I found him dead in his bed. Why did he do it?" she sobbed.

She doubled over as she cried. Doctor Kate waited patiently then said, "Andrea, I am so sorry your father killed himself and you had to find him. I am so sorry you had to see your father like that. I know that although he had his issues, you were also a daddy's girl. I'm so sorry," Doctor Kate said again. She questioned how much anyone in Andrea's life had ever apologized to her for her experience. She moved closer to Andrea. As she sobbed, Doctor Kate moved closer again.

"Can I hug you?"

Andrea nodded affirmatively through her low hung head and flowing tears. She blew her nose as Doctor Kate put her arms around her and held her close. The harder Doctor Kate held Andrea, the harder Andrea sobbed. Doctor Kate let Andrea cry in her arms for 20 minutes. *She clearly needed this*, Doctor Kate thought to herself. *This woman has never had a soft place to fall. As difficult as she has been, I will be her soft place to fall* she thought in this moment.

Session 4

"Andrea. Ready?"

"Yes, I'm ready." Doctor Kate noticed Andrea's very different demeanor. She no longer had the hard shell, but instead she was meek, almost childlike.

"How are you today?"

"I'm okay. I'm sorry about all that silliness last week. I mean I totally overreacted."

"What do you mean you overreacted?"

"All that crying was so dramatic. I mean, you aren't my mother. You shouldn't have to cradle me like a baby to stop my tears. So, I am sorry. I'm stronger than that. It won't happen again."

"Andrea, I understand your discomfort with being so vulnerable with me last week, but let me tell you, no apology is needed. I thank you for finally letting me in. I wanted so badly to understand what you were afraid of and now I know. You weren't being weak. That took a lot

167

of strength to reveal to me that your Papi committed suicide and you found him. Please don't think that I believe that is weakness. I actually believe that's very courageous."

Andrea listened intently to every word as Doctor Kate spoke. *She has such a way with words*, Andrea thought. *Maybe she should have been an attorney; she could have been a master negotiator with skills to make every one think they were on the same side.*

"Thank you for saying that. It's weird because I never talk about that and when I left last week, in a weird way, I felt better."

"I'm assuming that you don't talk about that often. Am I correct?"

"Yes, indeed. That would be correct," Andrea said.

"That's why you felt better. I think it is very possible that since I told you about the bipolar diagnosis that you have been trying to fight back that memory and those emotions. I also wonder if that has also contributed to your irritability lately as well."

"No, no. People just piss me off," she said dryly.

"No," laughed Doctor Kate, "I mean, since you and I have been meeting, it seems like your irritability in general has been pretty bad. If these thoughts of your dad that have been pushed down for almost twenty years had resurfaced, it makes complete sense that you would be more irritable."

"Do you think I am going to end up like my father?" she asked with the return of the child like tune.

"No, I don't. You have done something that your father was not willing or able to do. You are seeking treatment."

Session 5

It had been about three weeks since Andrea had revealed her secret. She was surprised that in the last session, Doctor Kate didn't ask more questions about the situation. She simply told her she was courageous, and then listened to Andrea ramble on from one tangential thought to another. Andrea had learned to trust Doctor Kate. If anyone had asked her six weeks ago how she would feel about her therapist, she would have bet anything that she would have something negative to say, but she didn't. She knew Doctor Kate was patient and kind but she now also knew that this woman was not dumb or weak by any means.

"It's been two weeks Andrea. How are you?"

"I'm doing pretty well. I mean, given everything."

"Anything new happened over the last few weeks?"

"It seems like every time I come here something is new."

"That's true."

The two laughed together—one laughing because she was beginning to realize that she was the common denominator in her own hot mess of a life. She then questioned if Doctor Kate's laugh was for the same reason.

"How are things at work?"

"As far as work goes, things are great. We ended up settling a few cases, but this crazy White case seems like it will never end. That has me a bit stressed, but nothing more than normal. Okay, so seeing as I am lousy at the small talk, Jackie, you know, the bitch at work? I noticed a few weeks ago that she has been kind of smirking at me, right? Then in debriefing case meetings, which is basically like a staff meeting, she interrupts me and tries to make these digs at me in front of everyone. She has always been a fake bitch but this has been different. So three days ago, Frank and I went to happy hour and I'm like 'what crawled up Jackie's ass and died?' Normally, Frank is congenial with me and says things like, 'yeah I know' or something more mundane than profound. But this time he just totally changed the subject. This was *so* not him, so I said something else about her like she has fake tits or something stupid... you know, just trying to bait him. Again nothing. So finally I asked him what was up with this. The look on his face said it all."

"What did it say?"

"Doctor Kate, it said he is fucking Jackie!"

"Did he say that or are you jumping to conclusions?"

"It's so obvious."

"Well, what is your reaction to that? You and Frank had a good friendship, although it crossed boundaries once, it seemed pretty good."

"I guess when he realized he wasn't getting any from me anymore he went to on the office THOT. That means...."

"Oh, I know what that means. I have been thoroughly educated on THOTS."

"Well, then you know it's an acronym that stands for That Hoe Over There. Anyway, Jackie is desperate and I guess Frank's bald, fat ass is good enough."

"What do you mean good enough? You and Frank had a 'thing' before."

"Yeah, but that was stupid and it clearly had a bigger impact on me than him."

"What do you mean by that?"

"Nothing, anyway so the next day I went to lunch with Katie and told her about Frank and Jackie and she already knew! I think that pissed me off more than Frank hooking up with Jackie. Then Katie looks at me with this pitiful look and said, 'Dre, I didn't want to be the one to tell you but everyone is saying that the time you were off was because you were in rehab for a cocaine addiction and that you went psycho and that's why you had to go.'"

"Wow, how did you respond?"

"What do you mean how did I respond? I was pissed. I went off. I told her she was the dumb bitch that I was doing cocaine with the only time I'd ever done it! She started crying, got mad and left. She didn't even leave me cash for her part of the check. So I paid the check and went back to work. From the parking lot of the restaurant until I hit the 37th floor I felt like people were looking at me. Then the next day or the day after that, I don't know which, my allergies were crazy so I kept wiping my nose. I noticed people looking at me every time I wiped my damn nose. It has been insane. I feel like a paranoid crackhead. I really don't know if it's me or them at this point."

"Do you believe it is true that people are talking about you? Maybe Katie exaggerated this?"

"No, this place is like high school. Everyone is so dramatic. I mean look at the crap we deal with all day, it's toxic. They feed off this kind of stuff. So I totally believe they think I was in rehab for cocaine. The problem is, is which is worse—being in rehab or a looney bin because they think I tried to kill myself? Rehab is like a fad these days. Saying you want to commit suicide still makes people think you need a straitjacket. But no one's smart enough to realize that if I was actually in rehab or in trouble for cocaine, my license to practice law would be up for review."

"Andrea, you seem to be reporting this information as if it is no big deal. I mean there is no emotion as you are sitting here talking to me about this."

"I don't know. I feel numb. I guess I used them all up last week," she smirked, only half kidding.

"You said that as a joke, but I think you mean it. I think you have decided to no longer be vulnerable so you have detached from identifying and feeling your emotions."

Andrea sat silently for a while. *Damn that was deep*, she thought. She didn't make a conscious plan to do that, but that's exactly what she had done. She learned after her father's suicide that it was easier to just not feel.

"I wonder if you learned how to detach emotionally after your father's suicide," Doctor Kate asked as if she had a crystal ball right into Andrea's mind.

"I don't know," Andrea stammered. I mean, after Papi left, I had to keep living. I knew that I didn't want to sit around and cry all day like my mother."

"So, what did you do?"

"I figured out a solution. I like solutions."

"And what was the solution?"

"I went to work. I worked at the school after hours as a tutor, and I worked at Dillard's after that. I didn't want to feel like I couldn't live any more. After Papi, I felt suffocated by my mother." She clenched her manicured hands and popped her fingers. "She depended on me for everything and I hated it, but I did it. I never wanted to be in that position."

"What position?"

"Like a typical Mexican woman. A stay at home mom who depended on a man. Mexican women are very dedicated to their men and their families. They do everything for the man. And the men, they are good providers—most of them. But I knew after Papi died that I had to provide for myself. I didn't want to be the mercy of any man."

"Is that why you always made a point to tell Daniel how much you didn't need him?"

172

"I didn't always tell him that. I mean, I did love Daniel at one time. He just stopped liking me, then loving me. We just grew apart."

"So, you had a reaction when I made an interpretation about Daniel?"

"Well, yeah, all you know are the bad things I said and did to him. I was really good to him at one time."

"I didn't say that you weren't. I was simply curious if your mother's dependence on your father and then his death caused so much fear and uncertainty for you that you made a decision to never be vulnerable—that kind of vulnerable—with a man."

Andrea sat in silence for a moment, soaking it in before saying in a voice so low it was almost a whisper, "I don't know... maybe."

"You don't have to know now," Doctor Kate said softly. "Just think about it for me. So, let me switch gears on you. What's going on with the kids?"

"They are doing really well. I FaceTime them almost every day, and Daniel and I meet halfway every other week for me to hang out with the kids. He lifted the supervision as long as he is there with us. It has been okay."

"Okay?"

"Yeah. Okay. I mean, who I am kidding? I was not put on this earth to be a mother. I'm no good at it. I wouldn't want me to raise me. They are better off with Daniel. He has the nurturing thing down. I just wished we lived closer so I could see them more."

"Are they planning on moving back any time soon?"

"I think so. Daniel has been very secretive about their plans. I think he's worried about the divorce. He knows I am a good attorney and have good representation and I think he is worried about it."

"Is he right? Should he be scared or cautious about a divorce?"

"At first I would have said yes! Hell yes! It was the principle of the matter, you know? Like it was a competition, where I felt like 'I know you're not leaving me,' kind of thing. But now, I know he is better for the kids, so at least for custody, unless he is a real jerk, then I am okay with him having the kids as long as he comes back to the city."

"What made you come to this realization?"

"Hell, I don't know. Maybe the therapy has finally started working!" she exclaimed.

They both shared a laugh.

Session 6

"Andrea, this is Doctor Kate. I'm calling because you have missed your last two sessions. Please call me and let me know how you are doing and when you would like to reschedule," Doctor Kate hung up the phone with concerned thoughts that either Andrea may have hit a bottom again and become suicidal again, or that she had given up on therapy all together.

Andrea woke up to her phone vibrating. She reached toward her night table feeling around for the phone. Her hand knocked over two bottles of prescription pills, and accidently tipped over a half empty bottle of Budweiser. "Shit," she mumbled, frowning at the smell of stale beer.

The previous night she had been on a high. Sitting around the house night after night was not providing the stimulation she needed; she deserved. She dressed, grabbed her clutch and headed out. There was a bar that Andrea used to frequent before her and her coworkers started to go to The Road Bar. An Irish pub called Murphy's. It was small, and there was a bartender there named Mark who used to always hit on her. She liked him, but she would flash her ring and say, "It's a no-go, bro, you know I'm hitched."

On this night, she found herself reminiscing about Mark pulled into the small parking lot of Murphy's. She adjusted her cleavage and lipstick in the car, then stepped out and headed for the door. As soon as she reached to open it, it swung open.

"Mark!" she smiled. She had expected him to maybe be working, not leaving.

"Dre? Is that really you?" Mark asked, smiling. He was in his late forties, tall, white with a farmer's tan, and had a really broad chest, like he lifted weights in his spare time. Andrea had always remembered that about him.

"Hell yes it's me. I came to visit, have a drink…," she winked.

He turned to the guys that were following him out. "Hey guys, I'll catch up with you," Mark said, glancing back at Andrea, who had worn her sexiest heels and made sure to arch her back a little. They sat in a booth and ordered shots of Jameson with Irish Car Bombs.

"This used to be your drink of choice," Mark laughed, knocking back a shot with her.

"I know. I missed coming here, I was hoping I'd see you," she confessed, looking at him dead in the eye.

"It's been a while, how's the law?" he laughed, watching her lick her lips.

"The law's still the law," she sighed. "But there are still some naughty things in the grey area that make right and wrong all blurry," she teased.

He looked at her left hand and she noticed.

"Still hitched, I see?" he lifted his brows.

She cursed herself for forgetting to take them off. "It's complicated, but you know, I remember you used to ask me that a lot."

"I did," he laughed. "I certainly did. I always had this...thing for you. I'm not going to lie, it didn't matter to me if you were married."

"Does it matter now?" she asked, lowering her voice to almost a whisper.

He switched his seat to her side of the booth, touching her thigh. "No," he said in her ear as he gently kissed it. It was exactly what she wanted. This thrill of an almost stranger, but with enough familiarity to make her feel truly desired, gave her a rush that hit harder than the cocaine with Katie. They both took large gulps of their drinks and he led her by the hand through a back door of the bar. They were in an alley behind the old brick building.

Andrea, remembering a hot image she'd seen in a movie, dropped to her knees and loosened his belt and pants. A flash of Daniel came into her mind. *Fuck him,* she thought. *He deserves this...or not knowing this. I deserve this,* she told herself as she began to take Mark into her mouth.

"God, those gorgeous Latina lips I've always wanted to feel," he moaned, wondering why she'd decided to come after him on that night, but not letting it distract him.

"Wanna feel the other ones?" she asked, pulling her skirt up over her hips and bending over against the wall. He pulled her thong to the side and began to work on her. She thrived off of every second of it. It was the perfect drug for her. She felt so sexy, so goddess-like, so perfect.

Now as she squinted in the light of the following day, the smell of stale beer reminded her of the previous night. She found the phone and clicked the side button. When the screen lit up she winced at the brightness of the screen, squinting her eyes to see it. Her head was pounding. She noticed that she had missed three calls. Two from the Katie and one from Doctor Kate. Katie had sent several text messages after the last phone call.

The first one read, "Girl, where are you? The partners are having a meeting and Jim came and specifically asked me for your calendar. He said you didn't show yesterday and he wanted to make sure you were ready for the hearing tomorrow."

Then she saw the subsequent, "Okay, why are you not responding to my text?"

The next one was more abstracted in importance. "You have to come in and see Frank. What an asshole. He is feeling himself since he started fucking Jackie."

"Okay now I am getting worried. Frank said you may be back in a psych hospital??? What is he talking about?" At the sight of the message, Andrea sat up and felt the adrenaline of anxiety rush through her body.

Here we go with this crap again, she thought. She got up feeling the pulsating move from her head all the way down to her toes. Everything was pounding. It was 11:00 a.m. and just standing made her feel like her body was dead weight. She didn't get it. She had been doing pretty well, but then overnight it was like a train had hit her. She hadn't left the house the last two days except to go out. She couldn't think straight. Her mind was racing 120 miles a minute. She couldn't work like this. She felt exhausted and restless all at the same time. *This has to stop. Whatever it is, has to stop. It's time to own your shit*, she thought.

An hour later she had made herself shower and brush her teeth. She pulled on a pair of black yoga pants and a tank top. She responded to Katie's text telling her that she was at home with a migraine, and she had no idea what Frank was talking about. She then opened her email and sent a quick message to Jim apologizing for not being present in the office. She assured him that she worked from home yesterday and would do so today. She said her migraine headache had caused her to need to sleep in and take it easy to ensure she was ready for the trial tomorrow. She felt her head become lightheaded as she pushed send. Her breathing became shallow as she thought about the hearing. She knew she had done absolutely no preparation and she guessed Jim knew it to. She knew she was on borrowed time with Jim.

****

"Thank you so much for squeezing me in today. I'm sorry I didn't call or cancel my last two appointments. I will make sure to pay you for those missed sessions before I leave today. Doctor Kate, I need your help. I can't keep doing this."

"Tell me Andrea. What was going on for you to miss your sessions?"

"The first session I was feeling really good. I just didn't think I needed it. But the second session was different. I was so down and so depressed I couldn't physically get out of bed. I slept right through the appointment."

"Well, I am glad that you called me back today. I was getting very concerned about you."

"Were you really, or are you just saying that?"

"Why would you think I am just saying that?"

"Because it's just your job. I mean this is how you make your money. It's like I am paying you to like me."

"Is that what you think? You are paying me to like you?"

"Kind of, yes."

178

"Who says I like you?" Doctor Kate said with a smirk. Andrea had been looking down and looked up suddenly to clarify.

"I hope you are kidding."

"Well, I must admit Andrea. You do make connecting with you very difficult. I wonder if the way you push me away is the way you interact with everyone in your life. I think you intentionally keep people away because you are so afraid of being hurt. And I get it, trust me I do. The last person you felt connected with left you. You had to see him in the worst way possible. I can't imagine what that felt like. Then, as if that wasn't enough, you were left to figure out life on your own after that because your mother basically checked out. You were alone. Alone feels safe for you, but it is also very lonely, isn't it? You and I both know that you are not living like you want to live."

Through quiet weeps, Andrea admitted that she had been very angry with Doctor Kate for telling her she was bipolar. She admitted that she was angry and resentful at Daniel for being so perfect and making life and parenting seem so easy. She was angry with her mother for abandoning her. She was really angry with her father for killing himself and leaving her to find him. She talked about being angry with her Lala (short for abuela) for making her stay in the same town and having to listen to the other kids tell her that her Papi was crazy and that he should have been wearing a strait jacket. Other kids told her that maybe if she wasn't such a fat-ass, or a bitch he wouldn't have had to kill himself to get away from her.

"Other kids said those things to you Andrea?"

"Yes, and that was just the stuff that was nice."

"I am so sorry you had to go through that. I am so very sorry. You didn't deserve any of this. You did not get what you needed from the moment your father died and that affected your emotional growth and your perception of the world. Tell me about Lala. Was she nurturing or supportive during this time?"

"You would have to know Lala. She is a strong Mexican woman, you know? She really is the backbone of my mom's family. She did the best she could, but she just didn't believe in this. She would always say, 'No seas llorón'. That means stop crying and suck it up. When you hear that enough times you start to think that tears are for the weak and if you are sad you are weak."

"Did that make you stop crying?"

"In front of her it did. But really, it just made me think I was weak. I spent so much time alone crying."

"Often the messages we get about expressing our emotions can taint or even halt our emotional development. So, with the trauma you experienced in addition to the messages you learned about emotions made you turn to denial of your own emotions."

"Ha," she laughed knowing that the words Doctor Kate was saying were true. "Am I crazy?"

"No."

"Is there something wrong with me?"

"Wrong? No, but you have a condition that needs treatment. And you do have past hurts that have to be healed if you want to live life differently."

"So, what do I need to do? I am ready to get better Doctor Kate."

"Andrea that is probably the best thing I have heard all day, from anyone. Let's get you better."

"Call me Dre please. Andrea is formal for me. Tell me what to do and I will do it. I promise."

"Okay Dre," Doctor Kate said, recognizing Dre's first attempt to connect with her since their first meeting which seemed so long ago. "First we need to get you an appointment with a doctor to begin medications. It will be very important for you to take the medication as prescribed and take it every day."

"Medications? Will they make me feel like a zombie? I have to be able to think on my feet doctor and can't be zoned out."

"I understand, but with the right medication it will not feel like that. These medications are designed to level you off. You should not feel those symptoms of hypomania and then sudden big shifts into depression. That should level off. You should also feel a bit of relief from the anxiety. It really should make you much more functional. Simultaneously, you and I have some work to do. We have to begin to process your emotions and then develop your emotional regulation skills."

"I don't understand all that. I mean, I understand what you're saying, it's just—is that possible?"

"Absolutely, I do it all the time. If you trust the process and do the work you will be surprised how far you can progress. Let's talk about your goals. What do you want?"

"I want my family back."

The surprise on Doctor Kate's face was unmistakable.

Cori

Session 1

Sunday night was a mess. After the kids were in bed, when Cori came from her room, the house was dark, and felt peaceful. *I miss these days,* she thought. *When it was just Stephen and me and the house was quiet. When we had no other responsibilities but ourselves and our jobs.*

She went down the stairs and into the kitchen. She could see the lights from the television on, as she rounded the corner. Stephen was on the couch watching some program on MSNBC. She didn't see how he could watch that stuff. Politics was not her thing and the current political climate was more repulsive to her than it had ever been. She opened the refrigerator and quickly noticed Stephen's six pack of beer that was purchased earlier in the afternoon was down to two. She shook her head, not having the strength or interest to entertain those thoughts. She grabbed a yogurt and at that time Stephen noticed her.

"Hey babe, how ya feeling?"

"I'm okay. Thanks for putting the kids down." The truth was that she was not okay. She was really not okay at all and she knew it. She lived in constant fear that something would happen to her parents or husband would make another *mistake* and she would have to go through that grief all over again. She lived in fear for her marriage. She had been pulling away from Stephen and he knew it. She lived in fear that he didn't love the kids.

She lived in fear that her medical practice would start failing. She lived in fear.

She climbed the stairs back to bed and clicked on the television. She scrolled through the television guide hoping for something mindless yet entertaining. She found a show on renovating homes and thought that was a good balance. As she lay with her eyes focused on the television screen her mind wandered. She went through her patient schedule for Monday. Mondays were always so busy, and she hated Mondays. Mondays were full of medication refills, acute illness that had gotten worse over the weekend because they were untreated, and high emotions because people tend to wreak havoc on the weekends then would come in to see her for a pill that would fix their problems. *If I had that power to prescribe a pill to fix emotions, I would be in a much better place,* she thought.

As the night progressed, she tossed and turned. She could hear the television playing the next renovation show and the next after that. She noticed Stephen had not yet come to bed and began to worry that he was intoxicated and passed out on the sofa. She worried that the children would find him like that in the morning. Trying to push out those thoughts, she pressed her eyes shut and drifted off to sleep.

Her breathing slowed. Everything slowed. She was in the car in with a young child. He was singing along to the songs on the radio as she drove. As they drove and sang songs she could see something approaching them in the distance. The sun was in her eyes but she could make out enough to know that the car was on the wrong side of the road. Everything sped up and the car drove right into her. The windshield immediately shattered, the car jumped, rolled, and bumped down an embankment. She reached behind her for the little boy. She could hear his cries in the distance. "Sister, sister! Help me. Sister!" She screamed with terror at the realization that the little boy was Ben!

"Cori! Babe! Cori! Wake up, it's me. It's me, wake up. You must be having a nightmare."

Cori woke to Stephen cradling her in his arms. As she opened her eyes she noticed she couldn't see anything. Stephen's voice sounded muffled. All she could hear was her heart pounding. Her vision came to and she saw Stephen's face. She felt his skin on hers.

"It's okay baby. I got you. Are you okay? You were screaming!"

"I'm okay," she said quietly. As she lay whimpering in Stephen's arms, she couldn't shake the thought of *I'm not okay*.

****

"Doctor Cameron. Hi! How are you? So nice to finally meet you. Please come on back."

"Oh no, don't call me doctor. Please, call me Cori."

"Okay Cori, It's so great to finally meet you in person. Of course, I hear your name a lot with all of the patients we share and the communication between our offices to collaborate care. We should have met a long time ago."

"Yes, we should have," Cori agreed but for completely different reasons. "Doctor Kate, will this be any kind of conflict of interest for you? I don't want to put you in a bad position at all. It's just that the patients I send to you tell me how wonderful you are and frankly I don't really know who else to see."

"No conflict for me. So let's jump in. Tell me what brings you in."

"I have anxiety. I always have, but it's getting worse. It's beginning to impact my life."

Cori went on to share the story of her brother and sister-in-law's death. She talked about her difficulties raising their children and she talked about her worry over Stephen's sudden increase in drinking and possible infidelity. "I think that pretty much sums it up."

"You are under a lot of stress Cori. Tell me about you and Stephen. Did you two want children or had you decided not to have children?"

"We tried actually, for several years. I had three miscarriages during that time. Two early in the first trimester, but the last one was the worst. I was five months along and lost the baby. Since that time, we have not been pregnant again."

"I'm so sorry for your loss. I can't imagine that experience."

"Medically, it all made sense to me. The placenta had become detached from the uterine wall. They discovered this at the sixteen week sonogram and I was put on light duty then on bed rest. By twenty-two weeks, termination was the only option. I understood it."

"You know, I noticed how you jumped right into doctor mode when describing that experience. Is that how you have had to cope with it?"

"I guess," said Cori, looking almost embarrassed.

"So, you two have not been pregnant again? Tell me about Stephen, how was he during this time—meaning was he supportive or distant? How did he handle it?"

"Stephen is awesome. He is very attentive and very supportive. Like I told you about last night when I had my fill of the kids, he just handles it. He is so strong. He's so confident. He's everything I am not."

"I see." She studied Cori's face for a moment. "Why do you look so sad when you say that?"

"Because I think he deserves so much better than me."

"When did your self-esteem issues begin, Cori?"

"Sheesh! From the day of conception."

"So, as long as you can remember?"

"Yeah...I always felt different, I just never fit or belonged anywhere."

"Well clarify for me because earlier you told me you had a stable loving home, a good childhood, good friends, and obviously a good education. Now you tell me you never fit?"

"Yes. I had all of that, but I was always on the outside looking in. I was born into a loving family, but I was different. I had friends, but I was always the last invited."

"I see. What made you different in your home Cori?"

"I always felt so nervous around people, so I just stayed quiet. I was almost invisible."

Session 2

"So, tell me your thoughts our first session," Doctor Kate prompted as she sat in her therapy chair across from the sofa on which Cori chose to sit. Doctor Kate made a subtle note that this was a different location than where Cori sat the first time.

"It was interesting. I definitely said more than I thought I would. I remember taking the psych rotation in med school and I do so much counseling at work, you know? But I have to be honest, being on this end is very different. I was conflicted actually. On one hand, it felt like a good release but on the other hand, I felt very exposed."

"What part of what you talked about last session made you feel the most exposed?"

"Definitely the part about Stephen's drinking and my self-esteem."

"Tell me why those things in particular made you feel exposed."

"Because my self-esteem is so low. Most people assume that if you are a physician, you have a nice home and nice cars that everything in your life is good. And don't get me wrong, for the most part my life is good, but I just have these moments."

"And what about your husband's drinking makes you uncomfortable?"

"Because his drinking only increased once my niece and nephew moved in. I think he is drinking to deal with the burden of them and really the burden of me. He doesn't look at me the same. He used to have this look. I can't explain it but it was like when he looked at me he was hanging on every word I spoke. Sometimes I would catch him looking at me randomly. When we would make eye contact he looked...happy. He doesn't look like that now. His eyes don't look happy."

"What is your fear in your marriage with Stephen?"

"I fear that he has realized I'm not as strong as he thought. I fear that he will not want to deal with my baggage. I fear that he will finally admit to himself that I am a burden for him—that me and my brother's kids are a burden. I fear that he will be out one evening for happy hour and find someone that has less *issues*, as he calls them."

"I understand what you are saying, but I guess I am not sure about what in his behavior leads you to have these fears?"

Cori paused for a minute and responded by telling Doctor Kate about the Bachelor party. As she told the story she felt short of breath, and her body began to heat from the inside out. She continued, feeling, unable to stop talking... Once, he had gone to a happy hour with co-workers after work, and when he told Cori where he was, being as transparent as possible, she drove over to the restaurant, walked up to the bar, and slammed her wedding rings down on the wooden surface in front of him. He was with two other male coworkers and they all remained speechless as she stormed out. He had told her the truth but those feelings—those heart pounding and racing, stomach dropping, adrenaline flooding feelings—forced her to do things that Cori knew she shouldn't do. And that wasn't the only time she followed him, snuck on him, and accused him. It was more frequent than she liked to admit.

Doctor Kate speculated that Cori might be projecting her self-value onto her husband. They discussed the increase in Stephen's drinking and her association with him cheating. Cori explained that she didn't mind alcohol in moderation. But with everything that had transpired and now trying to cope her brother's accident, she has developed a real fear of drinking to excess. Doctor Kate and Cori discussed Cori's need for control and how it impacted her marriage.

"The need for control or to always be in control is common among people with anxiety. Your experience of your then boyfriend cheating, and now your brother and sister in law being killed suddenly shook your security and I assume made you feel very uncertain and unable to predict life in that moment. Now your husband's increase in drinking may be a trigger for your need for control. Have you discussed your concerns with Stephen?"

"No, I haven't. He knows it bothers me. That's part of the reason why I don't understand why he is getting worse."

"So, then what do you do when you become agitated or unhappy with his drinking?"

"Mostly I will just sigh and try and let it go. Sometimes I will make a comment in a roundabout way, but here lately I just get so angry that I just blow up and we don't speak for a bit."

"That sounds a bit passive aggressive to me. I wonder why you don't feel comfortable telling him how you truly feel in the moment?"

"What's the point in starting a fight? He will give me some lame answer about it relaxing him or that it was in the past, and if I say anything after that it will be an issue. It's easier just to say nothing."

"It doesn't sound easier. It sounds more stressful to me."

"You just don't know my husband. We have been there and done that. I just get so mad I end up going crazy. I really don't like being disrespectful to him."

"Do you think that truly expressing yourself means that you have to curse at him or be disrespectful?"

"Not necessarily but those are the only words I can come up with when I am pushed to that limit. It's just better if I don't say anything at all. I learned that lesson too…a long time ago."

Cori started to recount her life.

Session 3

"Sister! Sister! Help me. Sissy Please! Grab my hand!" Cori reached for the hand, but before she could grasp it he feel down, far down, into darkness. Cori jolted out of bed. She was drenched in sweat and she was panting. She reached over for Stephen, wanting to cuddle next to him and feel safe again. He wasn't in the bed. She looked toward the bathroom to see if the light was on in there. Since he started blood pressure

189

medication he would get up several times a night to urinate. All was dark in the bathroom. She reached for her cellphone which was on the charger on the nightstand. 2:45 a.m. burned into her eyes from the screen. *Where is he?*

She had gone up to bed before him but he said he would be right up. She must have fallen asleep as soon as her head hit the pillow. She crept downstairs not wanting A.J. to wake. He was such a light sleeper. She saw the light from the living room television and she went over to the sofa to find Stephen breathing heavily in a deep sleep with his phone on his chest. *Should I?* she thought. *I told myself I would stop this*, but as she stood over him, her heart pounded; she couldn't resist. She just had to know for her own sake. *Just a quick peek to make sure he is still being faithful.* As she stood over him reviewing the messages he woke up and glared at her.

****

"Good morning Doctor Kate," Cori stated, more exhausted than she had been. She almost cancelled the appointment that morning. She had gone back and forth about continuing therapy. She knew she needed it, but since she started it three weeks ago she seemed to be worse. She was having awful dreams, she was always nervous, and she couldn't stop thinking about her past.

"The last few days had been really hard. I actually almost cancelled this appointment and my clinic today."

"You don't look like you are feeling well. Tell me what's going on."

"I have been having these dreams... these nightmares. They are different every time but it's the same theme every time. I am with this little boy who I don't recognize but as we face the accident he is crying

190

for me to help him and I can't. He seems to be my brother, but he doesn't look like my brother did as a child. I can never save him. It's killing me. I go to sleep, and the dream is there. I wake up and I can't shake it."

"How often are you having these dreams? They sound pretty scary."

"Some are more terrifying than others. At least two to three nights a week. One night, Stephen woke me up and said I was screaming. Last night I woke up in a panic, sweaty and out of breath."

"Where was Stephen last night?"

"He was on the couch. Passed out cold," she said with clear irritation.

"Okay, we can discuss that in a bit. When did these dreams begin?"

"They have been on and off for several months but have just increased in frequency in the last three weeks. Since I have been coming to see you."

"I wonder if it could symbolize loss of your intimate connections?"

"What? That doesn't make sense. He is calling me his sister in the dream. It's clearly Ben and not Stephen."

"I understand that but are you sure it doesn't symbolize both losses?"

"I haven't lost Stephen. He is still very much there."

"Hear me out for a second. You and Ben had become very close and you lost him, right? Then the next male you were close to was your husband, and you feel as though you are losing him or losing control now with his increased drinking. You have pulled away from him and you are constantly fearing that he will stray."

Cori sat there in silence. A strange feeling crept into her gut and the taste of salt filled her mouth. Her body felt numb and her ears began ringing. She felt paralyzed. Cori sat in silence. No thoughts. No sounds.

"You think that I am pulling away from Stephen. And… you're right. We had it so right at one point. How could it all feel so wrong now?"

"What feels wrong?"

"Me. Him. I look at him and I feel nothing. Sometimes I feel like I don't know him anymore. Sometimes I feel like I don't even like him. I feel alone and suffocated all at the same time. I just want to go. I just want to run. I don't want to do this anymore. I don't want to do him. I don't want to do A.J., and I don't want to do Lexi. I know this makes me a horrible person. I just can't. It's too much. I am on the verge of losing my practice, too. I just can't."

Another moment of silence followed. *Wow.* she thought. *I have never really understood it when my patients have said that 'they are at their wits' end. This is it. I think I am having a nervous breakdown.* Cori looked up at Doctor Kate with blood shot eyes. Doctor Kate could see the dark circles under her eyes. They had not been there before. Doctor Kate could see the look of defeat. Cori suddenly stood up and reached for her purse.

"Wait, where are you going?"

"I can't do this. Talking has just brought all of these emotions to the surface. Every week I just end up feeling worse. Even though I wasn't happy before I was at least functional. Now, I can't even function. I can't imagine how far down I would be if I continued on. I need to leave. I have a full clinic this afternoon."

"Cori, if I may just say. I know it feels really bad. I know emotions that you have worked hard to push away have come flooding to the top. But you know what? They were under the surface anyway. It was only a matter of time before they came out. You are burned out. You are depressed and you are anxious. Please sit down. Let's finish talking."

"Unless you have some kind of magic pill, then I don't think so. I do thank you for your time and I don't mean to be rude. I just can't handle this. Emotions are not my strong point."

"I don't have a magic pill but emotions are *my* strong point. Please sit. I know it is probably scary to admit that you are overwhelmed. You are in an occupation that says suck it and deal with it. But this is not something you can just suck up. That's what you have been doing. You have been just sucking up what life has thrown at you and now you are overwhelmed. You haven't healed from past experiences. I often tell people that our bodies are like those big plastic bins that we store our junk in. Well, you know when you first buy it, it's organized and everything in it has a place and you can snap the top on, no problem, but the more you put in there the harder it becomes to put the top on. Things in the bin become cluttered and somethings may be bent out of shape or even break. If you continue to add things the top will no longer fit and what you once had is now an unorganized mess. That's how our emotional regulation process is. If we don't organize the experiences as they come our regulation process becomes an unorganized mess and we lose our ability to 'put the top back on' so to speak."

"I understand that in theory, but it's been like three weeks and you haven't given me anything to do with it."

"First you have to identify what emotions you have that are under the surface and unresolved." Cori sat in silence with a blank look on her face.

"Worthlessness and sadness are the major ones."

"What emotion is underneath the worthlessness?"

"Shame, if I had to guess."

"Exactly. Shame is a feeling associated with inadequacy."

"Okay and sadness is your other emotion?"

"Yes."

"Okay then the next step is to own your feelings. You have been avoiding or hiding your feelings. Tell yourself that you feel ashamed and sad."

As they continued Cory finally admitted that she had never felt worthy after Stephen's indiscretion with the stripper.

"From that point on," continued Cori, "I doubted everything about me; not just about how I look, but if I was smart enough, a good enough girlfriend, a good enough lay, just *good enough*. While Stephen and I were split up, I had sex with several different men. One night I had a threesome at the urging of one of the guys and slept with a woman. I never could fully shake that. I mean I never thought I would do that; at least not being forced to do it by some guy."

"Did you feel coerced?"

Cori thought back to that experience. After she saw the video she was determined that men would desire her the way Stephen seemingly wanted that stripper. She began to wear extensions that went down to her waist, fake eyelashes, tight jeans, and bright red lipstick. The immediate attention from men was intoxicating. She met James, a football player at UT. He couldn't keep his hands off of her. They had had sex several times, even multiple times in one day and she had become comfortable with him and even comfortable with her sexuality. They met up one evening as planned and he arrived with another girl, someone she didn't know. Her initial objections were chastised by him and her. They made it seem like everyone had threesomes and it was no big deal. She eventually gave in. She had taken a few tequila shots, also at their coercion to loosen up, and agreed. She found herself enjoying the experience. Having a woman caress and gently touch her sensitive spots was more arousal than she had thought possible. The more aroused she became, the more James responded to her. The experience felt riveting; until the next morning. She looked around her apartment to find the remanence of her unexpected rendezvous, and her Baptist upbringing flooded her thoughts.

She could still smell the moisture between her legs and the undeniable smell in the air. As she showered, she couldn't stop her thoughts—so many thoughts, each one contradicting the last, each one racing through her mind. She prayed no one would find out.

A week later she found her prayers were not answered. She opened an email to find a tape of her head in between this random girl's legs pleasuring her with her tongue. You could hear the girl's moans in between James' commentary. The humiliation that followed was inexplicable. How could she possibly divulge this? As far as she knew, Stephen never found out and would never find out.

Tears streamed down her face she voiced this experience for the first time aloud.

Session 4

The next session was full of emotions. Cori was in between patients and was charting in her consultation room when she received a fax from the hospital. Mr. Ellington had been discharged after a two week stay and a diagnosis of a pulmonary embolism. He was to follow up with her in the next 48 hours. *Great*, she thought. *It would be easier if he would just find another doctor. Now he really won't trust me and will question everything I say. Who am I kidding? He won't be the only one to question every diagnosis I give him.*

After Mr. Ellington were two new patients referred by Ashley. *Validation*, she thought. Ashley had such a wide circle that pleasing her for such a small amount of time had paid off already.

As she went through the new patient visit with the first of the women referred by Ashley, it quickly became evident that Ashley sent them for the exact reason she feared. They, too, wanted Adderall. As she began to protest, each said almost word for word what Ashley had said.

Aggravated by the clear instructions to Ashley and continued manipulation, Cori just didn't have the strength to fight. She wrote each woman the same prescription, the same she wrote Ashley because for heaven's sake, she couldn't have them comparing notes on different dosages. She hurried through another woman from Ashley's group who wore too much make up to hide old acne scars, and had breasts too big for her body size, by not doing a physical or a complete history and provided her the prescription and asked her to follow up in three months. The visit lasted less than ten minutes.

She continued with her day on autopilot. Her thoughts continued to go back to the last session with Doctor Kate. She couldn't believe she told her.

Doctor Kate ended the session by speculating that her feelings of shame have just been compounded in her life and were now leading her to mistrust Stephen and pull away from him. *Why would I be pulling away?* She couldn't understand it. Doctor Kate had to be wrong about her speculation. What did she know anyway? She really hadn't been seeing Cori long enough to know her and she definitely didn't know Stephen.

196

She finished clinic early that day and headed home to make dinner reservations for her and her husband. She texted Vanessa, the teenager across the street, to come and sit for the kids. She was going to take her husband out on a date and end it with some steam between the sheets. It had been long overdue.

It used to seem like every night was date night for them; now she couldn't remember the last time they had been anywhere together on a date. She made a 7:30 reservation for Al Biernet's, their favorite restaurant and the home of many of their special date nights. She looked through her closet and found Stephen's favorite dress. It was a coral strapless fitted dress. He would always say he loved how it looked on her skin. She got the kids squared away with a movie and pizza and Vanessa would be there any minute. She showered and slipped into her dress. She slid her pink pedicured toes into the straps of her favorite nude colored heels. She heard the garage open and hurried to meet Stephen at the door.

She greeted him with a kiss, smelling the alcohol on his breath and choosing not to say anything.

"Hey babe. You look amazing. What's up with all this?" he asked looking her up and down.

"We are going out; just the two of us," she said with a flirtatious smile. She hadn't worn this smile in at least a year.

"We are? Well I was planning on watching the game but this looks much more like a win than some stupid basketball game," Cori could hear the excitement in Stephen's voice and knew that Doctor Kate was wrong. She wasn't pulling away. They were just as close and connected as ever.

****

The next morning Cori woke up without an alarm. What time is it, she thought, *Oh my gosh it's 8:15?* The house was quiet. She looked around and saw the remnants of Stephen's morning routine. He must have dressed and taken the kids already. She hustled to dress and get out the door.

She arrived at the clinic ten minutes late, which had a tendency to increase her anxiety. *Relax*, she thought to herself as she entered the building. The door chime signaled her entrance and her tardiness. Doctor Kate came around the corner.

"Good morning. I'm glad you made it. I was beginning to think you stood me up."

"Sorry I'm late. I had a rough night."

"What happened?"

Cori told her of the date night she planned including intentionally wearing his favorite dress. When Stephen had come home, he had been already drinking.

"During dinner his phone was on vibrate and I could hear it vibrating constantly. He couldn't concentrate for all the vibration. I finally had my fill and told him to check his phone. He refused, telling me that was just enabling me to control him and invade his privacy. He kept telling me that he was not doing anything shady and the more he said it the more pissed I got. He started knocking back drinks. I finally said something and he went off. We started fighting right there in the restaurant. In the car, he called me an uptight bitch and said that I was boring. He said that if I was half the freak I was while we were on a break, we wouldn't have this issue. I asked him what was wrong with him and he said it was me.

He said I had been unbearable since my brother died. I asked him if he was cheating and he said no. I don't believe him. He has never been so cruel. There has to be someone else."

Tears were streaming down her face. Her mascara began to smear under her eyes and they stung from the makeup as she wiped them.

"We fought until about 3:30 in the morning when he finally just left. He left the house and I haven't heard from him since. All I can think of is that he is with *her,*" she finished. Her mind danced back to seeing that he had taken the kids to school, so she knew he had to have been there, but she just couldn't reconcile the issues at hand.

Doctor Kate expressed her empathies which seemed to only set Cori off. She became very agitated, raising her voice, telling Doctor Kate that this whole time she was becoming convinced that she was the problem in marriage to only come to understand that it was not her. It was Stephen and his fake ass façade the whole time. "I mean you kept telling me it was me that was pulling away. I guess you were wrong. This whole time it was him," Cori said as her voice began shaking.

Doctor Kate sat patiently until Cori's temper tantrum was over.

"Well, I don't know that I agree with that. I think you may be taking the victim role here. I wonder if you often take that role. I think that both of you were having some issues and instead of being honest you bot swept it under the rug and know things have blown up."

"Play the victim? I have worked my ass off and fought for everything I have ever accomplished. If I were playing the victim, I wouldn't have half of these accomplishments."

"Cori, playing the victim emotionally has nothing to do with academic or financial accomplishments. You and Stephen had what appeared to be an idealistic marriage, but you two never seemed to encounter any difficult times in the years you have been together. Your brother's death multiplied by having to parent his two children has been a big change for you two individually and as a couple. You didn't seem to communicate honestly either of you about the challenges you were feeling. You pulled away and internalized. Stephen seemingly began drinking more to numb his feelings; and all the while this issue of fidelity has been rearing its ugly head and never been resolved."

"Well now I disagree with you *Doc*, Cori motioned air quotes when she said doc, intentionally demeaning Doctor Kate's profession. She gathered her things and stormed out of the office.

Cori sat in her car and listened to three voicemails she had gotten while in session. One from her mother, 'just checking in'. Another from her girlfriend from med school confirming a lunch date for later in the week. The last was from a number she didn't recognize; a number with an Austin area code. The Texas Medical Board, the caller said to call her back as soon as possible.

Session 5

Cori had spent the last two-and-a-half weeks constantly worried. She had finally gotten around to returning the call from the woman at the medical board. The woman had a soft sympathetic tone as she informed Cori that she had received a board complaint on behalf of the family of Mr. Ellington. The board was requesting his complete medical record and would be conducting and investigation of his case and a possible audit of medical records of different patients.

Over the next few weeks, Cori waited in limbo to hear from the Texas Medical Board. She hired an attorney whose retainer was more than one semester of medical school tuition. She was not sleeping or eating. She was

200

trying to hide her stress from her office staff, Stephen, and the kids. She and Stephen had still not spoken more than a sentence at a time since their date night.

Days were long and the nights were longer. Her attorney had advised her to ensure she was practicing evidence based medicine at all times and to ensure adequate documentation. This only appeared to increase her anxiety as she ruminated over the number of Hydrocodone and Adderall prescriptions she had been passing out over the last few months. She thought of how many diagnoses she had altered and symptom profiles she created to try and cover her tracks.

Surely the medical board would see through this. It was just a matter of time before her career was over. It was a matter of time before her marriage was over. And very possibly a matter of time that her chance at motherhood was over as she had not even tried to engage with either child since her last blow up where she called A.J. a baby and called Lexi a bitch. *What the hell has happened to me*, she thought.

****

"Hi Doctor Kate. It's good to see you," Cori looking slightly embarrassed.

"Hi Cori. I am happy to see you again. Tell me what's going on."

"Stephen moved out last weekend and I am under investigation by the Texas Medical Board. As it turns out, you were right. I bet you hear that a lot don't you," she said smirking, laughing to choke back her tears.

Sophie

Session 1

"I'm not sure why I'm here," Sophie stated. I'm fine. I think I just got overwhelmed.

"How long have you felt overwhelmed Sophie?"

"I think I just didn't eat enough last week."

"Since I went to the doctor, everything has been fine."

"I'm happy to hear that. Can you tell me a bit about what has had you so overwhelmed?"

"I have twin boys and I'm a stay at home mom. I think sometimes it just gets to me but honestly I'm good. I don't think I need to be here. My husband would lose it if he knew I spent $100 just to talk about my feelings," she smirked. "My feelings are fine and they don't matter to anyone anyway."

"Sophie, that's an interesting statement to make— that your feelings don't matter to anyone anyway."

"I didn't mean anything by it. I just meant that I'm not a weak person. I went to one of the best college prep schools and subsequently to Princeton after all," she rolled her eyes and with the wave of a hand dismissing the prestige of those accomplishments.

"You're sending some mixed signals."

"My life is full of mixed signals. Tell me this Doctor Kate, what is me being here answering your questions going to do for me? I mean, I see the women on TV going to their shrinks, and they say it helps but does it really help? Are you going to tell me how to run my life?"

"Well no, I don't tell people how to run their lives. First, we see if there are any conditions you are dealing with like depression or anxiety. If there is something like depression, we begin to treat it with medication if you want. The other, and most important part of the therapy is to begin to help you process and heal any past hurts that may be influencing your thoughts or behaviors. We also will work on having effective emotional regulation by teaching how to respond in more appropriate and healthy ways to emotional situations."

Sophie's look was cautious but somewhat intrigued. "And that works?"

"Yes, it does, very well in fact."

"Well, I know I don't want any medication. That is over the top. I don't want a pill that either makes me zoned out or feel numb."

"I understand that. A lot of people choose to not take medication and that's okay. But some conditions do need medication to help control them. I don't know if you have one of those or not, but I am more than happy to give you my recommendations if you want to continue with today's session."

Hesitant but knowing something had to change, Sophie agreed. *This is my last hope,* she thought. She liked Doctor Kate. Doctor Kate was easy to talk to and seemed very patient. She looked at Sophie with empathy, not pity. Sophie didn't feel judged...*yet*, she thought.

Sophie went on to complete Doctor Kate's evaluation. She answered question after question. No she didn't sleep well. No she didn't have an appetite. No, she couldn't concentrate. Yes, she felt guilt—a lot of it. Yes, she was irritable. Yes, she cried often...often was an understatement. Yes, she worried all the time. Yes, she had lost pleasure in things...everything. All of this began shortly after she had the boys were born, she remembered. Yes, it had all gotten worse with time. She told Doctor Kate she felt trapped, like she would suffocate at any moment.

She told Doctor Kate that her husband was a hard worker and she admired him. As Doctor Kate pressed, she became a little defensive.

"Doctor Kate, my husband is a good man. A good, hardworking black man. He doesn't cheat, *although he does incessantly like other women's pictures,* she thought deciding to keep this to herself. He doesn't lie. He has a job in fact he works hard to support me and the boys. He is good to me."

"Does he support you emotionally, Sophie?"

And with that Sophie's eye welled up and the tears streamed. The flow became a solid streak down her face. She sobbed uncontrollably. Doctor Kate sat patiently and waited for Sophie to gain her composure.

"Tell me Sophie."

"I hate this. I hate my life. I hate myself. I have become a shell. Most of my days I'm on autopilot. Some days I don't even shower and comb my hair. This isn't how I imagined my life. I was not raised like this. I'm just wasting away Doctor Kate. Somedays I think my boys would be better off if I wasn't here. My husband could remarry a woman who was happy to stay home and clean, cook, and take care of the kids."

"You've lost yourself Sophie."

"Was I ever found? I don't think I ever knew who I was. I went from my parents controlling me to a controlling husband."

"That's pretty powerful."

"Yeah I've never told anyone that. I don't want you to think that I want to kill myself and put me in some nut house."

"Are you concerned that I think that?"

"Yes, don't you all think that of your patients?" she laughed, only half joking

"No, Sophie we don't. If that was a symptom or an issue you had we would deal with it appropriately."

"Well, I don't. I'm just saying."

"I understand. I also understand that your recent behavior has hit a head. I think your natural defenses have broken down and that's what led you to go to the ER. Let me explain a bit. You have a condition called post-partum depression. Have you heard of that?"

"Sure, it's in every parenting message board I've ever read."

"Yes, it is. What happens is mothers can often feel these symptoms, lack of sleep, energy, guilt, sadness, not wanting to bond with their baby, everything that you discussed earlier. This can happen after birth. If there is no treatment, the symptoms can get worse over time. That's what happened to you. I think you began feeling these things and because society tells us that giving birth and having a new baby is a joyous time, then you never acknowledged the problems you were having. Things got worse over time and this led to your recent ER visit.

"Hmmmm...do you really think that's what happened to me?"

"I'm pretty positive Sophie, but the good thing is that we can treat it. You can try medications if you want and I will be more than happy to talk with your primary care doctor or obstetrician to discuss my thoughts. Otherwise, you and I can try weekly sessions for a bit and see if we can help you feel better."

"Honestly, I still don't see how talking about this would make me feel better."

"Well that can be difficult to understand until you are in the process"

Sophie made an appointment for early the next week. As she drove home she wondered how Will would respond to this. She knew she had to tell him what the doctor said to justify spending $100 every week. He would surely react hatefully.

****

Sophie just completed the third attempt to put the boys to bed.

"You know you could come in here and help me. They listen to you," she snapped, jarring Will out of whatever basketball game he was watching. Will turned and looked at his wife from his armchair.

Since her recent "issue", he thought he was doing a good job helping out. He was reaching his limit though. He didn't understand why she wasn't already better. She had the visit the other day with the doctor, but he didn't ask what happened. He was told that the visit was to make everything okay again, but he couldn't see what had improved...to him, it actually seemed to be worse than it was before.

The boys finally settled after Sophie gave them each a dose of melatonin.

"We have to talk," she blurted as she plopped in the old recliner across from him. He clicked the game on silent but kept his eyes on the television.

"So, you know I went to see Doctor Kate a few days ago right?"

"Yeah I thought everything was going to be better after that expensive-ass visit. All she seemed to do is stir you up even more."

"Are you serious right now? I'm trying to talk to you seriously."

Will glared at her blankly. "Well...say it."

"She says I have a condition called post-partum depression. She says that I will need to come back to her weekly for a few months or so until my symptoms go away, or I learn to manage them."

"A few months? What are you talking about symptoms? This is just in your head. You have been watching to many of those housewives shows, watching those crazy chicks going to their shrinks. That whole thing has just become a fad. We can't afford that."

Sophie's eyes welled up again. She knew Will had trouble understanding emotions but she had no idea that when it came to her and her health he could be so cruel.

"I'm going back on Monday and every Monday after that," she said more defiantly than she ever had.

"Like hell you will. You better find some way to pay for your looney visits then because I'm not busting my ass for you to go lay on some couch, pretending to have problems that you don't have."

Session 2

"Sophie. Good to see you again. Come on back"

Sophie followed Doctor Kate back to the familiar room. This time she noticed family pictures on Doctor Kate's desk.

"You have kids?" she asked quietly, wondering what Doctor Kate would think of her obvious short comings in the parenting department.

'I do. I have three children and they are a handful," Doctor Kate smiled.

"Do you have a nanny? You know, since you work?"

"No, we don't have a nanny. We use a great daycare."

"My husband doesn't believe in daycares. He says you shouldn't have children if you are going to pay for someone else to raise them."

"Yes, a lot of people feel that way. I believe daycares can be good for children as far as the learning and socialization they experience. But that's my personal opinion. Perhaps because I was a daycare child myself," Doctor Kate mused.

"A few weeks ago I told my husband, Will is his name, about this great Montessori school the boys could attend part time and I thought maybe I could find part time work. He wasn't up for it though.'

"You seem disappointed that he wasn't up for it."

"I was. I still am. I told you last week I feel stuck. But I feel like a horrible mother. I feel like I don't want to be around my children some days. That's so awful to say out loud."

"No, I don't think so. I think it's normal Sophie."

"You do? Will would crucify me if I said that to him."

"I think it's a normal part of parenting. People don't tell us before we have children how difficult it would be. I think that's because if we really knew no one would have children and the human race would be in danger of becoming extinct," Doctor Kate humored.

Sophie gently smiled, realizing the joke, but also knew that if someone told her how her life would be right now she would have chosen differently.

"I love my boys Doctor Kate. I just don't know what to do to get them to behave. We go to the park and playdates and other moms make it look so easy. Will's mom seemed to do everything so right. He compares me to her all the time. I just can't figure it out. What am I doing wrong? What is wrong with me?"

"Do you often feel like you are doing everything wrong Sophie?"

"Gah…really? Everything is always my on me. I can never get things to go the way they are supposed to. That is nothing new."

"So you felt like this when you were younger then?"

"All my life."

"What was your mother like, Sophie?"

"Oh goodness, Doctor Kate. How much time do we have?"

Sophie had not thought deeply about her childhood in years and there was a reason for it. Growing up as a biracial child was difficult. Her mother was Black and marrying a white man in the 1970s, although accepted, was not popular in the south. Black kids told Sophie she her skin was lighter than a paper bag so she must think she was better than them. White kids looked at Sophie's hair and wanted to touch it. They called her hair an afro and called her names like Oreo and mutt.

Sophie remembered one day in the second grade she came home and crying because her teacher pointed her out and told everyone she was from Africa so from that point on all the kids called her Sophie the Niger, the country in Africa instead of the word they all knew not to use. Sophie came home and told her mother about it. Her mother insisted that she stop crying at once because crying was for babies and she was no longer a baby. The next morning Sophie's mother went up to the school and confronted the teacher in front of the entire school. Her mother made such a scene that the principal threatened to call security. The kids stopped calling her Sophie the Niger but didn't speak to her the remainder of the school year. Sophie quickly learned that telling her mother her problems only made them worse. Her mother was so quick to confront people. Sophie hated conflict and stayed away from it at all costs.

Sophie's father was a sweet, gentle spirit. Much like Sophie. he was from a well to do family from South Carolina. The Bonhums were a well-known family, with prominent business all over Charleston. When Jimmy's parents heard he was marrying a Black woman and moving to Texas, they thought their oldest son had lost his mind. They sent him to Princeton to get an education not to get caught up and trapped by some jezebel! Even worse, he left Princeton and ended up at Texas A&M to complete his education, breaking with family tradition. The jezebel had made him do it. Sophie overheard this statement one evening when her mother was ripping into her father about an upcoming visit from his mother. As time passed Sophie's grandmother Bonhum seemed to let go of those issues and really embraced Sophie. She would make comments about Sophie needing to come out of the pool so she wouldn't get any darker. She would make comments about Sophie's hair feeling more like wool than silk, but overall she was nurturing and loving—more so than Cordelia was.

Sophie loved her Nana Bonhum and credited her with the only happiness she felt as a child.

"Sophie, it sounds like you received a lot of confusing messages about your value as a child. What race do you identify with now?"

"No one has ever asked me that. I honestly feel like I have to say Black because of my mother and my husband. But I really don't know. I mean I have this light skin and these light eyes. But it's funny because I look just like my father. I really don't feel like I belong to either race."

"Tell me what you think of yourself."

"I used to think I was a pretty good person."

"And now?"

"Now I don't. I feel…like I suck...honestly."

"Will gives me crap all the time about what I do and don't do. My mother has pretty much cut me off. She hasn't spoken to me in weeks."

"Really? Why haven't you spoken to your mother in weeks?"

Sophie recalled the story of brunch, things that led up to brunch and how she left her mother sitting at the table because her mother was once again laying into Will. She told the doctor how she felt stuck in the middle. Cordelia never thought Will was good enough and Will knew that. Sophie was the one now not feeling good enough.

"Your feelings of not being good enough make complete sense to me, Sophie."

"They do? You don't think I'm just sitting up here complaining?"

"Not at all. You have just told me that as a child you didn't fit in society and you didn't even fit into your own home. Your mother never nurtured you and wanted you to behave in a certain way. She didn't encourage you to be an individual. Your father although you knew he loved you was very distant from you. The only one you felt loved from was your Nana Bonhum and she often reminded you that you were different. Now you have married a man that, much like your father, is not emotionally available or plugged into the home life and he constantly reminds you that you are different as well."

With that, Sophie began to cry.

****

Sophie picked up the boys from her neighbor's house, making sure to put on extra concealer before going to ring the doorbell. She had cried the only way home. No one had every understood or summarized her life like that before. She was still overwhelmed by the experience, but knew she had to keep moving; at least until next Monday.

"Mommy!" they squealed in unison.

"Hi babies! Let's go get you guys some dinner."

She drove the boys through the Chick-fil-A that was close to the house. She knew Will would be angry that she chose fast food, but she didn't have the energy to care

"Hi, two four-piece kid's meals with lemonade please, and a grilled chicken salad."

She had not eaten all day and was still not hungry but knew she needed to eat. The last thing she needed was to have another episode. Will would definitely have her locked up if that happened.

Sophie heard the garage door open as the boys were getting out of the bathtub. She dried them off and put on their matching puppy dog pals pajamas. She handed them each a book, and turned to go into the living room. She nearly bumped into Will coming around the corner.

"Hey babe. I don't smell any dinner."

"That's because I didn't cook. Me and the kids had Chick fil-A"

"Chick-fil-A?" he questioned as if he had misunderstood her.

"Yeah. I didn't feel like cooking so we grabbed some food on our way home."

"Home from where?"

"Doctor Kate's. I had another appointment."

She noticed the energy in the tiny house grow tense and the air immediately stifled.

"So, you went back huh? And you didn't bother to cook. So, what am I supposed to eat?" He said dryly and more of a statement than a question.

"I don't know; you can make a sandwich."

Will turned and marched into the kitchen and began immediately to bang cabinets around as he made a ham sandwich with no condiments and nothing but bread because there was nothing else in the house. Everything he touched, he slammed, making Sophie twitch slightly with the noise.

Sophie clicked on the television and curled on the sofa. Will came in and sat in the recliner across from her. "See? I knew you could do it," she said sarcastically.

"Sophie don't start with me. I'm trying to be nice and cool about this."

"Cool about what?"

"I'm warning you Sophie. I'm trying to bite my tongue but you're gonna make me say something."

"Say it Will. I don't give a shit anymore," she said rolling her eyes.

Will was taken aback. He had never heard Sophie speak to him with such disrespect. That was one thing they established early in their relationship. He was the man and the head of the house. Sophie was to never speak to him in a disrespectful tone and until this moment she had abided by that.

"I'm only going to warn you one more time woman. Stop while you're ahead. I'm not taking any more of your disrespect."

"Woman? Who the hell do you think you are taking to like that? I'm sick of you treating me like I'm some dumb servant of yours. I'm sick of sitting in this house all day and waiting for you to come home so I can pretend to be happy to make your plate and clean up after you. I'm sick of running behind you like some attention starved puppy dog! Things are going to change, and they are going to change now!"

"I don't know what has gotten into you, but I do know one thing; you're not going back to that nut job doctor. She has you thinking you are something you're not. Don't let some white woman get you in trouble."

"She's not even white. She's Black."

"That's even worse. Some Black bitch who thinks she is better than everyone because she has a degree is going to fill your head with some bullshit about what you deserve."

"First off she's not doing that, and this isn't about her. This is about the way you treat me. You don't listen to me. You don't care about me. You just want your needs met."

"My needs?!" he screamed, his voice now booming through the tiny house. "What needs of mine are getting met? When's the last time you gave a brother some head? If it was about me getting my needs met I'd be getting my dick sucked, and not having to beg you to fuck once a month."

"You make me sick. You're an asshole, Will."

"Whatever. I don't know what you want from me. You better start appreciating me, I know that. What other brother would slave all day and let his woman sit up in here and watch TV all day? You don't cook, don't clean, and you sure as hell don't take care of the kids. They are bad as hell and that has everything to do with you."

"Me? Maybe they're bad because you once you get home you ignore them. You sit up watching some stupid game or flirting with girls on Instagram! Yeah you didn't think I knew did you. I know you spend all your time looking at those THOTS. And you expect me to suck your dick after you have been liking pics from those hoes. You're disgusting. You disgust me."

With that Will got up, grabbed his keys, and left. He slammed the door so hard that a canvas of the family fell to the ground.

Session 3

"The fight was horrible, Doctor Kate. The worst one we have ever had."

"What happened that lead up to the fight?" she asked curiously. Doctor Kate had long ago realized that Sophie was not the type to initial fights, especially not with her husband.

"I was pretty upset when I left here last week, and I just couldn't, you know? I couldn't listen to him bitch and complain about anything. So, after I picked up the boys, we got fast food. I didn't get any for him. He came home and got pissed. I got pissed. I called him an asshole and he left."

"Do you think you were pissed when you left here?"

"Pissed at him, yes"

"So, maybe not getting him any dinner was passive aggressive?"

"Maybe."

"Tell me why you were upset when you left here last week?"

"Well, I had just never realized how controlling he was. I knew my mom was controlling but not him. My mother had tried to tell me for years but I didn't listen. Probably because I thought she was trying to run my marriage. And he would tell me that she interfered too much. I believe him. But after you said that stuff last week I realized that he is controlling and I'm not myself with him. I don't work because he doesn't want me to. I cook every night because he wants me to. Everything I do is because he says so. I don't fit in this marriage."

"What do you mean don't fit?"

"A couple of months ago, before I started coming here I looked in his phone and saw what he was doing."

"What's that?"

"He's constantly on social media looking at pictures of women. Slutty-looking women. THOTS." Sophie smirked as she remembered finding the pictures.

"THOTS?" Doctor Kate asked, thinking of Andrea.

"It's an acronym that stands for That Hoe Over There," Sophie laughed a bit, observing Doctor Kate's oblivion to urban slang. *She clearly doesn't watch The Housewives of Atlanta,* Sophie thought.

"Oh yes, I've heard of them," Doctor Kate smiled knowingly.

"I just means a slutty-looking woman. Anyway, I never said anything to him when I first found the crap. It wasn't until I had lost it in the fight that I told him I knew."

"What did he say?"

"Nothing. What could he say? He just left. He didn't even come home that night. I still have no idea where he was. Probably with one of those thirsty bitches," she muttered under her breath.

"I'm sorry what?"

"Hey may have gone to one of those thirsty…that means desperate…women who he talks to online."

"Where did he say he was?"

"At his mother's house. I don't know if I can believe that though. I don't know what to believe anymore.'

"Sophie in our first session you told me he was a good man and didn't cheat. Now you're telling me you question it. Help me understand."

"I wish you could help *me* understand. I mean I already had found those pictures when I first came here. And I *did* think he was a good man. I didn't want you to think he was just some low-life…typical Black man that is sorry, you know?"

"Do you want to me to believe he is a certain way or do you want to believe it?"

"I needed to believe it I guess."

"Is he not what you thought he was?"

"I don't know. It's like since I have been coming here he isn't like I thought or wanted to think. The scary part is neither am I."

Over the next three weeks Sophie continued her visits with Doctor Kate. They soon became the highlight of her week. She got about an hour and a half away from the boys. Her neighbor agreed to keep them every week without pay. She said she and her husband enjoyed having them over. They were a sweet older couple who didn't get to see their own grandchildren as much as they liked. After the third week in a row of Ms. Sharon keeping the boys, she finally asked Sophie where she was headed off to every Monday afternoon at 2:00 p.m. Sophie was hesitant to tell Ms. Sharon that she was indeed in therapy. Ms. Sharon was what Sophie and Will called an old black church lady—the ones that arrive fifteen minutes late to the chapel and strut down front wearing a hat so big no one behind them could see anything. She knew Ms. Sharon would tell her she just needed to pray about it.

"I have a standing hair appointment Ms. Sharon," Sophie lied unable to think of any feasible explanation. As she kissed the boys good bye and drove always she questioned how believable that was considering her hair was always a mess and looked the same when she arrived as it did when she left. She would have to think of a reasonable answer for the next time. She pushed that thought out of her mind and thought of all the things she would have to tell Doctor Kate this week.

Session 6

"Hi Doctor Kate," Sophie said almost too excitedly. This forty-five minutes had become sacred to Sophie.

217

The only time she got to be herself. She could say whatever she wanted without being corrected, criticized, or judged. She had even cursed on occasion and Doctor Kate encouraged her to use the language she felt in the moment.

"Sophie, so good to see you this week. You know Sophie, I have really come to look forward to our sessions. I feel as though you have really acclimated to therapy. It seems like you have really let your guard down with me." Doctor Kate reflected the difference she noticed in Sophie's willingness to talk.

"I have really come to enjoy our time Doctor Kate. You are actually the only one I think understands me."

"Well, tell me what's going on this week. "

"Well, you know I told you in the last session that I had made up my mind to start looking for a job? Well, I did. I put together a resume and I have submitted it to a little firm downtown," Sophie said excitedly wanting Doctor Kate to be proud of her.

"You did!" exclaimed Doctor Kate with the expression and tone Sophie so badly needed.

"I did. I haven't heard back yet though."

"That's ok. The important part is that you have done it. Do you feel empowered now?"

"I do…kind of. I'm sort of freaking out about what Will is going to say when I tell him I'm looking for jobs."

"You haven't told Will Sophie? Why not?"

"Because I can't. He won't understand. It will just start another fight. We have been fighting so much I just can't bear another fight right now."

"Fighting a lot?"

"Yes," she said sheepishly. "We have actually been fighting about you."

"Oh," Doctor Kate replied, surprised and a bit taken aback at the idea of it. She knew it could happen with clients, but each time it sort of jarred her.

"Yeah he says since I have been coming to see you that I'm different and he doesn't like it."

"Different how?"

"He says that I'm talking back and I'm more combative than I used to be. He actually gave me an ultimatum. He told me to stop coming or he I would have to choose."

"Choose what, Sophie?"

"Basically, you or him. He says you're a feminist, and you are putting all this crap into my head. He says it has ruined our family and that I was just fine before I started coming."

"Hmmm....What do you think about what he says?"

"Well, I do wonder if he is right in a way. I mean things are very tense at home."

"I can understand that. I can assure I am not a feminist though, Sophie," she said with a quirky smile. "There is nothing at all wrong with feminism or feminist therapy. I just don't practice it. I do practice developing a healthy self-concept and self-efficacy. Self-efficacy is your belief in your ability to confidently handle things that come into your life or to set goals. I think the difference you two are noticing is that your self-concept and efficacy is changing."

"So, you think I am becoming more confident?"

"I do. Over the last few sessions, you have told me how you are now questioning if you want to stay be a stay at home mom. You have told me that you are beginning to set boundaries with Will as far as your responsibilities for the household. For instance, you no longer cook on the weekends. You have even told me that you have put the boys on a strict bed time schedule.

All of that shows improvement in your abilities to be more independent."

"I think that's right Doctor Kate. I feel like I should be more than what I have been. I hated myself. I hated my life. I still have no idea what I want, I just know it had to change. I just don't know what to do about Will. It's like he despises me now."

"What do you mean?"

"He barely talks to me. We don't spend any time together at all. You know you said to put the boys on a bed time schedule so that he and I could spend some time alone. Well, the boys now go down at 8:00 p.m. sharp. Once they are in bed, Will disappears either in front of the television or leaves the house and doesn't come home until I am sleeping. When I ask him where he goes he just tells me away from me because he doesn't know me anymore."

Doctor Kate nodded in understanding. "What do you think of that?"

"I think he's right. He doesn't know me anymore. He knew me as he had created me. Now that I am changing, he doesn't know me. Hell, I don't know what I am changing into myself. It's kind of scary."

"It is scary. I agree. What do you want?"

"I want to be happy."

"What does that mean?"

"I have no clue really? Maybe like you, you know? I want to be able to go to work and have a family, too. I want to take cute family pictures and put them up in my office. I want to talk to my husband in the middle of the day and find out what he's doing. I want to go to soccer games on the weekend. I want my parents to come over for Sunday dinner." The smile on her face quickly faded and tears streamed.

"What made the tears come?"

"Because I realize this will never happen. Will is getting ready to leave me. Once I tell him about the job, he's gone. My mom still isn't talking to me. When I call, *if* she answers, she just hands the phone to my dad. My dad will carry on a superficial five-minute conversation about the boys or some case he's been working on before he chokes out a 'we love you' and he hangs up."

"You sound very lonely."

"I am. I guess that's why I look forward to coming here, but maybe it was a mistake to come. We really can't afford it. It's made my marriage worse and my mother still refuses to talk to me."

"I can see how it looks that way. Each family has a dynamic. Each member plays a certain role in the family. This happens in the happiest most functional families to the most dysfunctional families. In dysfunctional families when one person begins to get healthy, it changes the dynamics in the family. Other family members often do not respond to this change very well at all. But as the member that is getting healthy remains consistent in their behaviors they dynamics will often change and improve as a result. My point is this: as you get healthy the family as a unit can become healthier. This could really improve your marriage if Will is willing to work though the change."

"And that's where the problem lies. Will doesn't like change."

"Do you think he is committed to the marriage?"

"Yes, I think so. I mean I know he doesn't believe in divorce."

"So, then maybe with time he will adjust. Do you think he would be willing to come with you to a session?"

"Absolutely not! That's out of the question. He blames you anyway, so I would be scared to even have him come."

"Okay I understand, but let's just put that on the back burner. The offer remains open if you ever want to broach the topic with him."

"Let's go back to you parents now, let's talk about your mother in particular."

"What about her?"

"Has she ever cut you off like this before?"

"Not like this. She has gone a few weeks without talking to me before but normally as soon as I break down and call her she will tell me all the ways I am wrong and have hurt her. After she gets all that out, she eventually becomes her old demanding self."

"So, why do you think this one is different? Is it all really because you left her in the restaurant?"

"I think she believes I chose Will over her, honestly."

"She has always said family comes before anyone and when I left to go home to him I think she flipped."

"Family comes first? Will is your family."

"Not to her. Will was a mistake to her. She never wanted us to marry. Like I've always told you she thought he was beneath me. She never considered him family. The really bad part is that she was right about a lot of stuff about him. She told me he would be controlling and I wouldn't be happy. I never believed her then. But she was right. He is controlling and I haven't been happy since I quit my job and had the twins," Sophie confessed with a defeated sigh.

"I understand all of that but why do you think she has had such an angry reaction to this all?"

"Because it reminds her of herself."

"What do you mean?"

"My dad is my mother's second marriage. She was married to another man before she met my dad. A Black man. He didn't have a good job and that was *when* he worked. My mother was working her way through

222

college when she met her first husband. When they married and moved in together, she got pregnant really fast and she quit her job. He started smoking weed and playing video games all day. She supported the household. One days she confronted him, it started an argument. As I've told you, my mother doesn't back down from a fight. She slapped him and he hit her back. When he did that, she fell. When she got to the hospital they told her the baby's heart wasn't beating. It wasn't because of the fight though, it was just a weird coincidence. He told her it was her fault and that she wasn't strong enough to even bare a child. He ended up leaving, her saying she couldn't perform even basic womanly duties. After that she swore off Black men. She met my father and my guess is that she felt like she could walk all over him, so she married him."

"Your mother told you all of this?"

"Goodness no. My auntie did—the night before my wedding. I was crying to her because my mother was being so awful to me and to Will's family. She told me it wasn't my fault and that's when she explained all of this to me."

"I see. So your mother hates Will because he reminds her of her first husband. She is projecting all of this onto you?"

"Projecting, like putting it on me? I want to understand," Sophie asked through sniffles.

"Projection is when we hate something about ourselves, but we identify in someone else and tell them we hate it in them. Your marriage to Will reminds her of the weakness she felt when she married her first husband. She projects her anger at you and Will. She sees him as an abuser and she sees you as weak. But it's really about her not you or Will."

"Dang, Doctor Kate. That's deep!"

"Yes it is. It's funny how our past can influence us, isn't it?"

"Hell yes it is! So ,what do I do with that?"

"You have to remember that first of all you are not weak. You never have been. You also have to know that you are not your mother. Will is also not your mother's first husband. I think you should send your mother a letter. You apologize for walking out in the restaurant. Let her know that you were not choosing Will over her you were just not in a place where you could receive that information."

"Wait. You want me to *apologize* to *her*?"

"Hear me out for a second Sophie. You are simply apologizing for walking out on her. You tell her you should have expressed your feelings instead of walking out. You aren't apologizing for how you felt, but instead how you responded to your feelings. You then tell her that you would like to meet and talk with her. You tell her that you understand if she is still hurt and that you both need to talk and try and mend the hurt that exists between the two of you."

"You think that will work?"

"I do think so. I think that she should have reached out a long time ago. I always believe that if an issues exists between a parent and child it is up to the parent to fix it. However, your mother does not have the emotional maturity or emotional intelligence to do so. You now have the emotional maturity so I think it would be a good thing to do for you."

"What if she doesn't respond?"

"Well, then she just doesn't and you and I will find a way for you to heal this hurt so you can continue to grow. I think she will respond though."

"Okay I guess I can do that, but don't be surprised if I say I told you so. Now what do I do about my marriage?"

****

Sophie sat in the parking lot of Doctor Kate's office and composed a text to her mother. Doctor Kate was right. It was time to put all of this silliness aside. Her mother would surely be happy to know that she had applied for a job; a real job.

Mom, I know you are still upset with me. I am really sorry I walked out on you a few months ago. I need you right now Mom. I miss you and the boys miss you. I know you are hurt and so am I. Can we sit down and talk about it over dinner? My treat.

She pushed send and fought back the tears. She needed her mom back on her side. As crazy and controlling as her mother was, she always felt safe with her and now she felt unsafe and alone.

Later that night as she fed the boys, Will walked through the door in his dusty, sweaty clothes. He kissed the boys and headed straight for the shower. *Uggghhh,* she thought. *I have to tackle this beast too.* If her marriage was going to survive, it couldn't survive like this. She made Will a plate and put it into the oven, setting the temperature to warm so it could be ready when he finished his shower. After the boys finished eating she put them in front of the television for an episode of Mickey Mouse Clubhouse before their 8:00 p.m. bedtime.

As the boys danced to the theme song, Will came around the corner in his pajama pants and shirtless. She remembered how she used to love to lay on his chest and rub her hands down his abdomen, feeling each muscle. She remembered the life they had before children. They would meet at home after work and pop open a bottle of wine. Before the night was over they were in the bathtub or shower half-drunk off wine and making love. She would often be so out of breath as they

225

climaxed together. Their love was almost animalistic. She would wake up feeling ready for round two and most often round two would happen before the sun even came up. Now she couldn't remember the last time they had sex.

"Honey, come sit down I have your plate ready."

Will looked at her curiously. She hadn't called him honey since before the last big blow out, and she had definitely not fixed his plate.

"Did you poison my food something?" he asked jokingly to break the tension.

It worked. Sophie smiled a little and said, "We have to change things between us. I know you're not happy, and neither am I."

"I told you have been different since you started seeing that shrink. I don't like it Sophie."

She immediately felt herself tense up. She had grown protective of Doctor Kate, but more so she felt frustrated that Will could not see the positive changes she had made.

"Well Doctor Kate has really helped me realize a lot of things. I wish you would just listen instead of judging me."

"I'm not judging you; I'm judging her. I think she's got you drinking the Kool-Aid. You never talked to me like you do now before you started seeing her."

Sophie took a deep breath to calm herself. She felt the irritation starting to grow. She reminded herself that when her irritability was quick to come on it was symptom of depression like Doctor Kate said. Just then her cell phone pinged. She saw her mother's name pop up on the screen, then quickly disappear. *Not now*, she thought. She needed to focus on this conversation with her husband.

"You're right," she said, but before he could begin his righteous banter she continued. "After the twins were born I began to feel depressed and I lost myself. The depression started and I was too afraid to say how I was really feeling. I was too afraid to say that I didn't want to take care of them that I was unhappy and not feeling loving toward them. I was scared that you would be angry and that my mother wouldn't understand. Then I started thinking I wanted to go back to work and that would make it better. The few times I tried to tell you, you would dismiss me. I felt lost babe. I didn't know who I was. I spent my whole days crying and trying to hide it from you. I was miserable. I wasn't good enough. I wasn't a good mother because I didn't want to be with my children. I wasn't a good wife because the house was never clean enough or dinner wasn't ready. I wasn't even pretty to you anymore. Then I saw the stuff on your phone. The conversations with the other women broke me. I stopped eating; I stopped caring. I feel like I snapped."

Sophie paused to give Will a chance to digest what she was saying. She saw him look at his phone. He seemed genuinely surprised at the information that was pouring out her. He opened his mouth and before he could speak her phone pinged again. Another message for Cordelia. She paused and waited for him to speak.

"I don't understand Soph. So wait, you're saying that you don't want to be a mom or a wife?"

"I do Will. I just can't do it like I have been. Going to Doctor Kate has made me realize that I have always lived for other people. I lived for my mother while up until college."

Will rolled his eyes at the mention of Cordelia.

Sophie continued, "Then we got married and I began to live for you and now I live for you and the boys."

"We agreed a long time ago that you would stay at home and raise the kids. Now, you just want to change all that? That's not right."

"We agreed that I would give it a try, and I have, but I never agreed to be treated like a nanny, house keeper, and sex slave. When is the last time that you took me out on a date? When is the last time that you bought me flowers? Hell, when is the last time you even asked me how my day was or took an interest in anything I do?"

Will sat silently. "See, that's my point," Sophie continued, her voice down to almost a whisper. "And now I know that you are interested in other women. How do you expect me to react to that?"

"I only started that when you stopped wanting to give it up. I've never cheated on you. That stuff doesn't even matter. All I'm doing is just looking. Every man looks Soph."

"No every man doesn't disrespect his wife like that"

They sat in silence for a while, clearly at a state of impasse. Then Will spoke quietly, "So what do you want to do?"

"I want *us* back. I want me back."

"What does that mean? I can't read minds."

"I don't know she said quietly, I really don't know."

Session 7

"This has been a hell of a week Doctor Kate."

"Tell me."

Sophie groaned, tilting her head back. "Where do I start." Doctor Kate could feel a sense of overwhelm in Sophie's voice; somewhat alarming her. "I guess I will start with my mom. I sent her a text. Here let me get my phone so I can read it to you."

228

Sophie read the text message she sent to her mother verbatim.

"That was very authentic and heart-felt. How did she respond?"

"She basically responded by telling me how much I hurt her. She said I have hurt her for thirty years. She said she didn't raise me to become the woman I have turned out to be. She said she is at a loss of what to do with me. She said she pitied my children."

"That's pretty harsh"

"Yeah, but you know all I could think of is how much I'm *just* like her. Anyway I called her the next morning, and we met for dinner the following night. That was a whole other issue with Will, but anyway, we met and we had a very good conversation in the end. It started off more than horrible. I began by apologizing for my part and honestly hoped she would too but she didn't. She never will."

"How did you respond initially when it was horrible?"

"I was getting very angry and honestly wondered what the point was. I wanted to leave her sitting right there again. It would have served her right. Then I thought…what would Doctor Kate tell me to do? So I told her I understood where she was coming from. You know what's funny? As she sat there telling me how disappointed she was in my choices and what my life had become I realized that we are one in the same person. I could see that she did everything my father wanted her to do. She didn't have some great career. Yes, my father was from a wealthy family but my mother wasn't. She didn't work a day after they married. She was a stay at home mom and cooked and cleaned her fair share. I remember she wanted a house keeper and my father told her no because he believed a wife should take care of the home. It wasn't until I went to college that she got a housekeeper. As I look back on certain times, I even wonder if she was depressed. I don't remember her ever being just really happy."

"What did you do with that realization?"

"I told her that I loved her, and I understood that she wanted more for me than what she had. She wanted me to be able to be independent and but mostly she wanted me to be happy. I told her she was right; that I wasn't happy as a stay at home mom. And then I told her that I had been coming here."

"How did she respond to that?"

"She told me that my faith wasn't strong enough. She told me that it was the church that Will and I had chosen that had weakened my faith. She asked about your religious beliefs and warned me about trusting a nonbeliever. But as we continued to talk she told me that she could tell I was maturing and maybe coming here was helpful. Since then we have spoken on the phone every day. It's not perfect but I at least I feel like I have her back in my life—even if it is on her terms.

"Well, to me that seems like a small win. I think your ability to tell her that you understand where she is coming from and that you see similarities between you and her was phenomenal. To me that shows huge growth for you."

"It does?"

"Absolutely. When we met some time ago, your emotions were so high that you couldn't even begin to understand someone else's. You would concede just to keep peace but now you have gained such insight into your dynamic with your mother. Although the understanding doesn't necessarily change how your mother treats you, it will and can impact how you respond to her and that's a success!"

"Well, I wish I could say the same about Will. I think I have taken an L on this one."

Sophie recounted the conversation that she had with Will. She reported how she owned her diagnosis of post-partum depression and explained how this affected her behavior and thoughts.

"And did he understand?"

"I thought he was understanding. We had a great talk the first night. The talk ended with him asking me what I wanted and I told him honestly that I didn't know."

"The next day we didn't talk much about it or at all really, but on Friday evening I asked him if he had any more thoughts about it and he blew up. He told me that if I didn't know what I wanted, how the hell was he supposed to know. He told me that he thinks this is all fake and it's my way of telling him that I don't want to be married any more. He forbade me to get a job, saying that I knew what I was getting into when we got married. He told me he didn't want a wife who didn't want to be there and take care of him or his sons."

"Oh Sophie. How were you responding to this?"

"I think I was in shock. Our first conversation had gone pretty well I thought. He seemed to be really listening and concerned about what I was saying. But on Friday it was like a different person. He basically told me to go to hell and he left the house again."

"And you had no response to that?"

"No, I did. I packed up some clothes and the boys and I left."

"And?"

"And I left and I haven't been back. I can't do this anymore, Doctor Kate. I really can't. He's controlling and overbearing. I need to be me…whoever that is. So we left and stayed the night in a hotel."

"A hotel?"

"Yeah we stayed at the Holiday Inn. The boys loved it because the hotel had an indoor pool. I couldn't bear to hear my mother that night. I had my fill."

"What did Will say when he returned home and you and the boys weren't there?"

"At first nothing. No call and no text on Friday night. I'm not even sure if he came home Friday night. But on Saturday around 7:00 p.m., he texted 'Where the hell are you with my kids,' and I told him we would be home later. He never responded."

"So, where are you now?"

"Now I'm at my grandmother's house. I couldn't afford the hotel after that one night. I have been spending all of my little stash on our appointments so that's almost gone. I called my Nana and told her that the boys and I wanted to visit for a few days. She agreed happily so there we are."

"Where did you tell your mother you were staying?"

"I didn't. She doesn't know yet. I need to have a plan before I tell her. I told Nana that we would be there for about five days because Will was traveling for work and would feel more comfortable if we weren't home alone. She bought it, but now my count down begins. Four days and counting."

"Okay so let's come up with a game plan. Have you heard back from any of the jobs you applied to?"

"Yes, actually last week before all of this, the HR person at Pioneer called and asked me to come in on the 25th, but that's next week. I haven't heard back from any of the others."

"Okay, have you applied to any other jobs?"

"No, I haven't. I just don't know if I am qualified. It's been three years since I have worked. I honestly feel so behind. I don't think I would know where to start."

"That's fair I think. Do you have an old mentor or colleague from your last position you could reach out to? Maybe ask them to have coffee and let them know you would like to return to work and need to know what's changed since you left."

"Really? You think I should do that?"

"Of course. If you didn't burn any bridges, I think it's a good move. That way you are letting them know just in case a position is open there, but also if they have connections they could help you network. One of my life mottos is you have to tell people where you want to be and let them help you get there."

"Hmmm...I guess I could email Josh. He was my office mate. He was pretty disappointed when I announced my resignation. He called and checked on my a few times during my pregnancy but Will didn't like it and yanked the phone from me one day and told him to stop calling me."

"Wow, really?"

"Yep, that's just how Will was."

"You know, when you talk about how Will treated you, you don't speak with any emotion. As you now are in this place what do you think about it."

"Honestly, he treated me great at first. He never wanted me talking to other guys so that was my normal. I was naïve enough to think it made me feel special, not that it was a sign of weakness in him. I think he didn't start to treat me badly until all this depression crap kicked in. Part of me is angry at him but part of me doesn't blame him. I feel like I deserved it."

"Is that what he would tell you? You deserved it?"

"Well, I don't know if he would say those words but it was more like 'If you wouldn't do this, then I wouldn't have done or said that.' Why are you looking at me like that?"

"Well, because I just wonder if you have been in an emotionally abusive cycle for so long that you can't see it. I wonder if Will's voice of criticism has become your own?"

"You think I criticize myself because of him? I think I did that way before him."

"Are you feeling the need to protect Will right now?"

"Yes, I mean no. Why would I? I left him, remember?" Obviously irritated, Sophie asked "What is your point Doctor Kate? I hate when you ask questions but already think you know the answer."

"I know my answer, but that isn't what matters. What matters is your perspective. Your answer matters. I just feel like you have been controlled and manipulated for so long that now you excuse it and have come to doubt yourself as a result. I can imagine the confusion you feel because on one hand you are making very independent decisions and setting boundaries—you're even expressing your emotions in a very healthy way—but on the other, you are plagued with doubt and insecurity."

"Damn. That's pretty much it. How the hell am I supposed to know what's right then?"

"Well, I think this is part of your growth process. I think it is growing pains. I think you make decisions based on what you think is right in the moment. If you go with it and it doesn't seem right, then you do what you need to do to make it right. None of us ever know ahead of time if our major life decisions are the right decisions. We just have to hope it is and commit to it. That's not something you have done. You've relied on yourself to just make it right. Think about this over the next few days and we can pick up the discussion then."

Session 8

"Sophie! I have been thinking about you all week. Are you ready to begin?"

"As ready as I will be." Sophie followed Doctor Kate down the familiar hallway. Doctor Kate noticed something different about Sophie. No more yoga pants. No more sneakers. She wore a pair of form-fitted trouser skinny pants that showed off her slim waist line and her hips. She wore a shear tunic and a pair of snake skin pointed flats.

"You sure look beautiful today. What's the occasion?"

"I'm sick of looking like I just crawled out of the dumpster behind this office building," Sophie laughed.

"Well, whatever the occasion, it's nice to see you looking beautiful and smiling. You should smile more."

"I have just decided to fake it until I make it."

"Well sometimes that does work." Sophie took her normal place on the sofa across from Doctor Kate. "Well, you had to reschedule your appointment last week. I missed seeing you. Tell me what's been going on."

"Yeah, I had to cancel because I was moving. My boys and I got a tiny apartment in Pearland not too far from my parents' house. My Nana cosigned and agreed to pay the first two months' rent."

"Oh Sophie, you're kidding!"

"Nope, I did it!" she said and burst into tears.

"What happened?"

"Well I left the kids with Nana and one of my cousins last week and ran back to the house to get more things for the boys and Will and I had had a few words over the phone and over text. I didn't tell him I was going because I didn't want to take the chance he would be there. I got there and he wasn't there, as I figured. I was packing our things and went into the bathroom to grab another curling iron for my hair."

The sobs grew heavier so much so that Sophie had to pause and get herself together.

"I saw a used condom in the trash."

"Sophie," Doctor Kate said as Sophie sat slumped over with her hands in her head. "I'm so sorry. What did you do then?"

"I took a picture of it and sent it to him. Before I could finish packing my clothes he pulled into the driveway and blocked me in. I kept trying to make him move so I could just leave. He was yelling and I was yelling. I don't even remember what I was saying. Ms. Shanon from next door came out to see what was going on, and he yelled at her to get back in the house. I tried to push past him and he grabbed my arm and threw me against the car. He told me he fucked 'her' because I didn't satisfy him. He then stood there yelling at me. Then the police pulled up. Ms. Shanon must have called them. Will started yelling at the cops that this was a marital issue and none of their fucking business. The more they tried to calm him down, the more pissed he got. They wrestled him to the ground and handcuffed him. It was terrifying. They were yelling at him to stop resisting. He just kept fighting back. I stood there and watched in horror. With all these Black men getting shot by police officers, I just knew that was going to happen. I remember yelling out to him to stop fighting. I have honestly never seen him like this. The look in his eyes was so scary.

They handcuffed him and put him in the back of one of the cars and asked if I was okay. I told them yes, and please to just leave. One of them saw a bruise forming on my arm," Sophie raised her arm to show Doctor Kate. "He said that he was arresting Will for domestic violence." Sophie choked on her last words with tears.

She blew her nose and then sat in silence looking for Doctor Kate to say something. They both sat in silence.

Sophie stopped in the bathroom and splashed cold water on her face hoping the redness and puffiness would subside before she went to pick up the boys. They had dinner scheduled with her parents that night and she decided that they needed to know. She and Will had not lived in the same home for three weeks, her grandmother was paying her rent, and now her husband spent two days in jail and was now out, but was jobless.

Session 9

As she drove to Ms. Shanon's house to get the boys, Sophie was lost in thought. She could hear Will yelling, "What the fuck! Let go of me!" as the police wrestled him to the ground. She heard the policeman's baritone bass voice saying, "Stop resisting or you will get tased!" Telling Doctor Kate the story, she knew she left out one of the most important pieces. She just couldn't bring herself to tell Doctor Kate or anyone that before the police were called that Will had forced himself on her. Every time she thought of his sweaty body pressed against her, she felt dirty. She felt tainted. She felt violated.

The phone rang as she shuttered away that thought. "Hello?"

"Hi, Is this Sophia Jackson?"

"Yes ,this is she."

"Hi Sophia, this is James Newman, from Newman Designs."

"Hello Mr. Newman!"

"Sophia, I was calling to let you know that we were very impressed with your interview and your designs. It has been a long interviewing process, we know, but we are very pleased to offer you the level one designer position."

"Mr. Newman, that is very exciting. I am interested and would like to view the compensation package."

"Certainly. I will have my assistant send it over to you via email so you can begin looking. We will send out a hard copy today as well."

Thank you, Lord Jesus, she thought. It almost didn't matter what the offer was for as long as she could have a reason to wake up every morning. Now she and the boys could have a fresh start. *But can I handle it? What if I can't remember the right measurements and formulas?* she thought. The self-doubt that her mother and Will had so skillfully orchestrated and ingrained in her began to play out. As she turned the corner into her old subdivision, she realized that the self-doubt was not hers but instead her mother's voice. *I can do this*, she thought. *I have to do this. I need a win.*

Sophie put the boys down and opened a bottle of wine. She observed how easily the boys took baths and went to bed these days. Was it the stress of living in the home with Will they were reacting to? She loved her tiny little apartment. She had turned the master bedroom into the boys' room and she slept on the pull-out sofa her Nana bought her as a housewarming gift. She was sure to make the décor as peaceful and warm as she could. She no longer stressed about dinner or grocery shopping. The boys were just fine with eating Lunchables or fish sticks every night. She would balance them with fruit and green beans to make herself feel better about their nutrition.

As she listened to the quiet, she sipped her wine thinking of how much her life had changed in just a few weeks. For the first time, she felt a bit of joy. It almost scared her to feel joy. She grabbed her laptop and

238

opened the email with the subject line *Compensation Package*. Sophie read through the cover letter, quickly scanning for any dollar amount. At the end stated the amount, Sophie covered her hand and began to cry. She continued to read through the benefits; medical insurance for her and the boys, dental, vision, and even paid time off. She never thought she would be in a position to be able to provide for the twins. Now all their basic necessities would be covered. She got down on her knees and prayed. She never remembered thanking the Lord so much. She couldn't wait until 8:00 a.m. to call and accept the offer.

****

"There is so much to tell you, Doctor Kate."

"Great! Well, let's just jump in."

"Well, I got the job! So I'm afraid this will be my last session for a while. I really can't start missing work, you know."

"I'm excited to hear that. I am very happy for you Sophie! Why do you think this has to be your last appointment?"

"Well, because I just don't know how it will all work. I mean I don't get off until 5 every day and I have to get the boys from Ms. Shanon by 5:30."

"I see. And what about your lunch hour?"

"I would hate to do that. I always leave your office crying and I would really hate to go back to work with my eyes all puffy and my nose red," she laughed.

"Oh, I understand. I will tell you this though. You have made really great progress since I met you and I am really happy with where you are. I do think there are things that you still have to work on though. I'm not sure we have finished processing the situation with you and Will. I have noticed that you tend to minimize that incident. And you haven't spoken to him since and we haven't even really discussed that at length. My concern is these things will creep back up if we don't resolve them. So, I am more than willing to do session via video conferencing in the evenings for a while until we can get these things processed and healed."

"You would do that? Like how? FaceTime?"

"Yes, absolutely. We can do FaceTime or Skype. The important thing to me is that you complete treatment. You are facing a lot of changes right now and I think you need the support."

Sophie was a bit taken aback at Doctor Kate's offer. She never really felt like anyone had gone out of their way for her before and this was exactly that.

"Okay, then yes. I was a bit worried about how I would handle things without you," she admitted.

"Now, tell me about the job."

They talked for a while about her new position, what it entailed, and Sophie's anxiety concerning the job. Sophie told Doctor Kate about her mother's reaction when she told her about the position and the daycare she had established for the boys.

"It sounds like your relationship with your mother has improved since you left Will."

"Yes, it has, a little. She likes to control me still but that is not new. The only thing now is that she just bad mouths Will so bad; even in front of the boys. I am just in a place where I just don't want to talk about him; especially with her. I finally had to put a boundary and tell her to stop. I told her if she wanted to spend any time with the boys or me that she would have to refrain from bringing up Will."

"You did? How did she respond?"

"Oh, I think she was surprised at my audacity at first, but she just said fine and shrugged her shoulders. That was only two days ago so we will see if she sticks to it."

"Good for you for putting a boundary. That's great."

As Sophie realized the time she jumped up, set up an appointment for an evening the following week and thanked Doctor Kate. She ended the session early to run by her new office and sign the compensation agreement paperwork before heading to get the twins. *This is my new life. Life as a single mom; a working single mom,* she thought.

Session 10

Doctor Kate and Sophie had been meeting via Skype one night a week for a few weeks. Sophie looked forward to her time with Doctor Kate. She had grown to see the real value in therapy and the importance of her health; mental health. As she dressed for church that morning, she reflected on the place she was when she met Doctor Kate. She didn't like herself, she didn't like her marriage, and she didn't like her parenting—or lack thereof. Now, she was learning to let go of her marriage, Doctor Kate helped her with some parenting skills, and she was learning who she was, and she liked Sophia. She decided to drop the Sophie and live up to the name her mother gave her. Recalling that her mother always chided her for not living up to the true meaning of her name, she googled the etymology of it and was surprised to find that it meant not only Wise, but Holy Wisdom or Wisdom in the biblical context. When she realized this, she knew immediately what lied ahead of her.

She began to seek God and learn about the Bible. Growing up, Sophia's family attended church services on certain occasions like Easter, Christmas, Baptisms, or other events where it was customary for everyone to go to church. Religion for Sophia's family had always been about the "look" of it instead of the "living" of it.

She and the boys began attending New Life Fellowship, which was a non-denominational church that was close to her apartment. They had a great worship service and the boys loved the kids program because they provided donuts every week.

Sunday mornings were a chaotic blend of breakfast, getting the boys dressed and fed, remembering their Bibles and heading out the door. After church they would meet Cordelia for brunch then head home for the boys' afternoon nap. Much to Cordelia's delight, the boys would sit through brunch, and would hardly interrupt except for an occasional request.

Sophia began to like the routine of her life. Sunday church Monday through Friday work. It was structured, scheduled, and routine. Sophia had come to learn in her therapy that routine and structure was good for her and the boys. She felt safe and secure with her new routine.

Wednesday night was her call with Doctor Kate. She hurried to fix the boys dinner, give them their baths and settle in for the Skype call. "Doctor Kate!" she exclaimed, maybe a little too excited. "I have been looking forward to this week. I have so much to tell you."

"Great! Well then let's get started."

"Things at work are going really well. I was asked to join as a junior associate on an exciting project! We will be designing a new hotel that is equipped with entertainment like a bowling alley, ropes course, and movie theater."

"Sophie that sounds wonderful!"

"Oh, and that's another thing. I have decided to go by Sophia now. I looked up the meaning and it means Holy

Wisdom. I think it's time that I start at least portraying myself as having wisdom. Fake it 'til you make it, right?"

"Sophia, I think you have a lot of wisdom actually."

"You do?"

"I do. Okay, what else?"

"So, I think I told you that the boys and I now attend New Life Fellowship. I have decided to start understanding more about faith and spirituality. But there is something I don't really understand. I know your religion is important to you so I thought I should start by asking you, but let me know if it is too personal. Most people who are religious think that you don't believe in depression or anxiety and they definitely don't believe in therapy. I just feel like I have grown so much since coming here so I'm not sure what to think."

"That's a question that I get often," Doctor Kate said simply. "A lot of people assume that because I am a psychologist that I don't believe in God or that my faith is questionable. They also get confused because I am a Black woman and the Black community just doesn't do therapy. Most communities of color don't do therapy."

"Isn't that the truth," Sophia commented. "I can't tell you how many times my mother has said something like, 'Child just pray about you," then as I got on my feet she would say, 'see the Lord has been answering your prayers. That's all you needed,'" Sophia responded, rolling her eyes.

Doctor Kate smiled showing her amuse, but she went on to explain that psychology and religion are not parallels; rather, two separate entities that coexist on the same course, but instead they intersect. Individuals that use their faith as a foundation of their health, but also use modern-day interventions and treatments for mental health conditions tend to be much healthier.

"See, so psychology and religion really complement each other not compete with each other. In my practice, I believe that my faith gives me the strength and guidance to continue to deliver this service to my community."

"Okay, I think I get it now. You know what makes even more sense? Is that wisdom doesn't just have to be gained by reading the Bible or studying formulas and plans for work but that God will put people in my life like you that will help me grow as well," Sophia said as she had the first experience of peace with her life in that exact moment.

Vivian

"Hi. This is Doctor Katherine Cameron."

"Hello, my name is Vivian. I was given your card by a doctor. I would like to set up an appointment with you please."

"Absolutely Vivian. Just out of curiosity what doctor gave you my card?"

She hesitated for a moment, humming. "I don't remember his name. I went to the ER yesterday and they gave it to me there."

"Okay. Are you okay?"

"Yes, I am. The doctor there said I had a panic attack."

"I see. Those can be very scary, can't they? I have an opening tomorrow at 9:30 if you would like to come at that time."

"Well, okay but I don't want to inconvenience you. Whenever you have time is fine with me."

"No inconvenience at all Vivian. I am located at the address on the card. I will see you in the morning. Hang in there."

"Yes ma'am, I will. Thank you."

As Vivian hung up the phone she felt flush and her heart began to pump hard. *Why does this keep happening*? she wondered. Was it possible that the doctor's at the hospital made a mistake and she really could have had a heart attack? She had always heard that the EKG would not show any abnormalities unless you were currently having a heart attack. Maybe yesterday was the precursor and now it was really happening. She felt hot, then cold, and very dizzy. Her breath became shorter and at that time Joshua came bounding down the stairs.

"What's up mom? What's for breakfast?"

Vivian didn't respond…didn't even make eye contact.

"Are you still feeling sick from last night? Does this mean I have to eat cereal?"

"Josh, please!" she finally forced out. Unaware of the panic ramming through his mother's body, Joshua bopped into the kitchen to devour a half a box of cereal. *Get it together. No, call 911. If you do that you will only be embarrassed again. Maybe they missed something. How can I handle this?* she thought.

"Mom, I'm done with my cereal. I'm ready for school. Mom, what's wrong. Are you okay?" Joshua's questions seemed to flow out of him like that of a giant toddler.

"No, baby I'm not. I just don't feel good. I can't drive you to school. Call Jason and ask him to give you a ride."

"Okay mom. Are you going to be ok? Will you be able to pick me up?"

She sighed heavily, something he wasn't used to hearing. "Just call Jason and tell him I'm not able to take you or pick you up today. I will see you when you get home."

With that Vivian turned and made her way up the stairs with a wobbly gait. At the top of the stairs she paused to try and catch her breathe. She plopped on her bed noticing how heavy her limbs felt. She could feel every pulse from her toes to the top of her head. She could hear her quick shallow breaths and ringing in her ears. Then she remembered the medication she picked up. She tried to look at the bottle and read the directions but couldn't focus on that tiny print on the bottle. She wrestled the top off and quickly swallowed one pill.

Fearing that wouldn't be enough she went ahead and gulped down a second pill.

When Vivian woke up, everything was dark and quiet. She looked around for a moment trying to remember where she was and what had happened. Where was Joshua? What time was it? She located her cell phone by the flashing blue light indicating a message—or several. She missed a text from Joshua saying he was staying at Jason's for dinner. She missed a text from Carly saying that Joshua told her she was acting weird. She had also missed a call from Michael. What did he want?

Being able to focus she turned on the lamp and retrieved the prescription bottle. *Clonazepam. .5 milligrams. Take 1 pill every six to eight hours as needed.* This must be why she had been sleeping for 12 hours! It was 8:30 p.m. *Great*, she thought. Now she would not sleep all night.

Session 1

Vivian parked her car and sat trying to catch her breath before entering the building. Once she felt as though she could walk without stumbling, she opened her car door, balancing on the handle, straightened her clothes and entered. She heard footsteps coming down the hall and was quickly greeted by a woman in a navy blue pant suit and a big warm smile.

"Vivian? Hi. I'm Doctor Cameron, but most people call me Doctor Kate. Come on back."

Vivian entered the office and recognized the smell of the lemon grass diffuser. The room felt more like a spa than a therapist's office. She eyed the walls taking note of the three degrees all from the University of Texas at Austin.

She smirked—maybe that school could produce some functioning people.

"So Vivian, I am happy to see you today. I know you had a recent panic attack. How long have you been experiencing these?"

"Well, I didn't know it was a panic attack. I have had times that I have felt week or faint but nothing like that."

Vivian went on to explain that she has always stressed out about things very easily. She had been a worrier from the time she was a child. She even joked that she worried about worrying. When asked about her childhood, Vivian told Doctor Kate that she was raised in a strict traditional Vietnamese home. Her parents were good parents. They wanted good things for her and her brother. They wanted her to get a good education and learn how to be a good wife. Vivian shared stories of how she remembered worrying about making the right choice on her elective classes or her major. She bantered on about how she chose a technical major because her desires to be an elementary education teacher were dismissed by her family. Doctor Kate listened closely, hoping to gain an understanding of the origin of Vivian's anxiety.

"Vivian, tell me about your family a bit. Are you married? Do you have any children?"

"I do have children. I have two. Carly is nineteen and she is attending your Alma Matter, I see," Vivian said forcing a smile and gesturing toward the wall of degrees. "Joshua is sixteen and a sophomore at Memorial High School. He is a sweet kid. I think he has my spirit," she smiled softly to herself at the thought of her baby boy.

"And your husband?" Doctor Kate asked, jarring her from her thoughts of sweet Joshua.

"My husband and I are separated, and we are going through a divorce," she answered, avoiding Doctor

Kate's eye contact purposefully. She couldn't believe the embarrassment and shame she felt just saying those words out loud.

"Vivian, this is difficult for you to talk about isn't it?"

"Yes. I didn't get married to just get divorced. I mean it's been twenty years for heaven's sake—well this October would be twenty years."

"That's a long time to face an ending. It sounds like it was abrupt," Doctor Kate stated, making it sound like more of a point of observation rather than a question.

"Yes." Hanging her head low in a state of shame she continued, "My husband was having an affair with a younger woman. "

"Vivian, I'm so sorry you had to go through that. How did you find out?"

"You know, for someone as smart as he is he can be really clueless. He bought our son Joshua a new iPhone and it hooked up to his account. I regularly checked Joshua's phone to monitor his messaging and social media. I found these messages…actually *sexts* is what I think the kids call them. I was horrified, and I immediately confronted my son. He told me over and over that it wasn't his penis in the picture. He told me over and over he didn't know the girl whose breasts were splattered all over the pictures. I honestly didn't believe him. I mean he is a teenage boy and those were teenage breasts. When my husband got home from work I told him and showed him the pictures. His face turned so red it was like I could see the steam coming from his ears. I couldn't believe it. He didn't even deny it. He said he had fallen in love. He said he needed some space to clear his mind. It all happened so fast. It felt like the next day we sat the kids down to tell them. Carly was just about to graduate from high school. He moved out a week later into an apartment."

"It does sound like it all happened very quickly. Tell me in hindsight did you have any suspicion of his affair?"

"No. You know you hear all these sayings about women's intuition. That when women have to ask the question, then they already know. I never thought of asking any questions. I still can't understand if he is that good or if I was in denial. I don't know how I didn't see it. Now I just constantly worry about what else I'm missing."

"I could only imagine. Tell me how you reacted to this situation emotionally?"

"Well, I mean I cried a little but only when no one was around. I felt a little angry, but mostly I think I am frustrated because I don't know what I did that led him to this."

"Do you typically blame yourself for other people's behavior?"

"Is that blaming myself? I just think that if I was doing my part than maybe this wouldn't have happened."

"I hear that a lot. I tend to believe that fidelity is not about the spouse that is cheated on, but the spouse that did the cheating."

"What do you mean by that?"

"I think the person who is unfaithful has more issues than the spouse that is being cheated on."

"Oh, I never thought of it like that. I'm not sure I agree but it is something to think about."

"Who is supporting you through this? Do you have any family members or close friends?"

"My mom I guess, but I wouldn't say we were close."

"So, that is a strained dynamic then?"

"Yeah," she said. Doctor Kate noticed Vivian's effort to fight back the tears that were forming in her eyes.

"I see. So, does mom live around here? Is she local?"

"Yes, she lives just half an hour or less from me."

"I noticed the tears in your eyes when I brought up your mom. Can you tell me why you tear up when speaking about her?"

"Honestly? I blame her for my husband's affair. She introduced my husband to that... woman... or child is more accurate."

"Your mother introduced your husband to his girlfriend?" Doctor Kate said sounded as puzzled as the situation sounded.

"Well, kind of. She owns a nail salon and Carlie used to be one of my mother's most loyal clients.

"Carly? Your daughter? I'm confused Vivian," Doctor Kate did her best to remember the names of the loved ones of her clients. It made it easier to understand but also seemed to strengthen the connection between her and her clients. She questioned her aging and the effects on her memory.

"No Doctor Kate," Vivian said. "It's not you. You heard me correctly. My husband's new girlfriend has the same name as our 19 year-old daughter, but her name is spelled with an 'ie' not a 'y,'" Vivian said in a mocking tone. "I guess I might as well go ahead and tell you that she is also six months older than our Carly, too."

"Oh, Vivian."

"Yes, that's a slap in the face to our whole family right?"

Doctor Kate wanted to nod in affirmation but refrained and instead affirmed Vivian's feelings with her eyes. She had been practicing for ten years and some things still surprised her.

"But as my mother said, I shouldn't have married a white man."

"Oh, your parents frowned on interracial relationships?"

"Yes, they are so traditional; stereotypical Vietnamese traditional people. I am second generation, so you would think we would be Americanized by the time I came up in the household. They run off the traditions and values so much, so I think my ba and ong would be rolling over in their graves on my wedding day."

"I'm sorry who are your ba and ong?"

"Oh, that's what I call my grandma and grandpa."

"Oh okay, I'm sorry. I'm not completely familiar with the Vietnamese culture so you may have to educate me a bit," Doctor Kate said. Knowing client's cultures and values was essential to her practice and how she made interpretations. She found that inviting clients to share their beliefs was cathartic on some level.

Vivian fell silent and was caught in thoughts of her wedding day. She remembered waking up on that day to her mother, aunts, and cousins talking downstairs. She assumed the conversation was positive and everyone was finally as excited as she was. There had been discourse between her and her mother, but she knew the family's presence would alleviate her mother's concerns or at least quiet her judgements. Vivian pounded downstairs to realize how wrong she was.

She heard their native language being spoken. She stopped short of the kitchen and listened while she still had the cover of anonymity. She heard her mother saying that Michael was a "blue eyed devil", her aunt followed with the sentiment that he was only using Vivian for pleasure and when he was done with her he would toss her to the side and move on to the next.

She shuddered to think of the truth that came from those words. The rest of that day followed that a similar sequence. She dressed in the dressing room at the W Hotel in Dallas. Her mother and aunts helped her into her dress and did her hair and makeup. She was not comfortable with the subtle makeup, but they insisted that she look like a virgin bride and not a woman of the street. Her uncle walked her down the aisle and she never told anyone that under her veil, tears were streaming from the corner of her eye. She longed for her father to give her away in this special moment. That longing had been there for years. She realized then that she longed for the comfort and security only a man could provide; something she never had.

As Vivian drove to pick up Joshua from school, she realized that she couldn't remember how the session had ended. Did Doctor Kate give her homework? When was her next appointment? These lapses in memory happened a few times in the last week. She would have to tell Doctor Kate about it at the next appointment...if she could remember.

Session 2

"Hi Doctor Kate. I'm sorry I had to call regarding my appointment. I just couldn't remember when I made it for."

"No problem Vivian. Let's go ahead and begin."

"How has it been the last two weeks? Tell me, what the first session was like for you?"

"It was different. I liked it. It felt good to talk about some of this stuff."

"That's good. People often have different reactions to their first session or sessions. Some people feel good while others feel exposed or uncertain, so I always like to ask so we can address any questions or concerns."

"No, it was good for me. I'm not sure what's really wrong with me. I mean, I don't feel like I really understand why I passed out a few weeks ago."

"Yes, I didn't answer that question for you. Our last session ended a bit abruptly."

"It did?"

"Yes, do you not remember?"

"No not really," Vivian said, without meeting the doctor's gaze.

"Well, you had a panic attack during our conversation about your family and their disapproval of you husband. You don't remember?"

"Um…I do remember part of it," Vivian said slowly, trying to sift through her memories of the last couple of weeks. "I didn't tell you last week that I have been having problems with my memory. I have always had a great memory. Now I can't seem to remember when I had for breakfast or what I watched on television. I can't even remember conversations I had with my children! Recent conversations with them." Vivian and Doctor Kate sat in silence for a moment.

"I feel like I am losing my mind sometimes."

"Trouble with memory can be concerning, but you are seemingly a healthy woman and you told me last week you have no significant health issues so I really believe the memory loss is a product of your anxiety. For some people, when they feel anxious, the anxiety has a way of taking over our central nervous system. Then our cortisol levels, which is the stress hormone in our body, increases. This is the fight or flight response. When that happens, our memory structures in our brain tend to shut down and this can affect our ability to concentrate and our memory."

"So, am I losing my mind or I'm not, Doc?"

"You're not, Vivian. This is a natural response to stress, I think. I'm curious though about your panic attack when we started talking about your parents. Can we start there today?"

Vivian hesitated. "I suppose so." She paused and fidgeted with her nails. "I don't talk about my family; to anyone."

"Is it painful to talk about them?"

"I don't know if it is pain or shame."

More silence from Doctor Kate followed her comment. Doctor Kate used silence often as a strategy to move a conversation into a deeper level.

"Shame can often be painful."

Vivian nodded in agreement.

"I told you last week that my mother can be a bit difficult. What I didn't tell you is that I was raised by my grandmother. My mother's mom."

"I see. How old were you when you began living with your grandmother?"

"From the time I can remember. I used to call her mom. I remember one day my brother said, 'She isn't your mom, she is your ba,' which is grandmother. I was remember being very confused. I never realized that he called her Ba and I called her Momma."

"Did your brother live with her, too?"

"No, he lived with my mother. I didn't realize at that time that brothers were supposed to live with you. I didn't go to school or anything so it was just me and my grandparents all day. My mother would drop my brother off sometimes and we would play but I was too little to understand."

"How long did you live with your grandparents?"

"Until I was about thirteen, then my mom came for me."

"Do you know why you lived with your grandparents? Did anyone ever explain it to you?"

"At first they always told me it was because she was working. But when I got older my brother and I were fighting. He called me a bastard. I didn't even know what that was, but it had to be something bad. I told my mom and she got very angry with him. My brother seemed to never get into trouble, but this time he did. Well, when he got in trouble this made him even angrier and he told me I was the reason our mom and *his* dad got a divorce. I didn't know what he was talking about. I was always told my dad passed away when I was little. I told him he was a liar. I remember he said, 'I'm not lying. Dad left us because you are a bastard baby.' I cried and cried."

"Did you understand what this meant?"

"No, not until I finally moved home with my mom. I asked her one night and she told me that when she was married, she had an affair with the neighbor. She got pregnant with me. When her husband found out she was pregnant, and pregnant with a girl, he left her. She had shamed his name and his family. He refused to raise me and my mother said she was ashamed by me as well, so she sent me to live with my grandparents." Tears slowly fell from Vivian's eyes. "I've never told anyone that story. My children don't even know that. I have always told them that same lie; that my father passed away before I was born. I didn't want them to know that my mother had done something so foul, so against everything we value. My Ba raised me to value family and marriage. Anyway, I never knew my father and never had any hope of meeting him. My mother said that he moved away after he had a physical confrontation with her husband."

"So, you were born into shame."

Vivian nodded.

"And why then did you move back in with your mother at the age of thirteen?"

"Because my grandpa got sick and my grandmother couldn't care for us both."

"What was it like living with your mom after not ever living with her?"

"It was really hard at first. My mom and grandma are very different. My grandma was sweet and loving. My mother is distant and cold. She seemed to only pay attention when I made a mistake. Sometimes I felt like she hated me."

"And did she treat your brother with the same aloofness?"

"No way. He was the trophy child. Jack could do no wrong."

"That sounds very lonely."

"It was. I just wanted to move out so badly. She and Jack always blamed me."

"For what?"

"For whatever. They blamed me that we were low on money because I was an extra mouth to feed or needed something for school. My mom blamed me that we weren't part of the synagogue. Back then the Vietnamese community in Plano was very, very small. After my mother's husband left us we couldn't go back to the synagogue. I was blamed for everything and I couldn't do anything right."

"Last week you said that you were always high strung and anxious. Do you see any link into your family dynamic and your feelings of anxiousness?"

"I do now. I never knew what was going to make my mother mad or critical. I tried to do everything right and it never seemed to work. I can see why I get so anxious now."

"It also seems like you continue to carry the shame even to this day. I wonder if your husband's affair triggered your feelings of shame and worthlessness."

Tears streamed uncontrollably at this point. Vivian noticed a box of Kleenex and reached for a few. She wiped her eyes but the tears streamed faster than she could control. Her face became hot and began to tingle. She began to have difficulty catching her breath and she felt sweat roll down her forehead.

"Vivian," she heard Doctor Kate say, but it sounded distant and like an echo. "Vivian," Doctor Kate called again. "You are having another panic attack. I want you to breathe in through your nose and out through your mouth very slowly."

Vivian tried to follow the directions. Doctor Kate repeated them again.

"Keep doing that until I tell you to stop. Now imagine your lungs inflating and deflating." Vivian did as she was told. Her lungs expanded then grew smaller then expanded again and grew smaller. She noticed her breathing slowed down a bit.

"Now, Vivian, starting with your toes. Tighten your muscles and go slowly all the way up to your head. Now, beginning at the head, slowly release your muscles. Now do that again while still breathing."

Doctor Kate then instructed Vivian to close her eyes. Vivian breathed in a scent of lavender. With a few more breaths Vivian felt calm and more relaxed than she did when she entered the room forty minutes before.

"Now," Doctor Kate instructed calmly, "tell me what your body feels like."

"I feel exhausted," Vivian said.

"Yes, that's normal. Feeling tired after experiencing a panic attack can be a good thing. Your body has released that tense energy."

"What else do you feel?"

"My mind feels strangely slow and I feel relaxed."

"Very good. It was probably a very good thing that you experienced that panic attack in here with me so I could go through the relaxation and breathing techniques with you in the moment, so you could see how effective it is. I am going to give you a little card to keep with you that has these steps on it so you can practice them if you have another panic attack."

****

Vivian stopped to pick up Joshua and unknowingly two of his friends.

"Hey mom! Chris and Luke need a ride home. I hope you don't mind."

"Sure!" Vivian said in a familiar, accommodating voice. This time though she really didn't mind the additional two sweaty boys hoping in the back of her GL450. "Let's go boys."

As the evening proceeded she noticed that, although she felt a bit sore, she also felt relaxed. She prepared food for Joshua and even ate some herself. She drifted off to sleep with no worries of Carly or Carlie.

Session 3

Vivian had been sleeping great the past two weeks. She had not had a full-blown panic attack since the one in Doctor Kate's office a few weeks ago. She was set for another session that day. She liked going to see Doctor Kate, but the 45- minute meetings seemed to take so much out of her. In the third session, Doctor Kate discussed some options to help with her anxiety. She definitely did not want to take any of the medication Doctor Kate told her about. Crazy pills were not the way to go and there would be no changing her mind on that. Besides, she had always heard that acupuncture and diet were better to handle stress. She told Doctor Kate that she would begin doing yoga and go to a wellness center on the outskirts of the city that offered acupuncture as well as other energy and body work classes. She kept up her end of the bargain and had already attended two sessions at the center. She had to admit, she did feel a little less stress.

Arriving in the parking lot of Doctor Kate's office, Vivian felt some tension return to her body. Her twenty-minute drive over was consumed with thoughts of what the discussion would entail today.

She had come to realize that she had many old wounds and Doctor Kate was very good at getting her to expose them. She knew the conversation could go in a variety of ways—her mother, her husband, her daughter. *Pick one*, she thought.

"So, where do we start today?" asked Doctor Kate. She knew that Vivian worked hard in her sessions and in between. She wished more of her clients could be as reflective and insightful as Vivian.

"I was thinking about that on the drive here. I have really realized how many things have been bothering me. I always thought I had it together, but I think I was just in some crazy denial."

"Can you explain that to me?"

"Well, a few sessions ago you told me I was born into shame. That really made me think. I have always felt like I was a bad person and I have so many regrets, you know? But I think it's the shame I was raised with. I remember when I met Michael I felt like I finally felt like I met someone who really liked me. He would tell me I was beautiful and smart and he seemed like he meant it."

"How did you and Michael meet?"

"I had just graduated high school. I went to a friend's graduation party. I snuck out of the house to go. He was at the party. We started talking. I was so infatuated with him. He asked me to marry him a month later."

260

"And did you say yes?"

"I did," she laughed. "But we didn't set a date until he asked Gno. My grandpa said no, of course. He didn't want me married to a white man. Ba told me it was not a good idea, but she would support me anyway."

"What did your mother say?"

"She accused me of having sex with him. She said that she couldn't have her daughter whoring around with a white man, so I may as well marry him. We got married six months later."

"Your mother's reaction sounds very hurtful."

"It was. I knew Gno would be upset and I expected it. But my mom...." she trailed, holding her head down. "She was so mean. All I could think of was that she was such a hypocrite."

"I could imagine. Did you and mom ever have any discussions about her reaction to your engagement?"

"Oh my, no. We were never allowed to be disrespectful. I just put it behind me and went on. I think over time she really came to like Michael. He was really great to her. He wanted to take care of her. Right after Carly was born we started our business and it took off. I think she really started liking him when the money came rolling in. But it seemed to make our relationship better too."

"The success of the business made your relationship better?"

"Yes, because she didn't have anything to criticize me about finally. She would say silly things like I needed to lose the extra baby weight or that she didn't like my hair cut but that's all."

"Let's reflect on that now; the fact that as your income grew, mom stopped shaming you."

"I think she realized that I was able to do something that she could never do. I had a good marriage and a successful business. She never had what we had."

"What emotion do you feel when you say that?"

"Part of me feels angry but part of me feels satisfied. Like I finally proved myself to her and to everyone else."

"And how do you feel about her now, Vivian?"

"I feel resentful toward her. I know she is trying now with the whole divorce. But I do I resent her. I resent her for treating me the way she did, I resent her for having an affair, I resent her for introducing Michael to that little tramp."

"Does she know that you feel this way?"

"I think she knows that I hold her responsible for Michael's affair but we have never talked about the rest of it."

"At some point do you think you would be interested in inviting mom here and we could all talk about it?"

"She won't go for that. She thinks all of this is in my head. She tells me I just need to get stronger and forget all of this."

"A lot of people of color believe that same thing. It's unfortunate, but it's our reality. My offer stands. If you can ever get her to come with you, I would be more than happy to help you both try and resolve some of these issues."

****

A few weeks had passed since Vivian's last session with Doctor Kate. She could not shake the feelings she had revealed about her mother. She had never said to anyone or out loud that she carried so much resentment for her mother. She was having a recurring dream and she couldn't quite understand the meaning. In the dream, she was she was in Ba and Gno's home. She loved their home. It was quiet and cozy with the smells of old Vietnamese cooking. The walls were lined with old family pictures. Gno was sitting on the sofa reading a paper, but it wasn't written in English. She could speak some in Vietnamese but not proficiently. Gno was very into whatever article he was reading. Vivian stood over his shoulders trying her best to interpret the words written on the page but struggled to keep up. She would ask her gno what certain words meant that she couldn't understand. Finally, her ba called to her from the kitchen telling her in Vietnamese not to read things that were meant for adults. She said it was better if she didn't know everything. At that very moment, moment there was a knock on the front door and Vivian ran and stood behind Gno as he answered. They spoke some in Vietnamese and she could only make out a word here and there. She finally got enough courage to look at the man only to realize she couldn't see his face. She then looked up at her gno and she could no longer see his face either. Just at this moment she would wake up. Each and every time she would wake up before she could make out their faces.

She was driving Joshua to his last week of finals for the semester, pulling up to the curb she heard "Bye mom!"

"Bye sweetie. Good luck on your finals! I'll be here to get you at 3:20 sharp."

"Okay," and with that he slammed the car door.

I just can't shake that dream, she thought. *Why do I keep having it?*

She went straight to her Tai Chi class that she now considered herself a regular at. She had never been a regular at anything. She and Michael had gotten married so young and she became pregnant with Carly shortly after. Life after Carly came was full of doctor's appointments and play dates.

Carly was in kindergarten when Michael and Vivian decided to strike out on their own and begin an IT company that provided platforms for mobile apps, and soon they ran their own apps and the company took off. During this time Joshua came along, and Vivian was able to stay home with Joshua like she did with Carly, but this time she worked from home in between feedings and naptimes. Life was hectic, but it was a good life. Michael was very meticulous and a "by the book" kind of guy. He was promptly at home by 6:30 and they would have dinner as a family every night, watch a bit of television, then he would be off to work in his study until shortly before midnight when they would go to bed together.

She wracked her brain. Could the man knocking at the door be Michael? Why couldn't she see his face and what did her ba mean by saying they were discussing adult business?

Later that evening, Vivian cleaned the dishes for dinner and waved goodbye to Joshua from the front porch as he and his friend Ivan headed off to a graduation celebration.

"Be careful!" she exclaimed. She knew he was a good kid, but Joshua was a bit of a follower and graduation time was a rowdy time. She ran back in as she heard her cell phone ring the familiar FaceTime ring.

"Hey baby!" she smiled, excited that Carly actually initiated a phone call for once. "How are you?" As the camera came into focus she could see Carly's face and she searched to understand that look.

"Mom? I need you. Mom…I'm pregnant."

Session 4

"'You're WHAT?' I said, screaming into the phone. I kept repeating it over and over. When I stopped screaming all I could hear where her sobs."

"She apologized over and over. She told me it was an accident and that she didn't know what to do. I didn't even know she had a boyfriend or even a male friend she was spending time with. I don't know if I have ever felt so much rage and fear all at the same time, Doctor Kate," Vivian said, and Doctor Kate noticed that agitation in her tone. "I don't know how she could let something like this happen. We've had the talk. She knows about sex. She knows about condoms and birth control. I may be conservative, but I also believe in educating my children about things and this was one of those things!" she said, almost yelling by this point.

"Vivian, how did the conversation end?"

"I don't know. I just remember I started having trouble breathing. I know my hands got tingly and I dropped my phone. Cracked the damn screen. I can't remember what happened then, but at some point, I remembered the breathing that you told me about. I started to do the breathing and I did the muscle tightening thing. It worked. I sat on the floor in the kitchen and cried. I don't want her to go through this. She doesn't know what she is getting into."

"I understand your fears for Carly, Vivian, but right now she needs you. She is scared and uncertain, too. I think that after you leave today, you should call her and let her do the talking."

"What do you mean? Do you think I do all the talking?"

"I think that some of you parenting style is similar to your mom's. I think there have been times for Carly that there is very little space for her to express herself. I wonder if that is where the wild colored hair and piercings comes from? I also wonder if that is why your relationship with her has been more distant that you would like it to be."

"I'm not my mother, Doctor Kate. Far from it. I don't really know how to feel that you said that. I've told you things about my feelings toward my mother that no one else knows and I don't really understand why you are throwing that stuff back up in my face."

"My intention is not for you to think I am throwing your feelings toward your mom in your face. Not at all. My intention is to show you that this may be the time for you to have a very different reaction to your daughter than your mother has had with you. There are similarities with how you parent. Most people do some of what they experienced because it is what you know. For the most part in your situation, it hasn't hurt anything. But it has created more distance between you and Carly. I don't want that distance to grow any further. She needs you now, and I just encourage you to think about responding with love and patience as opposed to judgement and criticism."

Session 5

"So, how has the last week been for you?"

"I'm not going to lie. It has been really, really hard. I just can't stop thinking about what you said. I was upset when I left and was really angry and afraid that I was becoming my mother, but you were right. My reaction to Carly was exactly how my mother would have responded to me," she said, bowing her head in what seemed to be disgrace. Doctor Kate sat silently and waited for Vivian to continue.

"When I got home, I called Carly to apologize for my reaction. She didn't answer. So I kept calling and calling. I started to panic a little. I didn't know if this was the final straw that pushed her away. And the last thing I want is for Michael to come in and save the day."

"So, did she ever answer?"

"No, not that night. The next morning, I left a note for Joshua that said I was driving to Austin and I left. I got to her dorm room about 10."

"Oh, and how did she respond when she saw you?"

"She just curled up in a ball in my lap and sobbed. She just kept saying she was so sorry for disappointing me. She said she knew I was ashamed of her and she was ashamed of herself. We both cried for a little while. She looked awful, so I waited for her to shower then I took her to eat."

"That actually sounds very cathartic. Do you think that was a bonding moment for the two of you?"

"I do. I really do. But I have to admit I disappointed in her. I am ashamed."

"Tell me why you feel ashamed?"

"Over lunch, I asked her if she had told the father of the baby that she was pregnant, she told me that she wasn't sure who the father was. I just didn't know what to say. I asked her how she could not know. As soon as I said it, I heard my mother's voice. I asked her how it happened. Carly and I have never talked like this before so I assumed she wasn't going to tell me. But she told me that she had been sleeping with different guys since high school. She told me that she believes sex is a casual thing and it's not a big deal. Doctor Kate, she then told me she had slept with girls too. Sometimes she has slept with guys and girls at the same time," Vivian began to cry and she relayed the conversation. "I just don't understand what happened. What did I do wrong?"

"I can only imagine how hard it was to hear this. I'm sure that you still see her as your little girl and can't imagine how or why she is behaving this way. "

"I just keep thinking it is all my fault."

"Tell me how the rest of the visit went."

"I asked her if she was going to keep the baby. She told me she had been looking into terminating the pregnancy. She told me she found a place in Fort Worth that would perform the procedure."

"What do you think about that?"

"I don't know honestly. I mean, I don't want her to raise a baby. She isn't ready for all of that. But I am Christian and don't believe in abortions. I don't know what to do. She hasn't made a decision yet and I'm trying to let the decision be hers."

"Does Michael know?"

"NO, thank goodness. She hasn't told him yet."

"You mentioned early that you didn't want him to know. Why not?"

"Because he is so self-centered and self-serving. He will swoop in and act like we need him to solve this problem; like we need him for everything."

"That makes you angry?"

"Absolutely, if he thinks we need him for everything he shouldn't have taken up with that little whore."

"I understand. Do you think you and Michael and Carly should have a conversation about this?"

"No, but clearly you do," she said with a smirk.

"I do."

"Carly needs you both right now. I think you should let Carly know that it's time to tell her father and that you would like to be there when she does so you all can have a conversation. When is the last time you spoke with him?"

Vivian rolled her eyes. "I don't know I guess about six weeks ago. I had to sign some papers for the sale of the business so he called to tell me where to go to sign them, and that's another thing with the sale of the business, the divorce, and now Carly—that's just all too much."

"Too much for what?"

"To have to talk to him about."

"Yes, that's a lot, but Carly takes precedence here."

Vivian reluctantly agreed to let Carly know that she did need to tell her father and they should all talk. She sent Carly a text and slipped her phone back into her purse.

"So, now tell me about what's going on with the business and the divorce."

"Well, it's a mess. The guy who was originally going to purchase it lost funding so we were in limbo for quite some time. Now he supposedly found a new buyer who agreed to our price. That's why he called a few weeks ago for me to sign the original papers. Now I suppose he will be calling for me to sign the new papers. "

"How did you find out about the new buyer if Michael didn't tell you?"

"My mother."

"Your mother? She still talks to Michael?"

"Yes. She still speaks with Michael and Carlie."

"You're kidding, Vivian!" Doctor Kate clearly couldn't hide her surprise.

"No, I'm not. Now you see why I was so angry when you told me that I am like her."

"I am at a loss for words right now. How did you respond to her when she told you this?"

"The same way I always do whenever she tells me anything about them. I say okay mom; good to know."

"Wait, I'm confused. I thought your mother hated Michael. She didn't want you to marry him. I mean I know she began to accept him but I had no idea she continued communication with him."

"Yes," Vivian answered incredulously. "She just tells me that he is the father of her grandchildren and was a good man to me for many years. She says Carlie is a good employee, too."

"Is?"

"Oh yes Doc, Carlie started working for my mother," she said with a smirk.

PART IV
The Truth

Andrea

Session 7

Buying a new pair of shoes always made Dre feel better. Retail therapy had been her choice of therapy for as long as she could remember. She would often spend thousands of dollars on shoes, handbags, and makeup. Daniel would become so enraged when he would open the credit card statement. At times, her spending was out of control and deep down, she was aware, but it made her feel a euphoric rush. They had been in a financial bind once or twice in their marriage. Once she landed the job at Park & Zimmerman, money never seemed to be that big of a concern. She would roll her eyes as Daniel nagged and nagged about the finances. As she pulled out her credit card, she thought about the improvement she had recently made. Instead of buying four of five pair of Louboutins, she purchased one. *This is sensible shopping*, she thought. She had consciously traded in retail therapy for psychotherapy. It had been three weeks since she started on her medication. She reflected back on picking up the medication from the pharmacy. The pharmacist asked her if she had ever taken the medication. She said no. He then proceeded to go down the instructions followed by the side effects. As she listened to the side effects, she felt her heart racing. She could feel her face getting hot and wondered if he thought she was crazy. Abilify 10 mg mood stabilizer, Prozac 10 mg for anxiety and depression. Surely two medications made everyone think she was crazy. It made her think she was crazy, but none the less Doctor Stewart and Doctor Kate assured her that with the right medication she would begin to feel better.

She had to admit that in the three weeks she had been taking her medications, she did feel better. She no longer felt the need to curse out Jackie and Frank every time she saw them giggling. She no longer felt the need to follow those who cut her off in traffic and call them assholes to their face. She had not had any days where she could not mentally or physically get out of bed. So far so good! Maybe she could feel normal.

After finishing her shoe shopping, she stopped for a coffee and continued on to Doctor Kate's office. She told Doctor Kate of the difference she felt on the medication. She talked about her recent cases at work and the minor successes she was experiencing. Things had changed significantly for her at work and until now, she was unable to admit to herself that her performance was subpar, and people noticed. She was taken off the White case and the Smith case that was promised to her was given to another mid-level associate. She pretended these things didn't bother her, but they did. They hurt.

All she had was her career and now that was failing. She had lost her family and had been on the brink of losing her job and career. Rumors had circulated around the office about her "losing it". She was accidently put on a group text that consisted of Frank, Jackie, Jim, Katie, and one other associate. At first most of the exchanges were about hearings, motions, and occasional happy hours which she had no longer been invited to. Then the text exchanges changed:

Frank: Don't' ask Andrea. She will ramble on and on about things that are not important. She just likes to hear herself talk.

Katie: LOL. She has definitely become such a bitch. I tried to be friends with her because I felt sorry for her. It must be really hard to be aging that terribly but you still try to look and act young. She is beyond my help.

Jackie: LMBO! She is definitely a nut bag. Don't judge all Latinas because we have one looney in the looney bin.

Jim: Let's try and be professional. She has been a good attorney. Let's just hope she is going through a rough patch. Her performance has gone down but we are a team. But I agree that you don't need to ask her about this case. All of the progress should be documented in the file. Let me know if you need me to fill in any gaps.

Bitch? Looney? Nut bag? That's how her coworkers who once respected her thought of her now. The hardest part was that she had these exact thoughts of herself. She thought about responding to the text with something like, "Hey douchebags, I see where we all stand now. Let's see who gets the last laugh," but she refrained; *another effect of the medication*, she thought. She would show them. She was going to climb back to the top and see what they had to say.

"Sounds like this has been pretty hurtful for you?" Doctor Kate phrased this as a question as she often did, but Dre it was more of a statement.

"It did. I mean I would normally just get pissed. But hearing what Frank and Jim said was the hurtful part. I don't give a fuck about Jackie, and Katie is a whore. She has already moved from blowing Jim to blowing another partner. But I thought Frank and Jim had my back. Frank clearly just wanted a piece of ass. He is such a loser. Jim has always been like a mentor. He hasn't even hardly spoken to me since I missed that hearing a few weeks ago. I just thought out of everyone he would understand what I was going through."

"You don't think he understands?"

"No, I think he is just out for himself like everyone else in that goddamn place. I have decided that since I'm on my way back up I will just start my own practice. It will take a little time but I know I could be amazing. So that's my goal for the very near future."

"What's the near future?"

"By the fall. Definitely by the fall. I'm not sure how much I can take there. You know how it is Doctor Kate. Once you have lost respect for someone, it doesn't come back. They will always see me as a crazy bitch. That's fine but I will now be the crazy bitch that is sitting across from them, ripping their case to shreds."

Session 8

"Good morning, Dre. You look beautiful."

"Thank you! I have lost 15 pounds total so far! I feel great!"

"That's wonderful! Congratulations. I didn't know you were trying to lose weight. But I didn't mean weight loss that makes you beautiful. Your eyes look bright, your skin and hair look amazing!"

"Oh, thank you. I stopped drinking. I think that has helped everything, I know it has helped me lose weight and helped my skin from looking and feeling so dry."

"You stopped drinking? Wow. What made you make that decision?"

"Besides the fact that I was a hot ass mess?" she laughed. "Daniel and I have been talking a lot. He asked me to stop drinking. I agreed."

"You did?" Doctor Kate was clearly astonished. She felt more surprised that Dre would agree to any boundaries Daniel had set. She knew Dre had been making progress, but this was a clear indication that she was doing very well.

"I can tell you, since I have stopped drinking it seems like my anxiety has gone down. I know you want to say I told you so, Doctor Kate, but I don't want to hear that," she said with a chuckle. "You were right, damn it. Why do you have to be so fucking right about everything? Anyway, Daniel said I was a different person when I was drinking, and he was right, too. He said he hated the woman I had become. I was mad at first, but I realized I hated that version of myself, too. I thought about how you told me that I use anger as a coping mechanism. I just get pissed at people, so I don't have to change my behavior. That was another thing you were totally right about. This whole therapy stuff is good, but I tell you it sucks. It is surely the hardest thing I have ever done. It is not easy to look at yourself in a mirror and admit your faults when you have worked for 20 years trying to hide them, but I say it does somehow bring peace when you just own your shit and try to make it better. Crazy, huh?"

Doctor Kate looked at Andrea and just smiled. Andrea had been a challenge on many aspects, but this moment just reminded Doctor Kate why she became a therapist and even more so of why she stayed a therapist. "I am so very proud of your progress Dre. I am almost speechless. So, you and Daniel are back together?"

"Well, we are dating actually. I told him I want to court him. He is a good man and I think I need to make amends for my behavior."

"What about the kids?"

"School is out in a week for them. Daniel and the kids are moving back here. They are going to have an apartment not too far from the house. We will split the kids. I need to work my program. Once I have completed my program, then we will go from there. He wants us to do family counseling, too. He says the Zeke and Anna have had a really hard time. Zeke is pretty angry with me so I have some healing, as you say, to do, but I am up for it. I hurt my kids and I hurt my husband because of my own selfishness. It's time to fix my life. You know, if eight months ago you would have told me that I would go to see a shrink and take crazy pills, I would have cussed you out. Oh wait, I did cuss you out didn't I?" she said with a laugh.

This made Doctor Kate laugh, too.

"I'm sorry for the hell I was wreaking with you Doctor Kate. You have been a real blessing in my life. I hope you can accept my apology and not because it's your job and you have to but because you want to. I think we have bonded and I hope we will continue to work on me together?"

"Absolutely I accept your apology. You have done great work. I know we will continue to heal you and heal your family."

Cori

Session 6

"Hi Cori. How are you this afternoon?" It was a bit past 5 p.m., Doctor Kate's last session for the week. "So last week was an interesting session. You and Stephen had decided to split. Tell me what has transpired since then."

"Honestly, I mostly feel relief. I have been angry, at myself, and Stephen, and at Ben. I have been angry at Lexi and A.J. as well. I think that's where I was when I came to you. I was angry but I couldn't admit it. It seemed very stupid to be angry."

"Feeling angry with situations beyond our control is very normal. Especially when anxiety from overwhelm and self-doubt kick in. I think you doubted your abilities to be a worthy wife, parent and physician."

"I did. I have some things to admit to you that I was holding back. I had begun to do things. Act out I think. I am still doing some of these things and need your help to stop."

Cori proceeded to tell Doctor Kate about the missing Mr. Ellington's symptoms, calling Lexi a bitch, modifying charts to fit what prescriptions she was giving at the patient's request, and how she was using Xanax samples provided to her by pharmaceutical reps to help her control her anxiety.

"That is quite an admission Cori. Let's break it down."

"My life is falling apart in front of me. I am awaiting results of the investigation, so I am just in limbo. That has been so stressful so I just started using the samples to help me sleep. They work. They really do. But I am using them nightly now. I don't want to go down this path. Stephen won't hardly talk to me. Lexi hates me. It's even worse now. It seems like she has gotten bitchier and A.J. has become more of a baby. We have decided to put them back in therapy. I think Lexi is depressed. I'm not her mother and I never will be. I think right after the accident I thought maybe the kids were Stephen and my opportunity to have children, and that would make all the other stuff go away, but that thought came crashing down very quickly. I need help, and I am willing to listen.

Session 7

Cori arrived at work a little early. She had stopped taking Xanax and hardly slept the night before. She decided to head in early and catch up on some charts. A slight knock on the door stopped her progress. She looked up to see a postal worker holding a certified letter. She signed and feeling short of breath and dizzy ripped open the letter. She skimmed through the letter quickly to see the word in bold **probation.** The Texas Medical Board had decided that she had been negligent but not enough to revoke her license. Instead she had a period of time to improve and prove that she was a competent physician. The investigation was over.

"I'm on probation. That stupid Ellington case." Agitation turned into anger. She began to feel flush and remembered Doctor Kate's words. She used the cliché seemingly over taught and ineffective breathing techniques which to her surprise worked.

****

"Cori. Are you ready? You look quite beautiful in your hot pick blouse."

278

Cori silently followed down the darkened hallway. She jumped in immediately telling Doctor Kate of the probation status. She admitted embarrassment, humiliation, and shame for the first time. She had always felt them but could never say them.

"In the last few months Cori, your life has changed. You have significant stress and you have not made the best choices as a result. We have to now move you forward. It is time to set some goals and begin to trust the process. The vulnerability resulting from shame could be a signal for change. What are you telling yourself about the probation?"

"I think it's now going to make me more anxious. I mean I don't know how I will ever trust my opinion again."

"Or maybe we change the messages you tell yourself about probation. Instead of letting it validate your feelings of inadequacy; maybe you tell yourself this is a sign of growth and improvement. You did not lose your license; you are still a physician; now you are motivated to be a better physician. You have plenty of things to motivate you for change. Let's focus on that truth."

Cori sat and pondered. She had never thought of this in this way. As she sat silently lost in her thoughts Doctor Kate continued. It is very important that we begin to reframe your thinking. You anxiety had peaked and affected how you did your job and even had you making poor assessments and even writing prescriptions that should have not been written. At home you were consumed of thoughts of Stephen cheating but could never speak your truth out of fear of losing. You fear of losing your job, your husband, your kids has led you to this point. You have begun to create exactly what you fear. Let's stop this destructive cycle before you *have* lost everything."

Cori nodded in agreement, as tears streamed down her eye. Her anxiety had gotten completely out of control. Even as a physician she could not heal this herself. Her feelings of vulnerability and weakness were beginning to change to feelings of acceptance and hope.

"I have a few ladies that I have asked to join a group for group therapy. I think you would be a great addition to that group. Could I convince you to join?"

Admitting her issues to Doctor Kate was one thing but admitting them to a group of other women to simply judge her was just a bit much. Cori accepted the invitation but had no intention of joining.

Sophie

Sophia sat across from her mother watching her play trucks with the boys. Her mother was in yoga pants and a T-shirt, a rarity of clothing for her, down on the floor playing trucks with her grandsons. Sophia almost pinched herself to make sure she wasn't dreaming. She sipped her wine, *I never thought in a million years my mother would be laying on the floor in a tiny apartment built in the 1970s, playing trucks and laughing with the twins.* A feeling consumed her and brought her to tears. She knew this feeling very well now. It was joy. Tears used to mean sadness, frustration, and anger. Now there was joy mixed into the emotional pot. Over the last two months she and her mother had really tried to change their relationship. She could tell her mother was trying to back off. At times it worked but most of the time it didn't. Sophia would take what she could get though. Her mom was caught in a tickle fest with the boys then carried them off to their room for bed. The one thing they did agree on was a 7:30 bed time.

She returned from their room huffing and puffing. She poured herself another glass Pinot Noir and plopped down on the sofa across from her daughter. The twins have just been a delight dear. Now, Sophia was convinced she was hallucinating or that she had gone crazy.

"How was your session with Doctor Kate? It has been quite a while since you have seen her right?"

"Yes mom, Sophia said, hesitantly. Their communication had improved but was a long way from

Sophia feeling comfortable telling her mother about her therapy session. She still felt weird even saying the words out loud to her mother. Now, hearing her mother asking, seemingly genuinely about her session was just about all she could bear. "It was good mom. I know you think therapy is useless but I really enjoy it. Doctor Kate has been a saving grace to me."

Sensing the defensiveness in her daughter, Cordelia responded, "That's great honey. I can see how much you enjoy your time with her. I have even thought about seeing her myself. If she can make you feel so good, maybe I should try it myself."

Sophia couldn't help the look of pure astonishment on her face. When Sophia first began seeing Doctor Kate, her mother went on and on about how her problems were because she was not in the right church and she married a man that didn't believe in God. These were the problems that non-believers had. Now, here her mother was saying she may even consider seeing Doctor Kate? "I think that would be great mom. You know she understands how hard therapy is for Black women and people of color in general. I think it couldn't hurt. The boys and I are much happier since I started seeing her."

"Well, she got the gold star when she convinced you to leave that deadbeat. That's all I needed to know about her." And just like that Cordelia was able to once again steal the credibility of Sophia's work and minimize Doctor Kate.

"Mother, don't start. The fact that you could even say that to me tell me that you should really consider seeing Doctor Kate. Maybe we should see her together."

"Together? Why would we need to go together? We are very close."

"Mother," Sophia started, then immediately regretted saying anything at all. She knew now she had to say it and she feared her mother's reaction. "Doctor Kate has helped me realize how much our relationship has shaped how I feel about myself. Just think about it. I went from being controlled and dominated by you to controlled and dominated by Will."

Sophia winced as she said this last statement. Her mother was very sharp and would put the pieces of this insinuation together very quickly. She closed her eyes, sipped her wine, and waited for the wrath of Cordelia to ensue. Instead, there was silence. That silence was followed by more silence. Sophia opened her eyes to see her mother starring off into space. She saw tears in her eyes. "Mom? Mom. I'm sorry. I didn't mean to."

"No, you are right," Cordelia interrupted. "You are right. Will was not right for you. He was wrong on so many levels. The truth is that your father told me that numerous times throughout the years. I had convinced myself that he was wrong. You know I have always admired your father for his intelligence but he was controlling, too. I never told you but we were ready to divorce a while back. We went to marital therapy at his request. The therapist told him a lot of things. The therapist also said that your relationship with Will was very much like our relationship. I have never seen your father cry until that moment. Right then, he promised me that he would change; and he did."

****

Sophia sat listening with her mouth wide open. Neither of her parents had ever given any indication that their marriage was in trouble. She had no idea that they had gone to therapy. Was this why her mother had changed? She felt happy and betrayed at the same time. She felt betrayed because her mother never told her any of it but had continued to judge her marriage with Will. She felt happy because if the therapist was the reason her mother was human now, she would take it.

Session 13

Sophia fired up her computer, ready for her session with Doctor Kate. She enjoyed their nighttime sessions almost more than the afternoon sessions. She found that she could process her day and went to bed feeling calmer. She heard the ringing of the Skype and ran back to the computer to answer the call. She settled on her comfy sofa ready to work.

Sophia spent the first part of the session telling Doctor Kate of her mother's recent admission. She felt like she was talking to a girlfriend rather than her shrink. Doctor Kate listened intently and then said, "It sounds like your mother's need for control was projected onto you. You then internalized that and entered a marriage with someone much like your mother."

Doctor Kate is so smart, Sophia thought. "Absolutely!" she chimed in. "No wonder my mother wanted me to leave will so badly. For her that would symbolize her leaving my father in a way."

"I agree. In a way, but the good thing is that it sounds as if you father's behavior did not escalate into abuse. He was willing to admit his problematic behavior and work very hard to be different. That is very important."

Sophie's excitement had fallen. Something had changed, Doctor Kate observed.

"Exactly. Will's behavior was getting worse while I was trying to heal. Not better."

"What do you mean Sophia?"

"Well, you know like the fight we got into before I moved out? We had never fought like that before. He

284

was like a different person—no he was an animal." Sophia's words trailed off and she was deep in thought.

"There was more thing that happened that night wasn't there Sophia. What happened? Can you tell me?"

Her eyes were dark and her face was blank. Before she knew it she was back in the bedroom; reliving that moment. Will had followed her into the home yelling and cursing. She tried to close the door on him but this made him angrier. As she walked down the hall to escape him he had grabbed her from behind and forced her into the bedroom. He threw her onto the bed and ripped her blouse open. He had unzipped his pants while shoving his fingers first inside of her. "You always get wet for me don't you baby."

She had pleaded for him to stop but he only became rougher. He inserted himself into her and pounded hard and deep. With every insertion it seemed to be harder and harder. Her cries and begging went dismissed. When he finished, he stood over her and told her *that* was what *good* wives did without being asked to.

She gathered herself and responded, "I don't know. I mean…nothing. Well, I don't know if it' nothing. Before the big fight started and before the police were called, Will forced himself on me. It's not a big deal really, I just can't shake it for some reason."

"What do you mean he forced himself on you?"

"He made me give him a blow job. I hate giving him blow jobs. He scared me and I did it. Then he ripped off my clothes and forced me to… well, do it. I told him I was I couldn't because I was on my period, but he didn't care. He did it anyway. It's just been so weird. I try not to think about it. But it pops in my head and I can't help but feel hatred for him."

"Sophia, you didn't tell me. I'm so sorry. Did you feel as though you couldn't share this with me?"

"I don't know. I didn't really know what to think of it. I mean he is, was my husband at the time. Does it really matter in that case?"

"Of course, it matters. If you were not willing and felt forced or coerced it absolutely matters. The most important part is how you felt and feel."

"I felt horrible at the time. I never thought Will was capable of anything like that. I felt angry. I told you I hated him and this was why. I felt…."

"Betrayed and violated?" Doctor Kate finished, feeling degraded and angry for Sophia. Sophia had worked so hard to get to a place where she could assert herself and this is how Will responded? Doctor Kate realized she had asserted herself into this situation, taking it too personally. She had to be careful to remain object, as if that was always possible.

"That's how I would imagine I would feel if it were me. I didn't mean to put words your mouth"

"No, that's exactly how I felt. I really couldn't process it until now. But if anything, it made me feel like leaving him was the right thing to do."

"I can't help notice that you refer to this as 'it'. I can only imagine how it must feel to talk about. Why do you keep saying 'it'?"

"I don't know what to say? I don't know what to think. Putting a label on it makes if more real I guess."

"What label would you put on it?"

"I don't even know."

"If it were someone else telling you that this exact situation happened. What would you tell them?"

"I would tell them they were raped and should press charges on the bastard," Sophia said as tears streamed down her face.

"Well…."

"You know it's always different when it's someone else's story. It's easier to make judgements and decisions."

"What's your story Sophia?"

Sophia pondered for quite a while before saying, "My name is Sophia and I was raped by my husband. I have two young boys and I despise the idea of them growing up thinking the way to exert your manhood is to strip a woman of her power. That makes you weak. I refuse to love or make a life with a weak man." Sophia and Doctor Kate sat in silence. Both recognized that Sophia never spoke in such power. Doctor Kate couldn't help but feel a personal victory.

"So, what now?" Doctor Kate asked for once not having an answer in head.

"So, now I find a way to heal. I find a way to continue to live my look at myself in the mirror. I find a way to not hate men. I find a way to move on from Will. I find a way to live my life. What that way is, I have no idea."

"The way that you are referring to is simple. The way is to know that you did not ever deserve the sexual assault you experienced. The way is to continue building your self-esteem and confidence. The way is to know that no matter what you will not surrender. The way is to know that your God will provide the path and you have to follow it. I hope I can be given the honor to be a part of your journey. I see big things in your future. You will have bumps and setbacks but I am very confident that you will see life and your purpose in the world very differently than you have ever before. I am considering beginning a group for women; a therapy group. As of now I have not entirely selected all the members but I think it would be great if you would attend. I hope you will think about it and agree?"

"No thinking needed Doctor Kate. I'm in."

Vivian

Doctor Kate was feeling exhausted, burnt out, and was fighting off a head cold as she pulled into her office parking lot. She saw Vivian's car there already. As she gathered her things to and got out of her car she saw Vivian still sitting in her car with her head on the steering wheel. Doctor Kate tapped on the window softly. Vivian jumped, clearly startled. She looked up and saw Doctor Kate.

They entered the office building and Vivian sat in the reception area as Doctor Kate prepared for the session. Vivian heard Doctor Kate clicking on lights and then sneezing blowing her nose. She heard the sink and was thankful that Doctor Kate was washing her hands.

"Vivian; I'm ready when you are" she called. Vivian noticed that this was the first time Doctor Kate did not escort her down the hallway. *Either she considers me a regular or she is not feeling it today*, she thought.

"You will have to forgive me," explained Doctor Kate. "I am fighting off a bit of a cold, but don't worry, I'm on antibiotics and I have plenty of tissues and Germ-X."

"No worries," said Vivian, secretly hoping she had Lysol too. Vivian was a bit of a germ-a-phobe, and it almost sent her into panics being around sick people.

"Well, let's start."

"Things are pretty good actually. I am feeling much better these days, thanks to you. I'm good, really."

288

"That's good to hear. Tell me why you had your head on your steering wheel when I pulled in this morning. I would have assumed you were tired or upset."

"I was just thinking."

"About?"

"Everything. Our last session, Carly, Joshua, the divorce. All of it. Carly told me two days ago that she plans to get an abortion. I have to say that I definitely did not react like *my* mother. I actually had no reaction. I mean, I know that sounds horrible, but I don't think it's a bad thing, really. She is 19. She is nowhere close to finishing college. She doesn't even know who the father is and let's just be real. If some young punk will have sex with a random girl whose name I'm sure he doesn't even remember, what are the chances that he will get the father of the year award? So, I just told her to make the best decision for her."

"This is a challenging situation Vivian. This is a big decision for a young person to have to make. I don't think it makes you sound horrible but I am curious about your lack of reaction. Did you not react because you feel numb or because you secretly want her to terminate the pregnancy?"

Vivian looked up, looking ashamed. "You know it's strange. I consider myself to be a balance between a liberal and conservative. I have known women who have gotten abortions and I thought for some of them I could understand. Others I couldn't. I always thought abortions were ok for other people to do if they chose, but not for me. Not in my family. Now I am facing this situation and I think that is the best option. Carly is not ready to be a mother and I am not ready to be a grandmother."

"I understand that, I do. It sounded like you put this decision totally on Carly though. Don't you think she needs your support during this time?"

"I honestly don't have the energy to support her right now. I am so angry with her for putting herself in this position. I don't even want to talk to her if I am being completely honest. What do you want me to do? You want me to hold her hand as she is aborting the poor helpless bastard child? I can't do that. Call me a bad mother. Call me *my* mother...whatever you want. I just don't have the desire or energy."

"Are you afraid that I will say you are a bad mother?"

"You did tell me that I am my mother remember?"

"I remember saying that your mother's tongue was critical and negatively impacted you. I said that at times you seem to do the same thing to Carly."

"Yeah, exactly. You said I am my mother."

"No, that's what you *heard*. I don't think you are your mother. I do think you should be aware of hurtful behaviors that you learned from your mother. I think we both know that you will support Carly through this. I think its ok for you to be angry with her and even express your disappointment. After you do that then you may feel more desire to support her."

****

Doctor Kate was sitting in her office catching up on her charting. After the third tone of the ringing phone she remembered her assistant was out of the office today. She looked at the caller I.D. and saw it was Vivian.

"Vivian. Hi. Is everything okay?" she asked. Vivian never called in between sessions. Vivian quickly explained that she was very anxious and need another session. Doctor Kate made a 4 p.m. appointment that day with Vivian.

Session 7

At 3:55, Doctor Kate heard Vivian walk through the door. Vivian was punctual as always. Vivian appeared anxious, but by the way she sounded on the phone Doctor Kate assumed Vivian would look much more disheveled than she did. "Are you ready?" Doctor Kate asked as she approached the reception area. Just at that moment, she heard her door chime sound again. Looking a bit startled she turned to see a tall, handsome gentleman dressed in an expensive button-down shirt and slacks come through the door. He looked right at Vivian then to Doctor Kate.

"Hello?" Doctor Kate said more of a question than a greeting.

"Hello, I'm Michael, Vivian's husband."

Doctor Kate could not hide her curiosity. "Michael, it's nice to meet you. I didn't know you would be joining us," she said as she looked at Vivian for an answer, but no answer came from Vivian. Vivian just stared back at Doctor Kate with a blank expression.

"Doctor," Michael began. I'm not sure how much you know about our marriage and our family. I'm sure you know we are in the process of a divorce. I have been doing a lot of thinking and reflecting, you know?"

Doctor Kate noticed Michael's face turning a deep shade of red.

"I have done some things that were not right. Vivian has done some things that are not right, but I want to come home. I told Vivian that I would like to work it out." Doctor Kate's eyes darted to Vivian as Michael was talking.

"Vivian?" asked Doctor Kate. "What are your thoughts of reconciliation?"

"I don't know. I just don't know." She turned and looked at Michael. "You have been sleeping with a 19-year-old. You told me you were so happy with her and that you loved her, and now you want to come back? Just like that you expect for me to open my arms, my house, and my legs back to you?"

"Doctor Kate, if you could please help us figure this out," Michael asked, almost helplessly.

"Vivian, tell my why you invited Michael here today?"

"I didn't. He told me he wanted to come. He begged me to come with me at my next appointment."

Doctor Kate asked Michael to step out of the room. She needed to get a sense of what Vivian wanted. It was clear Vivian was upset and confused, but Doctor Kate knew better than to let Michael possibly manipulate this situation and at the least change the dynamic of her relationship with Vivian. When Michael stepped out of the room, Vivian explained that Michael had been attempting to contact her for over a week. She finally answered his calls after her mother convinced her to give him a chance. Michael said that he wanted to repair their marriage. He came to this conclusion after fighting with Carlie for the last few weeks. He had finally noticed her immaturity when he was having a conversation with their Carly. He said they were fighting over the time he began spending on the phone with her.

He tried to tell Carlie that his daughter needed him. Their fight escalated and Michael ended up pushing her off of him. When he did that, she lost her footing and tripped. Carlie called her mother, who called the police. Michael had gotten arrested for domestic battery and spent the night in jail. It was in jail he realized that she was not the one for him. Vivian sat quietly and listened to Michael's account. She felt like she was in the *Twilight Zone*. This didn't even feel real. Was he serious? Should she really considering reconciling with someone who was clearly an idiot in a midlife crisis? Did he know what he had put her through? The sleepless nights, the crying, the self-doubt, the blame, the self-hatred she had developed, and the debilitating panic attacks. *Oh, my panic attacks. He had no idea. The audacity for him to all of a sudden stroll back in with his pressed shirts, designer socks and expensive cologne and expect me to just say yes as I had 20 years ago?*

Twenty years ago she couldn't have imagined life without him. He was her comfort and her security. He made her feel beautiful and sexy. He made her feel like a woman. She thought about the first time they made love. He knew she was a virgin and he was so careful and attentive. His touch sent chills of exhilaration through her body. As she climaxed for the first time in her life, tears ran down her face. He looked at her with confusion and caring. She folded into his arms and wept. The tears were tears of love and connection—feelings she never had before. She knew in that moment what they shared was special and no one else would have this connection. But now he had shared that with someone one else. A girl young enough to be his child, who shared the same name as their daughter; and just like that, with no apology, no acknowledgement of hurt, she was to say yes?

She felt rage. She felt anger. She felt love. Confusion set in. She told Michael that she needed to think. He *had* asked if he could go to her therapist with her. How did he know that? It didn't take much for her to figure it out. Ngoc. *She told Michael that I was in therapy,* Vivian realized. She was sure she told him that she was losing her mind and had a nervous breakdown because of the divorce. When he asked to go, she didn't say no, but she didn't say yes either. She had not said much of anything to Michael. He had been doing most of the talking.

"While he is talking, are you listening?" asked Doctor Kate.

"Yes, but I honestly don't have a thought in my head to respond. I have no idea of what I want to do. For over a year, he carried on this affair and I had no idea. Then he moves in with her and plans to propose? He just left me. He threw me out like garbage. Is this normal? Was it a mid-life crisis? Do men just expect you to come back after they put you through hell and back?"

Doctor Kate sat there quietly observing the anguish Vivian was in. "Do you feel the need to make a decision now Vivian?"

"I do. He is so persistent. He will not leave me alone. He calls and texts. He has sent so many flowers, I feel like I live in a cemetery. He won't let up, but you know what? He has yet to say he was sorry."

"Tell me what you think of that?"

"I think he is an asshole. You know, once our business began to really take off, this arrogance set in. And to be completely honest I didn't like it. He changed how he treated me. He began to treat me like I was his employee. He must have forgotten that I was the one writing the codes for the apps. He sold them, of course, but I was the backbone for the creation and design. None of that mattered to him thought. All that mattered was that he was making money. I never told you this, but I was never on the company payroll. He gave me what he called an allowance. That was so embarrassing. It was degrading. But I never complained. I was taught to just stay. And my culture says when the man comes back to reconcile, you do."

"How do you join your culture with American mainstream culture? What I mean is that you honor very traditional Asian cultural values, but you also have American mainstream values. Here, a lot of women would not base this decision on value, but on feelings. You are taking into consideration your tradition values. What do you do when your values and your feelings contradict?"

"I go with my values typically. But I haven't experienced a big contradiction. At least I don't think so. Well now that I think about it, my whole life is a contradiction with my values. Look at my situation with Carly. I don't know, Doctor Kate."

"I don't think you need to make a decision now. I think that if you decide to try, it's just that. It doesn't mean if you begin to work on your relationship that you both have to do the work. I think you both should be in therapy to see if this relationship is salvageable. Should we invite Michael in now?"

"I suppose, she said with a sigh. I am interested to see what he says to you. Be careful though, he is a smooth talker."

Michael joined the session and immediately began to explain to Doctor Kate how much he loved his wife. He said he knew he made a mistake but had come to his senses and wanted to repair his family. He talked about how their children needed them both at this time. He said that Joshua was close to leaving for college and the adjustment that would be for him because he was a naive child. He talked about Carly facing some very difficult decisions right now that would forever change her life. He talked about the empire they had built and that they had such a great partnership.

Doctor Kate then asked about Michael's relationship with Carlie. He professed his love for Vivian and stated it was over. Doctor Kate listened very carefully to what Michael was *not* saying. Something was missing. She knew it but was not sure Vivian knew there was more to this situation. Doctor Kate inquired into the ending of the relationship and Michael stated emphatically that he no longer had feelings for her. When asked about the contact between the two of them, Michael dismissed it saying that they were in the process of separating but it would soon be complete. As Michael bantered on, Doctor Kate focused her attention on Vivian. It appeared as though Vivian was hearing him, but she couldn't tell if Vivian was in or out. That would be for another session. Michael would have continued on for another hour or two, but Doctor Kate had other clients to see. She ended the session, inviting Michael to return independently, which was dismissed in a circular manner of reasoning. Vivian agreed to return at her next regularly appointment.

As they walked out together, Doctor Kate watched from the window. He watched Michael follow Vivian to her car and stand outside her door and talk more. He lowered his head into her window which Doctor Kate could only speculate was for a kiss. *He is definitely not telling the whole story,* she thought. And with that, her next appointment walked in the door.

Session 8

"Good morning! Last week was pretty intense. Let's jump in. How has the last week been for you?"

"A lot has transpired. After seeing you last week, Carly called me and told me she is keeping the baby. She went for an initial appointment at the clinic and they made her go for counseling. In the counseling session, she realized she wanted to keep her baby."

"Wow. What do you think about that?"

"At first I was very weary. She is so young and wild but something seems to be changing in her. She seems like she is at least wanting to think about making good choices in her life. Maybe this will be a good thing. I have been doing a lot of what we talked about and have been giving her support. I give her guidance, but I am very aware, mostly by her reaction, when I am being critical. She is even calling me now, which I think is pretty cool, so this will be crazy and difficult, but she is a strong girl. We will figure it out."

"Very good. I am so encouraged by your insight into your dynamic. And how is Joshua with all of this?"

"Joshua is so oblivious. He just wants everyone to be happy."

"Good. And what about you and Michael?"

"I have decided to try and make it work with Michael. I don't know what that means yet, but I have started by telling him what I think about him. I told him how angry I felt. I told him he had me the closest to hate I had ever been. I told him he had become an arrogant prick and I would not reconcile with that guy. And to my surprise, he admitted it and apologized. He has even agreed to go to couple's therapy and wanted me to ask you if you would see the two of us."

"Wow. That's surprising I have to say. I will see you both absolutely. I would like to meet with him individually first though,"

"Do you think I am making the right decision?"

"That I can't say. It's difficult because I don't know Michael, but I will say I do believe in the commitment of marriage and in some situations it is worth trying to reconcile. I do have one question for you. Do you believe that you have all the information that you need to move forward with him?"

Vivian looked up with astonishment. Her eyes were large and her mouth was open a bit. "Why are you asking that? Do you know something?"

"No, I just want to make sure you are making an informed decision. I think there is a huge risk for you to be reinjured in this situation. I think it is important that Michael be transparent; completely transparent and upfront in this process. You have done a great deal of healing, Vivian. You have worked very hard. You have not had a panic attack in several weeks and you have begun to find your voice. In fact, I'm creating a small group, I think you would be a perfect fit for it. The sessions would just be a few women together with me, going through a type of group therapy. You are in a great place to handle it but I am concerned. I want you to continue the work you have been doing no matter what you decide."

Vivian looked up sheepishly and said, "I'll think about it. I need to get used to being around other people again. I'd want to begin the couple's session very soon. I love him, Doctor Kate,"

Vivian sat in the silence for a long while before saying, "Carlie is pregnant."

. CPSIA information can be obtained
at www.ICGtesting.com
Printed in the USA
LVHW081303210219

608315LV00017B/371/P

9 781942 549369